CHRISTMAS AT
COLD COMFORT FARM

Stella Gibbons was born in London in 1902. She
went to the North London Collegiate School and
studied journalism at University College, London.
She worked for various newspapers including the
Evening Standard. Stella Gibbons is the author
of twenty-five novels, three volumes of short
stories, and four volumes of poetry. Her first
publication was a book of poems, *The Mountain
Beast* (1930), and her first novel, *Cold Comfort
Farm* (1932), won the Femina Vie Heureuse Prize
for 1933. Amongst her works are *Christmas at
Cold Comfort Farm* (1940), *Westwood* (1946),
Conference at Cold Comfort Farm (1959) and
Starlight (1967). She was elected a Fellow of the
Royal Society of Literature in 1950. In 1933 she
married the actor and singer Allan Webb. They
had one daughter. Stella Gibbons died in 1989.

ALSO BY STELLA GIBBONS

Cold Comfort Farm

Bassett

Enbury Heath

Nightingale Wood

My American

The Rich House

Ticky

The Bachelor

Westwood

The Matchmaker

Conference at Cold Comfort Farm

Here Be Dragons

White Sand and Grey Sand

The Charmers

Starlight

STELLA GIBBONS

Christmas at Cold Comfort Farm

VINTAGE BOOKS
London

Published by Vintage 2011

4 6 8 10 9 7 5

Copyright © Stella Gibbons 1940

Stella Gibbons has asserted her right under the Copyright,
Designs and Patents Act 1988 to be identified as the author
of this work

First published in Great Britain by Longmans, Green and Co. Ltd

Vintage
Random House, 20 Vauxhall Bridge Road,
London SW1V 2SA

www.vintage-classics.info

Addresses for companies within The Random House Group Limited
can be found at: www.randomhouse.co.uk/offices.htm

The Random House Group Limited Reg. No. 954009

A CIP catalogue record for this book
is available from the British Library

ISBN 9780099565697

The Random House Group Limited supports The Forest Stewardship Council
(FSC®), the leading international forest certification organisation. Our books
carrying the FSC label are printed on FSC® certified paper. FSC is the only forest
certification scheme endorsed by the leading environmental organisations, including
Greenpeace. Our paper procurement policy can be found at
www.randomhouse.co.uk/environment

Typeset in Bembo by Palimpsest Book Production Limited,
Falkirk, Stirlingshire

Printed and bound by
CPI Group (UK) Ltd, Croydon, CR0 4YY

To
Allan

Note

The stories in this book appear by courtesy of the Editors of *The Lady, The Bystander, Nash's Magazine, Penguin Parade, Good Housekeeping,* and *The Evening Standard.*

Contents

The Little Christmas Tree

Because she was tired of living in London among clever people, Miss Rhoda Harting, a reserved yet moderately successful novelist in the thirty-third year of her age, retired during one November to a cottage in Buckinghamshire. Nor did she wish to marry.

'I dislike fuss, noise, worry, and all the other accidents, which, so my friends tell me, attend the married state,' she said. 'I like being alone. I like my work. Why should I marry?'

'You are unnatural, Rhoda,' protested her friends.

'Possibly, but at least I am cheerful,' retorted Miss Harting. 'Which,' she added (but this was to herself), 'is more than can be said of most of you.'

The cottage in Buckinghamshire, which was near Great Missenden, suited her tastes. It had a double holly tree in the garden, and a well in whose dark depths she could see her own silhouette against the wintry blue sky. It stood in a lane, with long fields at the back which sloped up to a hill with a square beechwood on the summit. Halfway up the hill stood another house, Monkswell, a large, new, red house. Miss Harting used to look at this house and say contentedly, 'I feel like the gardener at Monkswell. This used to be his cottage, I am told.'

She furnished her cottage fastidiously with English china, English prints, chintz, and a well-equipped kitchen. For the first fortnight she played with it as though it were the dolls' house it so much resembled, but soon she began to work on a new novel, and, as everybody knows, the writing of novels does not allow time for playing at anything.

A quiet, pleasant routine, therefore, replaced her first delighted experiments.

Weeks went past so quickly that she was quite surprised to receive a letter one morning beginning, 'Darling Rhoda, you will come to us for Christmas, won't you, unless you have already made other plans' – and headed with an address in Kensington.

She got up from the breakfast table, where the steam from her China tea was wavering peacefully up into the air, and went over to the window and stood looking out.

'No, I shall stay here for Christmas,' decided Miss Harting, after a prolonged gaze out of the window. 'I shall have a chicken all to myself, and a little tree with candles and those bright, glittery balls we used to buy when we were small.' She paused, in her comfortable murmuring to herself, and added contentedly, 'It is really shocking. I grow more and more spinsterish every year. Something ought to be done about it . . .'

Her conscience quieted, Miss Harting went shopping in Great Missenden on Christmas Eve, wandering down the rambling bright-lit High Street with a big basket slung on her arm and her bright eyes dreaming in and out of the shop windows.

The long street was packed with people, and there was a feeling of frost in the air, but no stars, only a dense, muffling bed of cloud almost touching the bare beechwoods on the hidden hills all round the little town. In the butchers' shops the dangling turkeys were tied up with red ribbon, and hares were decorated with spiked bunches of holly and moon-mistletoe, and out of the warm caverns of the two wireless and gramophone shops poured rich, blaring music.

'Seasonable weather, madam,' said the poulterer who tied up Miss Harting's small but fat chicken.

'Going to be a regular old-fashioned Christmas, Miss,' said the old lady wrapped in a shawl like a thick, blacky-green fishing net, who packed up the silver glass balls and red and green lemons of fairy-glass that Miss Harting had chosen for her Christmas tree.

The old lady looked across at her with something more than professional interest, and enquired civilly:

'Was you wanting them for a Christmas tree of your own, Miss?'

'Yes,' murmured Miss Harting.

'Ah! Nephews and nieces coming down from London perhaps?'

'Well – no,' confessed her customer.

'Not your own little ones? Excuse me askin', but you can usually tell. I shouldn't have thought . . . Well, there now, I'm sure I beg your pardon. I oughtn't to have said that. Here's the toys, Miss. A happy Christmas to you.'

'Er – thank you. The same to you. Good evening.'

Miss Harting escaped, aware that the old lady, far from being embarrassed by her mistake, was taking her in from head to feet with lively, curious eyes and thought her a queer one. But Miss Harting was sure that her wildest guesses at the reason why the toys had been bought would come nowhere near the truth. In the circles in which the old lady's tubby person rotated, unmarried females did not buy Christmas trees, decorate them and gloat over them in solitude, however natural such a proceeding might seem in Chelsea.

Perhaps it was this breath of commonsense from the world of unimaginative millions that made Miss Harting feel a little depressed as she got down from the Amersham 'bus at the cross roads, and set out along the ringing frosty road to walk the last mile to her cottage. Her basket hung heavily on her arm. She was hungry. She did not feel in the mood for revelling in the bright, miniature prettiness of her Christmas tree. She almost wished she had gone to Kensington, as her friends had proposed. 'Good gracious, this will never do,' muttered Miss Harting, unlocking her front door. 'In the New Year I will go up to London and see people, and invite Lucy or Hans Carter or somebody to come down and stay with me.'

When she had eaten her supper, however, she felt better; and began to enjoy bedding the shapely little tree into a flower-pot and fastening the glass bells and lemons on to the tips of its branches. She stood it in the sitting-room window, with the curtains pulled back, when it was ready, and could not resist lighting its tipsy green and white candles, just to see what it would look like.

Oh! the soft light shining round the candles and falling down between the dark green branches! How pretty it was!

She stood for perhaps five minutes dreaming in front of it, in a silence unbroken except by the noise of a car that droned past along the unfrequented lane at the foot of her front garden.

Every year, ever since she could remember, she had had a Christmas tree, either bought for her by her parents, when they were alive, or by herself, with her own money. This year, it was as beautiful and as satisfying as ever.

Yet . . . was it? While she stood looking at it, she remembered the old lady in the little shop. The thought drifted into her mind that hers was a lonely, not to say self-conscious, way of enjoying a Christmas tree. She dismissed the thought impatiently, extinguished the little candles, and spent the rest of the evening profitably at work on her book.

In the night the snow came. She awoke on Christmas morning in that unmistakable light, coming up from the earth and shining between her curtains. All her loneliness and depression had gone. She felt as happy and excited as though she were going to a feast.

But when she had nibbled her breakfast, played Debussy's *Footsteps in the Snow* twice on the gramophone, stuffed her chicken and glanced more than once at her Christmas tree, whose bells glittered darkly against the snow, she found herself trying to feel happy, rather than feeling happy. It was eleven o'clock. The noise of bells was stealing in soft claps of sound on the snow-wind. She suddenly faced the fact that she was both lonely and bored; that eleven more empty hours yawned endlessly in front of her, and that she could do nothing to stop their approach and departure.

It was just at this moment, as she stood staring down at her fingers still greasy with chicken-stuffing, that there came a knock at the front door.

Miss Harting gave a great start.

'Oh!' she thought, with a rush of relief, 'perhaps it's some one come down from London to see me!' and she hurried out to the door.

But when she opened the door she saw no gay, familiar face from London. A little girl, wearing a red beret, stood on the doorstep, squarely yet somehow in a pose that suggested she might dash away in a second, looking up with large dark eyes into Miss Harting's surprised face. Two smaller children, in the same tiptoe pose, lurked in the background.

'Good morning,' said the red beret loudly and politely. 'We are very sorry to trouble you, but please may we take shelter in your house?'

'Shelter?' said Miss Harting, still getting over her silly disappointment that it was not a delightful visitor from London; and perhaps she spoke a little curtly. 'Because of the snow, do you mean? But –' she glanced up at the sky '– it isn't snowing. What's the matter? Are your feet wet or something?' (No one but a nieceless spinster would have asked such a question of a little girl on a snowy morning.)

'No, thank you,' said the red beret politely. 'It isn't that sort of shelter, and our feet are quite dry, thank you very much. But, you see, it is rather necessary that we should take shelter, because–' she looked up candidly into Miss

Harting's eyes '– some one is coming after us, and we want to hide.'

She glanced round at the two smaller figures, who both nodded violently as though she had pulled a string.

'Who's after you?' asked Miss Harting, startled. 'Are you playing a game?'

'Oh, no. *Truly*, it isn't a game. It's rather serious, as a matter of fact. You see, we have a cruel step-mother, and she said we weren't to have a proper Christmas tree this year, and Jane and Harry — these are Jane and Harry,' (jerking them forward and muttering, 'Say-how-do-you-do,' which they did, like two polite wool-clad parrots) – 'cried rather a lot—'

'I didn't, Judy. 'At's a story!' interrupted the other little girl flatly at this point in the narrative. 'And if you say I cried like a baby, I shall tell – you-know-what!'

'Oh, well then, perhaps you didn't cry quite as much as Harry,' conceded the red beret, darting a lightning grimace at her, laden with menace. 'But Harry cried all night. So we got up very early this morning, before it was light, and took some gingerbreads and hid in the woods until it got light, and then we ran down – I mean we walked a long way in the woods, until we saw your house, and as we were rather hung— I mean, we thought we would ask if we might take shelter here until our step-mother had stopped looking for us. That's what we thought, isn't it?' appealing imperiously to the woolly parrots.

'Yes, we liked your house because it was so *little*,' said Jane, accompanying her compliment by a smile of such specious yet goblin charm that Rhoda's heart contracted strangely.

Here Harry, who had been staring at her face, remarked 'Absolutely snow,' and pointed to the distant fields. He added, after another prolonged stare, 'You do look funny,' and began to run slowly up and down the path with his hands at his sides, puffing like an engine.

'Harry! That's rude!' cried the red beret, darting down on him. 'You mustn't mind him, please. He's only four and doesn't understand things properly yet. Besides, he isn't our brother. He's only a cousin.'

A pause followed; an awkward pause. The red beret and the woolly Jane gazed up into Miss Harting's face, too polite to put their request again into words, but with eyes full of pleading and hope.

She did not know quite what to do. She did not, of course, believe a word of the red beret's fantastic story. The red beret, with her over-persuasive eyes and tongue, had betrayed herself with her first sentence as one of those incurable romancers who are doomed never to be believed.

'She will probably earn a large income one day by writing best-sellers,' thought Miss Harting, who was now handicapped by having to struggle with the pangs of violent love at first sight. It did not seem at all shocking to her that the red beret should tell lies, but she did wonder very much whether the red beret had a mother, and if so, did she know of the daughter's capacities for inventing? It seemed to Miss Harting that these three needed looking after. In spite of their educated enunciation, their warm clothes and pretty manners, they had a lost look about them.

But, if they felt lost, why in the name of Father Christmas

himself should they choose her unromantic doorstep to be lost on? Taking another long look at their anxious faces, she sighed, and gave it up.

She said, cautiously (but a curious warm feeling of happiness began to invade her), 'Well, come in by all means, if your step-mother is as bad as all that. You can stay until you're warm, anyway. Jane – that is your name, isn't it? – is beginning to look blue. Er – you can see my Christmas tree, too, if that would amuse you.'

The two faces changed with incredible speed. They smiled, but Rhoda felt that was a smile of triumph, of success achieved, rather than one of gratitude. She was sure that only prudence prevented the red beret from saying to Jane, 'There you are, clever! I told you so!' and she became more than ever puzzled.

'Oh, thank you *very* much—' gushed the red beret.

'*Vewy* much,' came Jane's slower, fatter voice, in dutiful diminuendo.

'I'm afraid there are no presents on it,' warned Rhoda, opening the kitchen door. But there was no need for apologies. The three paused on the threshold, staring at the little tree, their faces solemn with pleasure.

'Oh, isn't it *pretty!* It's so *little!* It's like those little ones we saw growing near Barnet,' said the red beret. 'Daddy told us they were going to be Christmas trees when they got bigger. Oh, what pretty little bell-things. Oh, look Jane, a norange! all made of glass!'

'*Pretty!*' said Jane, intensely. 'It's the littlest tree I ever saw. May I touch it? Who is it for?'

'Er – it's for you,' said Rhoda, feeling very queer indeed.

Yet they were all warmly-clad, all well-fed and healthy. It was ridiculous to feel inclined to cry.

The three faces, incredulous, were lifted to hers.

'For us? Oo! Really? Can we play with it? Can I have the little lemon thing? Can we light those little cangles ourselves?'

'After lunch,' said Rhoda, who had suddenly become so full of bustling happiness that she could not keep still, and she began to tie on her white cooking overall with unnecessary energy.

'Is that your lunch cooking?' asked Jane, looking round the kitchen with polite interest. 'It smells nice.'

'Jane!' warned the red beret. She glanced appealingly at Miss Harting. 'Jane's only six. I'm nearly nine. Jane's rather rude sometimes. She's still fairly little, you see.'

'I suppose your cruel step-mother hasn't much time to teach Jane manners, either,' said Miss Harting drily. She was used, of course, to the type of grown-up person to whom ironical conversation is natural.

But in this case irony would not do. She realized it at once with extreme contrition, as the red beret stared up at her, wounded and rather frightened by her tone. She knelt down in front of her suddenly, and murmured, beginning to unbutton the reefer coat:

'What's your name? Mine's Rhoda Harting. Let me help you off with your coat. Will you please all stay and have lunch?'

'Oo, hooray! I'm so hungry,' shouted Harry, who had been poking at the bells on the Christmas tree and exchanging hoarse whispers with Jane.

'Thank you very much. We should like to. As a matter

of fact, we are rather hungry. I'm Juliet Woodhouse, but I'm us'herly called Judy,' said the red beret.

Rhoda carefully folded the little coat and put it on her Welsh dresser. 'I must cook potatoes,' she said.

'Oh, let me help,' said Judy, eagerly. 'May I fill the saucepan? Where is it?'

'We have maids at home to cook our lunch,' said Jane, mildly, watching these preparations. She had put her hat and coat on a chair, and now looked more than ever like a gnome. She had the shortest face and nose Rhoda had ever seen, framed in a streaked straw bob. Harry was red and round, and his voice was strident. He said little, but what he said was to the point.

'Is Jane really your sister? You are so fair and she is so dark — like Snow White and Rosy Red. Where do you live?' asked Rhoda, half an hour later, as she and Judy were laying the cloth. Her curiosity refused to lie down and behave politely, even though she was the hostess.

'Yes, she is, really. Oh, we live a long way away from here. I don't expect you would know it,' said Judy, vague as the organizer of a charity matinée. 'Look! Jane has dropped her apple core on your pretty rug. Do you mind?'

'No,' said Rhoda. Nor did she. The kitchen smelled of roast chicken, burnt fir branches (for they had, of course, lit the candles), hot wax, and raspberry jam. Rhoda, putting plates on the table, wondered if it were really only an hour ago that she had felt lonely and bored.

Judy was darting about the kitchen like an elfin actress, fastidiously selecting forks, making her fingers hover undecidedly over spoons and glasses, shaking her dark hair back from her face. Rhoda, watching rather sadly, thought she had seldom seen prettier or more self-conscious actions. She wondered more and more what Judy's mother could be like.

Amid a pleasant scramble Rhoda got the three of them seated at her kitchen table. The white snowlight lit up the two absorbed, innocent faces turned towards the window, and made a background for Judy's dark head. Rhoda looked round at the three of them, blessing the chance that had brought them to her doorstep on Christmas morning, and wondered, as she minced chicken for Harry, whether they would stay the night, who they could possibly be, and – a more serious thought – whether some poor mother was spending a terrible Christmas Day somewhere looking for them.

Yet, beyond her one question to Judy and Judy's casual avoidance of a direct answer, she could not bring herself to ask them bluntly who they were and where they lived. After all, they were her guests, though self-invited. They had thrown themselves on her mercy. She felt she could not take advantage of their childish state and behave to them as a grown-up person. She had to meet them on their own ground. It was delightful to have them at her table, filling her carefully-furnished kitchen with the noise of their merry voices and their polite laughter at her jokes and giggles at their own.

'Is this turkey?' demanded Harry, presently.

'No, darling; it's chicken. Don't you like it?' asked foolish Rhoda, anxiously.

'No. More please,' said Harry.

'You are silly, Harry,' said Jane. 'Saying "No, you don't

like it," and then asking if you can have some more. Isn't he silly, Judy?'

'He's only little,' from Judy, patronizingly. 'Don't worry him.'

'If we were at home we *should* be having turkey, but this is much nicer,' said Jane. Judy's foot stealthily knocked against hers under the table.

'No, Jane, we shouldn't be having turkey. Our step-mother wouldn't let us, would she?'

'No, I s'pose she wouldn't. She's very crool,' said Jane, influenced by the kick and by Judy's meaning nod.

Rhoda had decided that it was not quite fair to show her disbelief in the step-mother legend, so she joined in politely with—

'How disgraceful. Doesn't she even let you have turkey on Christmas Day?'

'No. She's *awful*, isn't she, Jane?'

'Yes, simply *awful*,' agreed Jane. 'Isn't she awful, Harry?' suddenly giggling into Harry's neck.

'Don't. Old man wiv scizzors,' said Harry, whose mind was evidently still at work on the pictures in the Nonsuch Blake at which he had been looking.

After Rhoda's little Christmas pudding had been greeted with cries of delight, 'Oh, isn't it *little!*' 'It's the littlest pudding I ever saw!' and eaten, Rhoda had to confess that she had no crystallized fruits or crackers, so they must light the Christmas tree again and then play games.

This suggestion was welcomed with rapture, and Judy, as the eldest, lit six of the little candles, and Jane and Harry lit the remaining six. Rhoda lifted Harry

up, putting her cheek for a moment against his warm
head.

Darkness was beginning to fall, and the snow gleamed in
its own ghostly light under the deepening blue of the sky.

Now the Christmas tree was all alight, the candles burnt
still and pointed against the green branches. Three little
faces were turned up to the tree, with the candlelight
making aureoles round their hair. They were silent, staring
up at the beautiful, half-despoiled little tree.

'Oh,' thought Rhoda, looking at them, 'that's how it
should have been last night! It looks *right* now, somehow.
Darlings . . . how glad I am I had it here, ready for
them . . .'

The entranced pause was broken by a loud knock at
the front door.

Judy flew round, her eyes dilated.

'Who's that? That's some one come for us! We won't
go! Tell them to go away! I *like* being here! I won't go
home!'

'It's Daddy,' said Jane, resignedly. 'I knew they'd find us,
Judy. I told you so.'

'I lit free cangles by myself,' said Harry, holding up the
stump of his match.

Rhoda, smoothing her fingers across her straying hair,
with a distressed look on her face, was halfway to the door
when Judy came flying down the passage after her, and
locked her arms round her waist.

'Don't tell! Don't tell about the step-mother,' she
implored in a frightened whisper, lifting a white, distorted
little face in the dusk. 'I made it up. I made it all up, and

Daddy said I was never to make anything up again – *ever*. We saw your little tree all lit up in the window last night, when Daddy was driving us back from London. We wanted to see your little tree. We've never had a *little* tree at home. Everything's so *big*. It's horrid. We haven't got any mother – Jane and I haven't. Promise you won't tell about the step-mother? Promise – promise!'

Her grip tightened round Rhoda's waist, her eyes, enormous with terror, stared up imploringly. The knock was repeated, twice, louder, and impatiently.

'No, darling. Of course I won't tell. I promise faithfully, Judy. Now let me go, darling. Take your arms away, there's a dear little girl!'

Judy darted her a look of passionate gratitude and flew back to the kitchen. Rhoda, her heart beating unpleasantly, opened the front door.

The man standing there saw a tall woman, silhouetted against a candle-lit passage, and noticed how white her hand was against the door handle. He took off his hat.

'Good evening. I'm sorry to disturb you, but I suppose you don't happen to have seen my two daughters and my nephew, do you? My name's Woodhouse. We live up at Monkswell. The three of them have been missing since just after breakfast, and their aunt's nearly frantic. The eldest girl's got on a red tam-o'-shanter, I believe—'

'Yes. They're in here, with me,' Rhoda interrupted the uncultured but pleasant voice, and stood aside to let him enter. Over his big shoulder she saw a long saloon car blocking the lane at the foot of her garden. 'Won't you come in? I'm so sorry . . . you must have had a terrible day. They've been quite safe, of course, but I couldn't get out of them where they lived or to whom they belonged.'

'Ah! Judy romancing again, I suppose.'

He came forward into the candlelight. Tall, middle-aged, prosperous; clever eyes, weak mouth, good chin. Not a gentleman. I like him. Rhoda's usually well-ordered thoughts raced confusedly.

'Judy should make her fortune out of writing best-sellers when she is older,' she said, stopping just outside the kitchen door, which had been carefully closed by the strategists within; 'but I am sure you will not scold her for romancing to-day. She is very penitent, and they have all been so good and so happy.'

'They had a Christmas tree the size of a house at home, and any amount of presents – all the usual things children expect at Christmas,' he interrupted, roughly. 'Why should they come down here, bothering you? It's intolerable. They get more out of hand every week. Their aunt can't do anything with them, and I'm away all day, and most week-ends. Especially Judy. She's the most shameless little liar— And yet, you know,' his irritable expression suddenly changed, and his face became cautious, intelligent, as though he were weighing a problem – 'it isn't just lying. It's something quite different. She seems to need it, somehow. I haven't the heart to be very hard on her. I'm worried about Judy. She wants some one to look after her.'

He paused. 'Their mother died when Jane was born. It hasn't been a particularly cheerful household since. I suppose they both need looking after properly.'

There was another pause.

★ ★ ★

In that pause, filled with the soft light of the candles now burning low on the little Christmas tree, and with silence, his unsatisfied, clever eyes took in the fineness of Rhoda's ringless hands, the subtle and tender modelling of her mouth, and the irony which looked out like an armed sentinel from her eyes.

But it seemed to him a sentinel who might be persuaded, one day, to lay aside its weapon.

'Well,' said Rhoda, lightly, at last, 'shall we go in to the children?'

Christmas at Cold Comfort Farm

It was Christmas Eve. Dusk, a filthy mantle, lay over Sussex when the Reverend Silas Hearsay, Vicar of Howling, set out to pay his yearly visit to Cold Comfort Farm. Earlier in the afternoon he had feared he would not be Guided to go there, but then he had seen a crate of British Port-type wine go past the Vicarage on the grocer's boy's bicycle, and it could only be going, by that road, to the farmhouse. Shortly afterwards he was Guided to go, and set out upon his bicycle.

The Starkadders, of Cold Comfort Farm, had never got the hang of Christmas, somehow, and on Boxing Day there was always a run on the Howling Pharmacy for lint, bandages, and boracic powder. So the Vicar was going up there, as he did every year, to show them the ropes a bit. (It must be explained that these events took place some years before the civilizing hand of Flora Poste had softened and reformed the Farm and its rude inhabitants.)

After removing two large heaps of tussocks which blocked the lane leading to the Farm and thereby releasing a flood of muddy, icy water over his ankles, the Vicar wheeled his machine on towards the farmhouse, reflecting that those tussocks had never fallen there from the dung-cart of Nature. It was clear that someone did not want him to come to the place. He pushed his bicycle savagely up the hill, muttering.

The farmhouse was in silence and darkness. He pulled the ancient hell-bell (once used to warn excommunicated persons to stay away from Divine Service) hanging outside the front door, and waited.

For a goodish bit nothing happened. Suddenly a window far above his head was flung open and a voice wailed into the twilight—

'No! No! No!'

And the window slammed shut again.

'You're making a mistake, I'm sure,' shouted the Vicar, peering up into the webby thongs of the darkness. 'It's me. The Rev. Silas Hearsay.'

There was a pause. Then—

'Beant you postman?' asked the voice, rather embarrassed.

'No, no, of course not; come, come!' laughed the Vicar, grinding his teeth.

'I be comin',' retorted the voice. 'Thought it were postman after his Christmas Box.' The window slammed again. After a very long time indeed the door suddenly opened and there stood Adam Lambsbreath, oldest of the farm servants, peering up at the Reverend Hearsay by the light of a lonely rushdip (so called because you dipped it in grease and rushed to wherever you were going before it went out).

'Is anyone at home? May I enter?' enquired the Vicar, entering, and staring scornfully round the desolate kitchen, at the dead blue ashes in the grate, the thick dust on hanch and beam, the feathers blowing about like fun everywhere.

Yet even here there were signs of Christmas, for a withered branch of holly stood in a shapeless vessel on the table. And Adam himself . . . there was something even more peculiar than usual about him.

'Are you ailing, man?' asked the Vicar irritably, kicking a chair out of the way and perching himself on the edge of the table.

'Nay, Rev., I be niver better,' piped the old man. '*The older the berry, The more it makes merry.*'

'Then why,' thundered the Vicar, sliding off the table and walking on tiptoe towards Adam with his arms held at full length above his head, 'are you wearing three of Mrs Starkadder's red shawls?'

Adam stood his ground.

'I mun have a red courtepy, master. Can't be Santa Claus wi'out a red courtepy,' he said. 'Iverybody knows that. Ay, the hand o' Fate lies heavy on us all, Christmas and all the year round alike, but I thought I'd bedight meself as Santa Claus, so I did, just to please me little Elfine. And this night at midnight I be goin' around fillin' the stockin's, if I'm spared.'

The Vicar laughed contemptuously.

'So that were why I took three o' Mrs Starkadder's red shawls,' concluded Adam.

'I suppose you have never thought of God in terms of Energy? No, it is too much to expect.' The Reverend Hearsay re-seated himself on the table and glanced at his watch. 'Where in Energy's name *is* everybody? I have to be at the Assembly Rooms to read a paper on *The Future of The Father Fixation* at eight, and I've got to feed first. If nobody's coming, I'd rather go.'

'Won't ee have a dram o' swede wine first?' a deep voice asked, and a tall woman stepped over the threshold, followed by a little girl of twelve or so with yellow hair and clear, beautiful features. Judith Starkadder dropped her hat on the floor and leant against the table, staring listlessly at the Vicar.

'No swede wine, I thank you,' snapped the Reverend Hearsay. He glanced keenly round the kitchen in search of the British Port-type, but there was no sign of it. 'I came up to discuss an article with you and yours. An article in *Home Anthropology*.'

''Twere good of ee, Reverend,' she said tiredly.

'It is called *Christmas: From Religious Festival to Shopping Orgy*. Puts the case for Peace and Good Will very sensibly. Both good for trade. What more can you want?'

'Nothing,' she said, leaning her head on her hand.

'But I see,' the Vicar went on furiously, in a low tone and glaring at Adam, 'that here, as everywhere else, the usual childish wish-fantasies are in possession. Stars, shepherds, mangers, stockings, fir-trees, puddings . . . Energy help you all! I wish you good night, and a prosperous Christmas.'

He stamped out of the kitchen, and slammed the door after him with such violence that he brought a slate down on his back tyre and cut it open, and he had to walk home, arriving there too late for supper before setting out for Godmere.

After he had gone, Judith stared into the fire without speaking, and Adam busied himself with scraping the mould from a jar of mincemeat and picking some things which had fallen into it out of a large crock of pudding which he had made yesterday.

21

Elfine, meanwhile, was slowly opening a small brown paper parcel which she had been nursing, and at last revealed a small and mean-looking doll dressed in a sleazy silk dress and one under-garment that did not take off. This she gently nursed, talking to it in a low, sweet voice.

'Who gave you that, child?' asked her mother idly.

'I told you, mother. Uncle Micah and Aunt Rennett and Aunt Prue and Uncle Harkaway and Uncle Ezra.'

'Treasure it. You will not get many such.'

'I know, mother; I do. I love her very much, dear, dear Caroline,' and Elfine gently put a kiss on the doll's face.

'Now, missus, have ee got the Year's Luck? Can't make puddens wi'out the Year's Luck,' said Adam, shuffling forward.

'It's somewhere here. I forget—'

She turned her shabby handbag upside down, and there fell out on the table the following objects:

A small coffin-nail.

A menthol cone.

Three bad sixpences.

A doll's cracked looking-glass.

A small roll of sticking-plaster.

Adam collected these objects and ranged them by the pudding basin.

'Ay, them's all there,' he muttered. 'Him as gets the sticking-plaster'll break a limb; the menthol cone means as you'll be blind wi' headache, the bad coins means as you'll lose all yer money, and him as gets the coffin-nail will die afore the New Year. The mirror's seven years' bad luck for someone. Aie! In ye go, curse ye!' and he tossed the objects into the pudding, where they were not easily nor long distinguishable from the main mass.

'Want a stir, missus? Come, Elfine, my popelot, stir long, stir firm, your meat to earn,' and he handed her the butt of an old rifle, once used by Fig Starkadder in the Gordon Riots.

Judith turned from the pudding with what is commonly described as a gesture of loathing, but Elfine took the rifle butt and stirred the mixture once or twice.

'Ay, now tes all mixed,' said the old man, nodding with satisfaction. 'To-morrer we'll boil un fer a good hour, and un'll be done.'

'Will an hour be enough?' said Elfine. 'Mrs Hawk-Monitor up at Hautcouture Hall boils hers for eight hours, and another four on Christmas Day.'

'How do ee know?' demanded Adam. 'Have ee been runnin' wi' that young goosepick Mus' Richard again?'

'You shut up. He's awfully decent.'

''Tisn't decent to run wi' a young popelot all over the Downs in all weathers.'

'Well, it isn't any of your business, so shut up.'

After an offended pause, Adam said:

'Well, niver fret about puddens. None of 'em here has iver tasted any puddens but mine, and they won't know no different.'

At midnight, when the farmhouse was in darkness save for the faint flame of a nightlight burning steadily beside the bed of Harkaway, who was afraid of bears, a dim shape might have been seen moving stealthily along the corridor from bedroom to bedroom. It wore three red shawls pinned over its torn nightshirt and carried over its shoulder a nose-bag (the property of Viper the gelding), distended with parcels. It was Adam, bent on putting into the stockings of the Starkadders the presents which he had made or bought with his savings. The presents were chiefly swedes, beetroots, mangel-wurzels and turnips, decorated with coloured ribbons and strips of silver paper from tea packets.

'Ay,' muttered the old man, as he opened the door of the room where Meriam, the hired girl, was sleeping over the Christmas week. 'An apple for each will make 'em retch, a couple o' nuts will warm their wits.'

The next instant he stepped back in astonishment. There was a light in the room and there, sitting bolt upright in bed beside her slumbering daughter, was Mrs Beetle.

Mrs Beetle looked steadily at Adam, for a minute or two. Then she observed:

'Some 'opes.'

'Nay, niver say that, soul,' protested Adam, moving to the bedrail where hung a very fully-fashioned salmon-pink silk stocking with ladders all down it. "Tisn't so. Ee do know well that I looks on the maidy as me own child.'

Mrs Beetle gave a short laugh and adjusted a curler. 'You better not let Agony 'ear you, 'intin' I dunno wot,' said Mrs Beetle. "Urry up and put yer rubbish in there, I want me sleep out; I got to be up at cock-wake ter-morrer.'

Adam put a swede, an apple and a small pot in the stocking and was tip-toeing away when Mrs Beetle, raising her head from the pillow, inquired:

'Wot's that you've give 'er?'

'Eye-shadow,' whispered Adam hoarsely, turning at the door.

'*Wot?*' hissed Mrs Beetle, inclining her head in an effort to hear. ''Ave you gorn crackers?'

'Eye-shadow. To put on the maidy's eyes. 'Twill give that touch o' glamour as be irresistible; it do say so on pot.'

'Get out of 'ere, you old trouble-maker! Don't she 'ave enough bother resistin' as it is, and then you go and give 'er . . . 'ere, wait till I—' and Mrs Beetle was looking around for something to throw as Adam hastily retreated.

'And I'll lay you ain't got no present fer me, ter make matters worse,' she called after him.

Silently he placed a bright new tin of beetle-killer on the washstand and shuffled away.

His experiences in the apartments of the other Starkadders were no more fortunate, for Seth was busy with a friend and was so furious at being interrupted that he threw his riding-boots at the old man, Luke and Mark had locked their door and could be heard inside roaring with laughter at Adam's discomfiture, and Amos was praying, and did not even get up off his knees or open his eyes as he discharged at Adam the goat-pistol which he kept ever by his bed. And everybody else had such enormous holes in their stockings that the small presents Adam put in them fell through on to the floor along with the big ones, and when the Starkadders got up in the morning and rushed round to the foot of the bed to see what Santa had brought, they stubbed their toes on the turnips and swedes and walked on the smaller presents and smashed them to smithereens.

So what with one thing and another everybody was in

an even worse temper than usual when the family assem-
bled round the long table in the kitchen for the Christmas
dinner about half-past two the next afternoon. They would
all have sooner been in some place else, but Mrs Ada Doom
(Grandmother Doom, known as Grummer) insisted on
them all being there, and as they did not want her to go
mad and bring disgrace on the House of Starkadder, there
they had to be.

One by one they came in, the men from the fields with
soil on their boots, the women fresh from hennery and
duck filch with eggs in their bosoms that they gave to
Mrs Beetle who was just making the custard. Everybody
had to work as usual on Christmas Day, and no one had
troubled to put on anything handsomer than their usual
workaday clouts stained with mud and plough-oil. Only
Elfine wore a cherry-red jersey over her dark skirt and
had pinned a spray of holly on herself. An aunt, a distant
aunt named Mrs Poste, who lived in London, had unex-
pectedly sent her the pretty jersey. Prue and Letty had
stuck sixpenny artificial posies in their hair, but they only
looked wild and queer.

At last all were seated and waiting for Ada Doom.

'Come, come, mun we stick here like jennets i' the
trave?' demanded Micah at last. 'Amos, Reuben, do ee
carve the turkey. If so be as we wait much longer, 'twill
be shent, and the sausages, too.'

Even as he spoke, heavy footsteps were heard approaching
the head of the stairs, and everybody at once rose to their
feet and looked towards the door.

The low-ceilinged room was already half in dusk, for it
was a cold, still Christmas Day, without much light in the

grey sky, and the only other illumination came from the dull fire, half-buried under a tass of damp kindling.

Adam gave a last touch to the pile of presents, wrapped in hay and tied with bast, which he had put round the foot of the withered thorn-branch that was the traditional Starkadder Christmas-tree, hastily rearranged one of the tufts of sheep's-wool that decorated its branches, straightened the raven's skeleton that adorned its highest branch in place of a fairy-doll or star, and shuffled into his place just as Mrs Doom reached the foot of the stairs, leaning on her daughter Judith's arm. Mrs Doom struck at him with her stick in passing as she went slowly to the head of the table.

'Well, well. What are we waiting for? Are you all mishooden?' she demanded impatiently as she seated herself. 'Are you all here? All? Answer me!' banging her stick.

'Ay, Grummer,' rose the low, dreary drone from all sides of the table. 'We be all here.'

'Where's Seth?' demanded the old woman, peering sharply on either side of the long row.

'Gone out,' said Harkaway briefly, shifting a straw in his mouth.

'What for?' demanded Mrs Doom.

There was an ominous silence.

'He said he was going to fetch something, Grandmother,' at last said Elfine.

'Ay. Well, well, no matter, so long as he comes soon. Amos, carve the bird. Ay, would it were a vulture, 'twere more fitting! Reuben, fling these dogs the fare my bounty provides. Sausages . . . pah! Mince-pies . . . what a black-bitter mockery it all is! Every almond, every raisin, is wrung from the dry, dying soil and paid for with sparse greasy notes grudged alike by bank and buyer. Come, Ezra, pass the ginger wine! Be gay, spawn! Laugh, stuff yourselves, gorge and forget, you rat-heaps! Rot you all!' and she fell back in her chair, gasping and keeping one eye on the British Port-type that was now coming up the table.

'Tes one of her bad days,' said Judith tonelessly. 'Amos, will you pull a cracker wi' me? We were lovers . . . once.'

'Hush, woman.' He shrank back from the proffered treat. 'Tempt me not wi' motters and paper caps. Hell is paved wi' such.' Judith smiled bitterly and fell silent.

Reuben, meanwhile, had seen to it that Elfine got the best bit off the turkey (which is not saying much) and had filled her glass with Port-type wine and well-water.

The turkey gave out before it got to Letty, Prue, Susan, Phœbe, Jane and Rennett, who were huddled together at the foot of the table, and they were making do with brussels-sprouts as hard as bullets drenched with weak gravy, and home-brewed braket. There was silence in the kitchen except for the sough of swallowing, the sudden suck of drinking.

'WHERE IS SETH?' suddenly screamed Mrs Doom, flinging down her turkey-leg and glaring round.

Silence fell; everyone moved uneasily, not daring to speak in case they provoked an outburst. But at that moment the cheerful, if unpleasant, noise of a motor-cycle was heard outside, and in another moment it stopped at the kitchen door. All eyes were turned in that direction, and in another moment in came Seth.

'Well, Grummer! Happen you thought I was lost!' he cried impudently, peeling off his boots and flinging them at Meriam, the hired girl, who cowered by the fire gnawing a sausage skin.

Mrs Doom silently pointed to his empty seat with the turkey-leg, and he sat down.

'She hev had an outhees. Ay, 'twas terrible,' reproved Judith in a low tone as Seth seated himself beside her.

'Niver mind, I ha' something here as will make her chirk like a mellet,' he retorted, and held up a large brown paper parcel. 'I ha' been to the Post Office to get it.'

'Ah, gie it me! Aie, my lost pleasurings! Tes none I get, nowadays; gie it me now!' cried the old woman eagerly.

'Nay, Grummer. Ee must wait till pudden time,' and the young man fell on his turkey ravenously.

When everyone had finished, the women cleared away and poured the pudding into a large dusty dish, which they bore to the table and set before Judith.

'Amos? Pudding?' she asked listlessly. 'In a glass or on a plate?'

'On plate, on plate, woman,' he said feverishly bending forward with a fierce glitter in his eye. 'Tes easier to see the Year's Luck so.'

A stir of excitement now went through the company, for everybody looked forward to seeing everybody else drawing ill-luck from the symbols concealed in the pudding. A fierce, attentive silence fell. It was broken by a wail from Reuben—

'The coin – the coin! Wala wa!' and he broke into deep, heavy sobs. He was saving up to buy a tractor, and the coin meant, of course, that he would lose all his money during the year.

'Never mind, Reuben, dear,' whispered Elfine, slipping

an arm round his neck. 'You can have the penny father gave me.'

Shrieks from Letty and Prue now announced that they had received the menthol cone and the sticking-plaster, and a low mutter of approval greeted the discovery by Amos of the broken mirror.

Now there was only the coffin-nail, and a ghoulish silence fell on everybody as they dripped pudding from their spoons in a feverish hunt for it; Ezra was running his through a tea-strainer.

But no one seemed to have got it.

'Who has the coffin-nail? Speak, you draf-saks!' at last demanded Mrs Doom.

'Not I.' 'Nay.' 'Niver sight nor snitch of it,' chorussed everybody.

'Adam!' Mrs Doom turned to the old man. 'Did you put the coffin-nail into the pudding?'

'Ay, mistress, that I did – didn't I, Mis' Judith, didn't I, Elfine, my liddle lovesight?'

'He speaks truth for once, mother.'

'Yes, he did, Grandmother. I saw him.'

'*Then where is it?*' Mrs Doom's voice was low and terrible and her gaze moved slowly down the table, first on one side and then the other, in search of signs of guilt, while everyone cowered over their plates.

Everyone, that is, except Mrs Beetle, who continued to eat a sandwich that she had taken out of a cellophane wrapper, with every appearance of enjoyment.

'Carrie Beetle!' shouted Mrs Doom.

'I'm 'ere,' said Mrs Beetle.

'Did you take the coffin-nail out of the pudding?'

'Yes, I did.' Mrs Beetle leisurely finished the last crumb of sandwich and wiped her mouth with a clean handkerchief. 'And will again, if I'm spared till next year.'

'You . . . you . . . you . . .' choked Mrs Doom, rising in her chair and beating the air with her clenched fists. 'For two hundred years . . . Starkadders . . . coffin-nails in puddings . . . and now . . . you . . . dare . . .'

'Well, I 'ad enough of it las' year,' retorted Mrs Beetle. 'That pore old soul Earnest Dolour got it, as well you may remember—'

'That's right. Cousin Earnest,' nodded Mark Dolour. 'Got a job workin' on the oil-field down Henfield way. Good money, too.'

'Thanks to me, if he 'as,' retorted Mrs Beetle. 'If I 'adn't put it up to you, Mark Dolour, you'd 'ave let 'im die. All of you was 'angin' over the pore old soul waitin' for 'im to 'and in 'is dinner pail, and Micah (wot's old enough to know better, 'eaven only knows) askin' 'im could 'e 'ave 'is wrist-watch if anything was to 'appen to 'im . . . it fair got me down. So I says to Mark, why don't yer go down and 'ave a word with Mr Earthdribble the undertaker in Howling and get 'im to tell Earnest it weren't a proper coffin-nail at all, it were a throw-out, so it didn't count. The bother we 'ad! Shall I ever fergit it! Never again, I says to meself. So this year there ain't no coffin-nail. I fished it out o' the pudden meself. Parss the water, please.'

'Where is it?' whispered Mrs Doom, terribly. 'Where is this year's nail, woman?'

'Down the—' Mrs Beetle checked herself, and coughed, 'down the well,' concluded Mrs Beetle firmly.

'Niver fret, Grummer, I'll get it up fer ee! Me and the

water voles, we can dive far and deep!' and Urk rushed
from the room, laughing wildly.

'There ain't no need,' called Mrs Beetle after him. 'But
anything to keep you an' yer rubbishy water voles out of
mischief!' And Mrs Beetle went into a cackle of laughter,
alternately slapping her knee and Caraway's arm, and
muttering, 'Oh, cor, wait till I tell Agony! "Dive far and
deep." Oh, cor!' After a minute's uneasy silence—

'Grummer.' Seth bent winningly towards the old woman,
the large brown paper parcel in his hand. 'Will you see
your present now?'

'Aye, boy, aye. Let me see it. You're the only one that
has thought of me, the only one.'

Seth was undoing the parcel, and now revealed a
large book, handsomely bound in red leather with gilt
lettering.

'There, Grummer. 'Tis the year's numbers o' *The Milk
Producers' Weekly Bulletin and Cowkeepers' Guide*. I collected
un for ee, and had un bound. Art pleased?'

'Ay. 'Tis handsome enough. A graceful thought,' muttered
the old lady, turning the pages. Most of them were pretty
battered, owing to her habit of rolling up the paper and
hitting anyone with it who happened to be within reach.
''Tis better so. 'Tis heavier. Now I can *throw* it.'

The Starkadders so seldom saw a clean and handsome
object at the farmhouse (for Seth was only handsome) that
they now crept round, fascinated, to examine the book
with murmurs of awe. Among them came Adam, but no
sooner had he bent over the book than he recoiled from
it with a piercing scream.

'Aie! . . . aie! aie!'

'What's the matter, dotard?' screamed Mrs Doom, jabbing at him with the volume. 'Speak, you kaynard!'

'Tes calf! Tes bound in calf! And tes our Pointless's calf, as she had last Lammastide, as was sold at Godmere to Farmer Lust!' cried Adam, falling to the floor. At the same instant, Luke hit Micah in the stomach, Harkaway pushed Ezra into the fire, Mrs Doom flung the bound volume of *The Milk Producers' Weekly Bulletin and Cowkeepers' Guide* at the struggling mass, and the Christmas dinner collapsed into indescribable confusion.

In the midst of the uproar, Elfine, who had climbed on to the table, glanced up at the window as though seeking help, and saw a laughing face looking at her, and a hand in a yellow string glove beckoning with a riding-crop. Swiftly she darted down from the table and across the room, and out through the half-open door, slamming it after her.

Dick Hawk-Monitor, a sturdy boy astride a handsome pony, was out in the yard.

'Hallo!' she gasped. 'Oh, Dick, I am glad to see you!'

'I thought you never would see me – what on earth's the matter in there?' he asked curiously.

'Oh, never mind them, they're always like that. Dick, do tell me, what presents did you have?'

'Oh, a rifle, and a new saddle, and a fiver – lots of things. Look here, Elfine, you mustn't mind, but I brought you—'

He bent over the pony's neck and held out a sandwich box, daintily filled with slices of turkey, a piece of pudding, a tiny mince-pie and a crystallized apricot.

'Thought your dinner mightn't be very—' he ended gruffly.

'Oh, Dick, it's lovely! Darling little . . . what is it?'

'Apricot. Crystallized fruit. Look here, let's go up to the usual place, shall we? – and I'll watch you eat it.'

'But you must have some, too.'

'Man! I'm stoked up to the brim now! But I dare say I could manage a bit more. Here, you catch hold of Rob Roy, and he'll help you up the hill.'

He touched the pony with his heels and it trotted on towards the snow-streaked Downs, Elfine's yellow hair flying out like a shower of primroses under the grey sky of winter.

To Love and To Cherish

Mrs Carter was brushing her husband's hat. She stood in the wide hall of Clevedene watching Peter's reflection in the hall mirror as he got into his overcoat. The brush travelled lightly, obediently, over the hat.

This was about the five thousandth time she had brushed Peter's hat, and it was going to be the last. They had been married nearly twenty years, and she was tired of it, and tired of Peter. Quiet, complacent, lacking ambition and the saving grace of discontent that makes for progress, he had turned from an individual into the type of a million husbands. Mrs Carter was going to live her own life.

The brush skirted the discreet grey band, paused and tapped the brim to shake out any possible grain of dust.

'Thanks, dear.' For the five thousandth time Peter took the hat. She turned to hang the brush on its brass hook.

Peter was transferring a letter and some other papers from his inner pocket to his overcoat, where he kept things that were unimportant. He did this with scarcely a pang . . . now. For years he had been quietly suppressing dreams, ambitious, adventurous dreams of being his own master and launching out on his own, because to indulge them might mean discomfort and danger for his wife. He had a safe job.

But his ambition refused to die. Starved, suppressed, argued with and 'rationalized', it was still there. That was why he had not torn up a letter from a cousin who offered him a partnership in a flourishing little business. It was bound to succeed, his cousin said.

Peter had turned down two offers of partnership in the last ten years.

Mrs Carter held up her face for the good-bye peck.

The front door slammed.

Upstairs in her bedroom a few minutes later, the lipstick followed the movements of her hand as obediently as the hat brush; over the thin lower lip, pausing at the corners where dimples should have been, painting a cupid's bow on the upper lip. On the underlip the stick paused, tapping hesitantly.

Would she pass for thirty?

A month ago she would have taken it for granted that she did.

But now she could see that there were discontented lines round mouth and eyes and her skin was faded.

Her near-beaver coat hung over the bed-rail, with her real snakeskin shoes at the foot to keep it company. On the bed lay a hat in the newest shape, tilted over her eyes, with a veil over it. She put on a new dark blue dress.

The clock said ten to ten. London lay in the valley below the suburb where the Carters lived, veiled in smoke the colour of a pearl necklace by day, glittering by night with millions of soft tiny lights. She had hung over the distant city from her bedroom window until the picture was burnt into her mind.

Now she was going back to it.

She took a last look at the letter for Peter – square, white, uncompromising, on the dressing table.

As she hurried through the clean, prim streets to the station she thought of the good job she had had twenty years ago. Rather a pioneer among her 'set' she had been, in those days.

The streets were full of women – women with Alsatians on leashes, women with shopping baskets, women with cars, and women with children, women going off to golf with other women because their husbands had gone to London to work . . . She was going to London . . . to work.

She had answered five advertisements, and had had replies from three. Her first appointment was at 11.30. Evidently they liked her subdued blue paper, her monogram and good address. The Carters' suburb was a nice place to live in . . . only it wasn't London.

When she had worked for Gregory Hardy and earned three pounds a week she had had opportunities for meeting interesting men. She had met Peter through the office.

Peter had been an interesting man.

Had he? Or had she married him out of panic fear of loneliness and always having to work?

Peter found his cousin waiting for him in his private office when he arrived. He hung up his hat and coat, glancing at the clock. Even sales managers of big firms couldn't afford to be nearly fourteen minutes late. Damn that train . . .

His cousin, smiling easily, his time his own now — he had looked in at his own office — asked if he'd come to a decision yet?

Peter asked him to wait. He had to read his morning's mail.

Mrs Carter dropped her chin on to her suede-gloved hand, watching London coming nearer. What was the use of a home your friends envied if your soul was crushed? It was different for Peter; he liked a quiet life. She wanted excitement, gaiety, interesting people.

The train drew into Charing Cross.

She taxied to Cannon Street. Messrs. Archer, Stone, and Mead, solicitors, lived at the top of these dingy stairs, up which she ran with the colour rising under her powder in ugly patches.

But — there were others! Other women, after *her* job, in the waiting-room. *And they were all young.*

Young, impudent eyes under those cute little turbans, which certainly were trying if you were over twenty. Figures slender with natural youth, not dieting and exercise.

The advertisement had said 'under thirty' but she had ignored that. These solicitor people wanted an educated, intelligent, confidential secretary, and she was both. Age did not matter. She had been sure she could make them see that . . .

Only now she was not so sure.

One of the slim little girls made room for her.

She sat down, too nervous to repair the damage to her complexion.

The door opened. A clerk said: 'Miss Holroyd.'

She got up nervously and crossed the room, conscious of critical young eyes.

She was entering a big, light, bare room. Facing a big man, sitting at a desk. A voice said:

'Won't you sit down, Miss – er –' (a glance at a list – so quick as to be almost unnoticed) '– Holroyd?'

She sat down, trembling. The light poured down from a high window full on her face. He looked across at her, impersonal, businesslike.

She had had some vague thought of enchanting her prospective employer with her personality, breaking the formality of the interview with a warm, intimate note. The poor little hope wavered and died.

'Let me see,' he began, looking at his list more openly this time. 'Your shorthand speed is a hundred and twenty, I think you said. That's a little lower than we require. The work here is heavy, and full of legal terms. What is your typing?'

Had she forgotten to say? What speed was one's typing, if one was an intelligent and educated candidate for a confidential secretary-ship? Gregory Hardy had never asked her that.

'I'm afraid I don't know,' she faltered, in her light, tonelessly refined voice. 'I'm pretty quick, I know. My late employer—'

'And your age, Miss Holroyd?' he interrupted. His eyes were now wandering curiously over the near-beaver coat, the little prosperous touches in bracelet and handbag.

'Thirty-one,' she said quickly. 'But that doesn't matter, if one is quick and willing, does it? I've always been told I'm young for my age.'

That was her little personal touch. She essayed a timid smile into his eyes.

'But this advertisement expressly stated that applicants must be under thirty, preferably twenty-five to twenty-seven,' he interrupted her. 'I am afraid you've been wasting my time and yours, Miss Holroyd. I can't offer you anything. Sorry you've had your journey for nothing. Good morning.'

He was annoyed. His hand moved over to the bell, pressed, and a second later the clerk entered, and held open the door for her.

She rose. She was angry, not ashamed. She, a married woman, had been treated like one of those little chits in the waiting-room! She swept out of the room, holding her head, in that too-young hat, very high. Her cheeks blazed, and her hands trembled. She never once looked at the girls in the waiting-room. She had no definite thoughts until she found herself outside in Cannon Street at a quarter to twelve.

There were the shipping people in Leadenhall Street. They wanted to see her at twelve-fifteen. She beckoned a taxi.

In the taxi she powdered her flushed face, repaired the line of her lips, avoided her own eyes. She tried not to see that letter, square and white and conspicuous, propped up on her dressing table.

In the end Peter had to ask his cousin to meet him for lunch, to talk it over.

The big room where they lunched was full of men talking things over, with steaks or omelettes (according to digestions) in front of them.

Peter had £2,500 saved; and his cousin wanted every penny of it. He said it would come back as three thousand . . . four thousand five hundred . . . and so on . . . in the second and third years of partnership. Peter was a fool to think twice.

But Peter was thinking twice; of the little car, Carrie's near-beaver coat, the yearly holiday, the subscription to the golf club, their pretty house ('my beautiful home,' Carrie called it to her acquaintances), their quiet, well-ordered life.

Carrie never seemed to want anything more ambitious . . . but she was different.

He shook his head as his cousin talked . . . as he had shaken it at every stir of ambition for the past fifteen years.

Mrs Carter found it worse at Leadenhall Street. The man was short and red and he barked at her. Before she knew where she was, she had been given a sheet of paper and told to take a shorthand test. The words – long, unfamiliar, technical words – flowed from his lips in a smooth steady stream . . . faster . . . faster . . .

'Oh, please!' she interrupted piteously. 'Can you go a little slower?'

He glanced up at her sharply, but slowed the stream down a little. He was impressed by the near-beaver coat and her prosperous air.

The words stopped suddenly.

'Now read back,' he said, and leaned back to listen.

But she couldn't. After the first few words there was nothing on the paper but a few meaningless scrawls. And she couldn't even put up a pretence at remembering. It was awful. Her voice faltered . . . died . . .

'M'afraid you won't do for us,' he was saying, with an undertone of satisfaction. 'Too slow. Must have a girl who can take notes very fast. What system do you use?'

She murmured the name of the system that had sufficed for Gregory Hardy's letters.

He shook his head.

'Out of date. Always use Wegg's here. Other may have been all right ten years ago. No good now. 'Morning.'

She was outside again. Half-past twelve.

Other women's children would be coming home from school now. She had never had any. She had always dreaded being tied down by children.

Back in the office, after lunch. Peter's cousin had left him irritably, declaring he was a fool. But the offer was still open. There was time. He could telephone and accept. No more catching the eight-forty; no more secret ache of suppressed ambition.

He picked up a morning paper. On the back page there was an announcement of a sale that afternoon; a gem of a Georgian house in Hereford. Later on, he might be able to buy a house like that . . . if he accepted. But the thing was a gamble, and he could not indulge himself in a gambler's throw, because of Carrie.

He sighed and glanced at the clock. Nearly three – the weariest hour of the day. Routine . . . routine . . . He bent his head over his correspondence as the typist came in with letters for signature.

Mrs Carter saw the letter again – square, white and conspicuous, propped up on her dressing table. She took

out the third reply, from the theatrical agent. He wanted
to see her at 5.15 . . . Hours to fill up . . . hours and hours.
No use going to the hotel she had planned to stay at that
night. She'd meant to ask Peter to send her things on . . .

She went into a tea shop and sipped some coffee. The
world was crumbling about her. London was too enormous,
too busy and cruel. There didn't seem to be much place
for women of forty-three who had tried to come back.
What was it she had said in her letter to Peter?

For twenty years our life has been a mockery of
happiness. I want to develop my individuality, to be free,
like other women, and live my own life. I want to
escape from this cramping, dull existence that is killing
me. It may content you, but it is death to me. You're
different . . .

She finished her coffee, paid her bill and wandered out
into the street again. She dropped into a cinema for an
hour or so, but saw little of the show. Doubt was beginning to creep over her. Suppose she couldn't get a job?

Ten past five, in Covent Garden. The atmosphere was
different here; more exciting. A girl ushered her in; a really
lovely girl, with stockings the colour of black grapes and
a black frock.

Mr Meyerstein wanted a gal to see the young ladies
who came after jobs in his touring companies. She must
be tactful – and here Mr Meyerstein blew a cloud of smoke
straight up above his head – and she must be firm and
smart. He didn't think Miss Holroyd looked the type. How
old was she?

Miss Holroyd was thirty-one.

'No, dear, you aren't,' said Mr Meyerstein, pleasantly, running his kind, shrewd eyes over her faded prettiness. 'Give it another ten years. Now you've wasted five minutes of my time, and I'm a busy man this morning, but I'll forgive you. Run along and don't do it again.'

Outside again, in Covent Garden. Her trembling hands straightened the hat on her forehead. She could see nothing now but the letter.

'YOU MAY TELEPHONE FROM HERE.'

It caught her glance as it hung outside a tobacconist's shop. She crossed the road, entered the shop. She gave her own number.

A pause. Her heart beat so that she could scarcely breathe. Suppose he'd come home early? Then she would have burnt her boats for ever and ever . . . there would be scenes . . . endless, awful rows, into which relatives and friends would be dragged.

'Hullo . . . hullo . . . is that you, Grace? Mrs Carter speaking. Oh, Grace, there's a letter addressed to Mr Carter on the dressing table in my room. You can't miss it; it's in a white envelope. I want you to put it in the top left-hand drawer of the dressing table, in my handkerchief case. Can you hear me?'

'Yes, ma'am. Put the letter addressed to Mr Carter on your dressing table in your handkerchief case.'

'That's right . . . don't forget. It's very important.' (The girl might be curious. Mrs Carter couldn't help that . . .)

She hung up the receiver and came out of the shop. It was half-past five. Time to get home and buy some mushrooms for dinner on the way. Peter liked them, and a good dinner might keep him from asking questions about the presumably idle day she had spent in town.

Peter Carter stopped to buy a bunch of late roses outside the station . . . a mute peace-offering because he had, for a day, thought of breaking up Carrie's safe, tranquil existence. After all, he had married her, and a man had to stick to his guns. Naturally, Carrie liked a settled life. She was getting on.

They met on the doorstep of Clevedene.

'Hello, dear.' He pecked at her cheek.

'Brought you some flowers.' And he thrust the tissuepaper wrapped, thorny, wet stems into her hand.

'Mind my frock, Peter. Thank you, dear. Had a busy day? I've got something for you, too. Mushrooms . . .'

The door of Clevedene closed.

The Murder Mark

It was vaguely noticed by those in Chesterbourne who noticed Mr Pavey at all that the old chemist's marriage was not a success.

It was not so unsuccessful that it could be called unhappy; but Mrs Pavey was discontented and inclined to despise her husband because he did not make more money, and his young daughter considered her father to be damp, dim and a back number.

Neither lady troubled to conceal what she thought about the head of the family.

Mr Pavey's business was not a consolation to him; it kept going, but that was all. The shop was in a narrow back street of the ancient Essex town and few customers found their way to it. Visitors and residents alike went either to the branch of a well-known firm in the High Street, or to Anders & Rockett, which had sold drugs in Market Square for some two hundred years. Between these two commercial poles languished E. Pavey, neither one thing nor the other.

And yet, unsatisfactorily though he was adjusted to love and work (as the psychiatrists would say) Mr Pavey had somehow managed to adjust himself to living, for he was not an unhappy man; indeed, his tranquil bearing and philosophic outlook were so marked as to increase his wife's and daughter's irritation with him.

'Anyone would think Dad didn't *care*,' was how they put it.

In fact, Mr Pavey was a Grand Master in that ancient and humble Lodge in which most of humanity is forced to enrol itself. He knew how to get the utmost out of the second-best.

The splendid rewards of life had marched by without sweeping him into their army of happily fulfilled beings; and now he was over sixty and the army would not march past a second time. However, there remained the loot scattered in its wake, and *there* he was a busy and contented gleaner.

He loved reading, and observing the odd, warmly natural habits of his fellows. He had an historical sense; he could feel himself strongly as a tiny part of old Chesterbourne's story. He loved to walk on a summer night to the ruins of the Roman camp above the town, and stand gazing down on the dim marshes, while he wondered how the scene had looked to a Roman soldier two thousand years dead.

He did not enjoy his food, because Mrs Pavey had a ladylike disdain for the art of cookery, but he enjoyed practising a little strictly amateur palmistry, and most of all he enjoyed his friendship with the writer of detective stories, Walter Niven.

Walter Niven was a Chesterbourne man, a solicitor who had become a celebrity late in life with a story called *The Test Match Murders*, which had walked easily into the delightful ranks of the minor classics. He created a detective who was also a professional cricketer, a likeable and credible chap without mannerisms, named 'E. R. J. Roberts.' Thousands of equally likeable and credible chaps at once took 'E. R. J. Roberts' to their bosoms, and so did their wives: and Mr Niven made a lot of money.

Nevertheless, he preferred to remain a private person, living quietly in Chesterbourne and increasing the modest pleasures of his home by sums from film rights, first and second serial rights, translation rights and dramatization rights, while Mrs Niven and the three young Nivens revelled in every halfpenny and second of his success.

Mr Niven had learned that people became self-conscious when they discovered that he was *the* Walter Niven, and began to pose and try to be interesting, with the disappointing result that they became far less interesting than they were before they began to try; so he never talked about his work, and trusted to his commonplace name and pleasant but undistinguished manner to conceal his fame. Usually it did.

Chesterbourne was proud of Walter Niven, of course, but it was a little disappointed that he did not 'look more like a writer.'

'You'd never think it, would you?' was how Chesterbourne put it. After a year or so it gave up behaving oddly in front of him and took him for granted, which was just what he wanted.

He continued to stroll about back streets, watching people and marvelling at them, and one evening he strolled into a chemist's to buy himself a comb and his youngest daughter some gelatine lozenges, of which she was fond.

Mr Pavey came out to serve him, carrying a half-open book called *The Secrets of the Palm*, and Mr Niven, attracted by the old chemist's tranquil expression and the piquant fact that so intelligent-looking a man should be reading a book with such a title, commented upon the volume. Thus their friendship began.

On two or three evenings a month during the winter Mr Niven would push open the door of the shop, setting its melancholy little bell a-tinkle, and the two would settle down in the room behind the shop to talk about history and palmistry, to please Mr Pavey; and once or twice in six weeks during the summer months Mr Pavey would push open Mr Niven's gate, with a laburnum in blossom above it, and the two would sit in deck-chairs in the garden talking about writing and cricket, to please Mr Niven.

They seldom talked about money, and never about personal relationships. Few women would have found anything worth listening to in those two middle-aged voices, cautiously expressing tentative opinions in the dusk.

One beautiful spring evening, the sad bell sounded as the door of Mr Pavey's shop opened, and in stepped Mr Niven, inhaling with pleasure the smell of ether (some one had just bought sixpennyworth to ease an aching tooth), scented soap and camomile flowers.

Mr Pavey came out from the parlour, peering into the dim shop with a half-open book as usual in his hand, and gave an exclamation of pleasure.

'Mr Niven! I thought you were in London. Can you stop for a bit? I'm alone this evening.'

'I got back this morning,' explained Mr Niven, stepping round the counter and following his friend into the parlour.

'And how's London?' Mr Pavey's tone was at once respectful and mocking, as a worldly-wise but virtuous uncle might ask after a rackety and beautiful niece.

'Very stimulating. Very exhausting.' Mr Niven lowered his square self into a chair. 'And very expensive.'

Mr Pavey's faint appreciative laugh floated from the kitchen at the back of the house where he was putting on the kettle. Mrs Pavey did not consider that her house-keeping money ran to sherry for the entertainment of visitors, though she knew that sherry was the proper thing to do. None better, but beggars can't be choosers, as she bitterly observed.

When the chemist came back with the tea-pot Mr Niven was studying the *Chesterbourne Echo*, which he had picked up.

'Nothing more about our friend "Jack,"' he remarked.

'And I don't imagine there will be, do you?' quietly answered Mr Pavey.

'No. I think the police want public interest in this murder to die down. Have you noticed that less and less space has been given to it? There was next to nothing in the London papers this morning.'

'You think the police are suppressing something, is that it?'

'Oh no, not necessarily that. But I think they want friend "Jack" to imagine that the fuss is over. Then he'll feel safe. He'll come out of his hole. And then . . . they'll get him.'

Niven bent down and put a spill between the bars of the sulky little fire, and lit his pipe.

'You see,' he went on, puffing, 'this isn't one of those

murders in which it's a help to the police to have the public on the look-out for a man.'

'Because they don't know what this man looks like?'

'Exactly. He might look like . . . you or me. There are a good many Jacks in England, I imagine. Two or three of them may even have a scratched wrist.'

'That's true.'

There was a pause. Mr Pavey said:

'But the police'll be carrying on with their usual routine behind the scenes, won't they?' His tone was admiring and a little smug; he seemed to be warming his hands at the glow of police efficiency and also recalling that he paid rates.

'Of course. Sifting every tiny scrap of information that might possibly lead to something definite, interviewing cranks, watching places . . .'

'Ah!' Mr Pavey's voice was a little dramatic under the pressure of his thoughts. 'It's said that they always come back to the place where they did it.'

'Then you'll have a good view when he does,' retorted his friend cheerfully, glancing upwards and over his shoulder, through the glass door of the shop.

Sunset lay faintly reflected across the blank window of a mean house directly opposite, where a white 'To Let' board stuck its head out of a black, sour area.

'They soon cleared out.' Mr Pavey's glance followed the writer's.

'I don't blame them.'

A pause.

'She was such a pretty girl,' said Mr Pavey suddenly. 'Millie – my wife, you know – said that she dyed her hair, but it was a lovely colour, very pale gold, and she always kept it so neat.'

'I know. I used to see her about, you know.'

'A pretty manner, too,' went on the old chemist pensively. 'It was a miserable business from the beginning . . . did you know the father?'

Niven shook his head. 'It all happened while I was in France.'

'Of course it did. I was forgetting.'

Silence again in the little, slowly darkening room.

'I suppose,' said Mr Pavey, 'when a lady . . . a girl who's gently born, I mean . . . takes to that sort of life it must be much, much worse . . .'

'Yes. She probably wasn't sorry to go.'

'And that being loyal to the man who killed her, not giving him away, I mean, that was part of her being a lady, too, I think. At least, I like to think so. A kind of nobility.'

'She probably loved him,' said Niven.

The shop bell rang and Mr Pavey went to answer it.

The writer leaned back in his chair with the tips of his fingers just touching, and stared into the heart of the fire while a deep fear and sadness for which there seemed no cause slowly crept over his spirit. It's the spring evening, he thought, and the ghostly light in this room from those windows opposite. Their last words, dealing with violence and death, seemed to float in the air like dark mist. He pulled at his pipe, steadily fighting the thought that his life was half-over, and meaningless at that; and the knowledge that the world was very, very old and would grow older.

It's a good thing, reflected Mr Niven, that I'm not the sort that spins two pages out of every mood I get. He sighed faintly and, rousing himself, glanced into the shop. The two voices there had been rising and falling for some time.

The shop was now brightly lit, and Mr Niven could see every object in it as clearly as though he were gazing into an aquarium.

The first object which he saw was a familiar one, yet so beautiful that as it broke upon his sight it seemed fantastic.

It was a long white hand, spread palm uppermost across the counter and showing pride in its own tapering beauty as plainly as pride is shown in the gorgeous tail of the peacock. Above it, gazing down at the hand with lowered eyelids and a slight smile on the lips, was a man's face, so pale that it seemed to glimmer under the shade of a fashionably square-crowned hat. Mr Pavey, bending over the hand, expressed interest and servility in the curve of his back as plainly as the man's lounging pose conveyed vanity.

That ought to be a wonderfully good-looking chap, was Mr Niven's first thought, but he isn't. There's something lacking. He's got all the signs of beauty – height, shape, features – but what is it that's wrong?

The writer stared coldly out of the darkness at Mr Pavey's unconscious customer, receiving the impression of his personality as indifferently as a mirror. Then, obediently, two words floated into his mind. Broken . . . stained. He nodded with satisfaction, staring. He looks as though a mainspring had gone somewhere, and as though he had been crawling through places that have marked him. Beastly-looking chap; pathetic, too, decided Mr Niven, shuddering suddenly as the ordinary human reaction to a personality suddenly replaced the detached curiosity of the writer.

Mr Pavey was moving. Unhurriedly, he turned his baldish head with a tortoise-like movement towards the dark door of the parlour, and called:

'Walter! Come here just a minute, will you?'

Mr Niven, obediently going forward into the light, felt mildly surprised. Mr Pavey had never before used his Christian name, any more than Mr Niven had addressed Mr Pavey as E (he supposed that E stood for Edward but had not troubled to inquire). This was a peculiar moment to choose. Was Pavey – well, showing off?

Mr Niven immediately suppressed this suspicion. Mr Pavey was not the showing-off kind. Nevertheless, the writer's manner was a shade cooler than usual as he glanced questioningly from one to the other.

'Such an interesting hand,' confided Mr Pavey cosily, looking up at Mr Niven. 'You can spare a minute to look at it, can't you? Your appointment isn't until half-past eight, I think you said?'

Mr Niven had no appointment. Nevertheless, he nodded. When given an irrelevant lead, follow it, was Mr Niven's rule. Often it led to a good plot or to some interesting sidelight upon human nature.

It suddenly struck him, as he made an appreciative mutter and gazed down at the beautiful hand, that Mr Pavey was giving him an excuse to slip away in a quarter of an hour if he wanted to, leaving Mr Pavey free to spend another hour reading the hand and discussing it with the obviously flattered and willing owner. Mr Pavey was an unusually sensitive and intelligent man, but palmistry (in which

Mr Niven had no faith) was his blind spot. If Mr Pavey really found this an interesting hand, it was no wonder that he called Mr Niven Walter and invented appointments for him. Everything but this hand and its alleged meaning would have gone out of his old head.

'Interesting, yes,' murmured Mr Niven obligingly, bending lower over the hand.

The stranger made a slight, deprecating movement. He had not said a word, and his lids were lowered so far over his eyes that he seemed asleep, while his thin, shapely lips were curved in that faint disdainful smile.

'I noticed what an unusual hand this gentleman has while I was counting out his change,' ran on Mr Pavey brightly, 'and I had the – the cheek, I suppose you might call it, to tell him what a wonderfully sensitive hand it is. My word, I said, there's some feeling there! and then I told him about my little hobby, you know, and asked him if he would think it a great impertinence if I gave him a reading. I'm sure you've been asked *that* before, haven't you, sir?'

The stranger inclined his head and the corners of his mouth twitched with self-conscious mischief, but still he did not speak.

'*Lady* palmists, I should think, must give you little peace?' suggested Mr Niven archly, wondering just how much this superb vanity could swallow.

This time a little laugh broke from the man as though against his will. He moved his wide shoulders.

'They *have* been known to ask me if they could – er – read my hand,' he said.

The hoarse, weak voice came as a shock to Niven; it

so carried on his first impression that some spring in this creature was broken. The ugliness of the ultra-refined accent was like the poor echo of some voice which he had once admired, and tried to capture for himself.

'And I expect you've had a good many readings, haven't you?' pursued Mr Pavey.

'Well, not so many as you might think. The fact is' – his tone grew confidential – 'I'm just a bit nervous of palmistry. Sometimes I think it's all rot, you know, and then one hears of a case when something's come true, and one wonders.'

He glanced at Niven as he spoke, and just for an instant the writer had the strangest impression that the large eyes meeting his own were a woman's.

'Sensitive,' nodded Mr Pavey. 'Impressionable' – he bent again over the hand – 'and a little too inclined to take other people's opinions seriously – look at the space between the first and second fingers. Very narrow. Not much independence of judgment, eh, Walter?'

Mr Niven nodded owlishly. The second appearance of his name almost made him jump. Mr Pavey's eyes shone behind their glasses as he looked up at his friend, expressing nothing but an eager interest in the hand which he was lightly touching with his rheumatic fingers.

'But that's counterbalanced by a good thumb,' pointed out Mr Niven indulgently, wondering why this hand with its pink nails should seem slightly repulsive to him. 'Plenty of will-power there.'

'And doesn't he need it, with such a sensitive hand?' demanded Mr Pavey, taking out his handkerchief and wiping his forehead as though he suddenly found the spring evening warm. 'Look at the pointed fingers and almond-shaped nails. Sensitiveness to – to beauty. That's what I read in this hand, sir. It's the hand of an artist. If it isn't an impertinent question, sir, may I ask if you're a painter?'

'Not by profession,' drawled the stranger, 'though I've done a bit of painting in my time, and writing, too.'

'And acting?' inquired Mr Niven respectfully, jerking his mind back from a wild canter after what sort of things this creature might write about. 'You're pretty talented all round, I should think, with a hand like that. It's almost pure Psychic, isn't it, Pavey?'

'Psychic and Conic,' corrected Mr Pavey. 'The trouble with this hand is that it has too many talents. Look at these lines under the Mount of Saturn, Walter.' (There he goes again! What's the matter with the old boy, thought Mr Niven.) 'Three of them – no, four. You could have expressed yourself successfully, sir, in four distinct branches of the arts. But that is just your trouble, if you will forgive my saying so. You have too many irons in the fire. You *will* not conserve and concentrate.'

'That's true.' The man nodded eagerly. His disdainful expression had vanished, and he looked what Niven thought of as avid. His bright eyes in their net of fine lines were slightly moist, and the curves of his mouth had relaxed.

'I get so many ideas for – for scenarios and stories that I don't know where to start first, and I end by going off with the crowd as usual' – he stopped suddenly and drew a quivering breath. Niven at once dropped his eyes from the instantly horrified face, and stared at the floor. He saw with distaste that the fellow's long brown suede shoes were broken. What the devil did he want, lolling there like some damned but vain-glorious ghost?'

'. . . and nothing gets done,' ended the stranger with a long, long sigh. He smiled at Mr Pavey, showing excellent false teeth.

'I knew it. It's all here.' The chemist gently touched the palm before him and bent his baldish head a little closer over the long, relaxed hand. Mr Niven, idly watching his old friend, observed a glistening on his upper lip and noted, without comment, that Mr Pavey was sweating.

There was silence while the chemist peered closely at the palm. Mr Niven yawned quietly, glancing at the clock. It was five-and-twenty past eight. Should he take the excuse offered by Mr Pavey and slip off to an imaginary appointment? He was beginning to lose interest in the tall man's hand, and he knew from experience that Mr Pavey might keep on about it for another three-quarters of an hour. There would be no peaceful gossip that evening.

Suddenly Mr Pavey said, without glancing up:

'Walter, what do you make of this?'

Nothing, E, thought Mr Niven, bending over that palm, which was becoming increasingly uninteresting to him, and examining the almost invisible cluster of tiny creases indicated by Mr Pavey's finger. He stared at it for as long as politeness demanded, then shook his head.

'Is that, or is that not, Walter, a Star on the Mount of Jupiter?' demanded Mr Pavey.

'I shouldn't care to say,' cautiously replied Mr Niven; 'but it's certainly in the right place.' Where that place might be he did not know, but again obediently followed the lead given by Mr Pavey.

'Is that a good sign to have?' demanded the man, glancing from face to face, and catching in his own eyes a spark of Mr Pavey's excitement.

'Good!' Mr Pavey dropped the hand he held, and straightened himself, looking earnestly into the man's face. 'My dear sir, it's a magnificent sign – the finest promise of luck a hand can hold. I'm not sure, for the moment, exactly what *form* the luck takes, but . . .'

'Any form will do, thanks,' said the stranger very bitterly.

'But we can soon find out,' went on Mr Pavey. 'Walter, will you just look up The Star in my *Secrets of the Palm*? You'll find it in the usual place, left-hand corner of the third shelf. Page 91, I think it is.'

Mr Niven docilely strolled back to the parlour to look up The Star.

What a piece of work is a man floated into his head as he stood by the shelf, looking for the book. What inexhaustible colour and variety in human nature!

No evening which had yielded so much sheer human interest could be called 'wasted'; and it would not be until he was at home, alone for a few moments before going to bed, that the familiar faint melancholy, born of the writer's detachment, would again invade his spirit.

Mr Niven's memory and fingers had, meanwhile, found page 91 for him, and he stared down at the page for a second without seeing it, as his thoughts wandered on.

Then he noticed that there was no reference to a Star. Only one paragraph on that page stood out, forcing itself upon the eyes in heavier black type.

He stared at it for what seemed to him a long time. Even after he had read it, he stared on. His mind took a

huge leap, like that from darkness into brilliant sunlight
. . . but his first thought was that Mr Pavey had gone a
little mad. That's what he meant me to see, of course, but
he's mad. It can't be. There's no proof.

What can I do?

His heart was beating a little quicker as he strolled back
into the shop. The man had taken off his hat, showing a
white forehead heavily lined, on which the hair grew
repulsively low.

'Can't you find it?' asked Mr Pavey placidly, looking up.

'Not that — no. No. It must be some other page, and it
isn't in the index,' said Mr Niven, speaking clearly and
carefully; but now every word he spoke and every loud
tick from the old clock high on the shop wall seemed
heavy with meaning.

'I'll find it,' said Mr Pavey, and he took the book. He
added: 'I don't want to push you out, but oughtn't you to
be off? It's half-past now.'

'So it is.' Mr Niven felt his own voice to be loud and
stupid as he glanced at the clock.

'This gentleman's coming in for a cup of tea,' said Mr
Pavey, lifting the flap of the counter. Mr Niven walked
slowly towards the door.

'Don't forget your hat,' smiled the stranger.

'Of course. Stupid of me.'

Then he had to go through the parlour again, find his
hat, pick it up, walk slowly out into the shop, and linger
courteously at the door while he said good night (*but why?
Why does he want to get rid of me?*).

'Oh, Walter' — Mr Pavey looked back over his shoulder
as he turned to go into the parlour — 'tell Carboy my set's

gone wrong again, will you? He might look in, if he can find time.'

'Right you are.' Mr Niven made a hearty gesture. Indeed, he was enormously relieved, because now he knew what Mr Pavey wanted him to do.

'Good night to you, sir.' He made a formal inclination to the stranger, who returned it with mechanical charm: that's what he'd expect an ageing buffer in a one-horse town to say, reflected Mr Niven, shutting the door. The spring air smelled sweet. The windows of the house opposite were now filled with the dead glitter from a street-lamp. Mr Niven walked crisply down the street until he came to a turning, then he began to run.

When he came back fifteen minutes later he approached the shop casually but cautiously, with his coat collar up and his hands in his pockets. One or two shops still sent their lights across the pavement, and Mr Niven, strolling idly, stopped before one of these and gazed at the window. Opposite was Mr Pavey's shop, and Mr Pavey was bidding his guest good night.

Mr Niven saw their two shapes reflected for a moment in a mirror outside the tobacconist's. He could even hear his old friend saying:

'Good night, sir, and a comfortable journey to Ireland. I think you'll find the hair tonic very good. I sell a lot of it. And the other stuff should clear up your insomnia in no time.'

The tall man's reply could not be heard. He had pulled his spotted silk muffler up round his chin in the fashion-able 'stock' style, and re-tilted his square hat. His silhouette looked extraordinarily hunched and sinister, like a gangster-vulture. But then, thought Mr Niven, there's nothing odd in that; all the young men try to look like gangsters nowadays and he *is* a young man; still under thirty, I should think.

The stranger walked quickly away. So quiet was this mean little street that Mr Niven heard his steps ringing on the pavement, with a strange effect of meaning and farewell. Going. Going. Gone – thought the writer; and as the tall, graceful shape receded down the street, Mr Niven slowly crossed the road to his friend's side. They exchanged a look, and Mr Niven nodded.

They stood in silence, watching that figure dwindling into the dim end of the street.

As they watched, a second figure detached itself from the night, so casually that it seemed at one instant to be part of the shadows in a doorway and the next to have become a man, and moved down the street after the first.

'There he goes,' muttered Mr Pavey. 'Did you have much difficulty with Carboy?'

'Not when I told him who I was,' said Mr Niven. 'And when he heard your name he seemed to think it was all right. You and I apparently aren't the sort to go after wild geese and red herrings.'

'No,' said Mr Pavey, who looked exhausted.

'All the same,' said Mr Niven very severely, 'I think you have sent a plain clothes' man on a wild-goose chase, and I shouldn't like to be you when Carboy finds out that you have. All I said was "behaving suspiciously." I couldn't tell the police that you wanted a man trailed because you found a murder mark or something in his palm, could I?'

'Mr Niven,' said Mr Pavey piteously, 'you don't think I

set a policeman on that poor devil because of a sign in his palm, do you? Mr Niven, palmistry's my hobby, but I wouldn't take that risk. I'm not a professional. I might have been mistaken. Oh no, I wouldn't have dared to do that. It was the *word*, Mr Niven. The *word*. I *had* to get the word murder *somehow* into your head without arousing his suspicions. I was terrified he might guess who you were, too. That – that was why I used your first name. I hope you didn't mind.'

'Of course I didn't mind,' growled Mr Niven, rather crossly. He had misjudged his friend so completely that he felt guilty, even in the midst of his other emotions.

'And then I remembered that paragraph about the murder mark, and the number of the page, and I thought that if you saw it . . .'

'Yes. Of course, the instant I saw it, I knew what you meant. All the same, you took a big risk, you know. I mightn't have tumbled to it. And even if you were sure I would tumble to it, you might have known I should hesitate to set the police on a man's track just because you saw a "murder mark" in his palm.'

'Mr Niven,' said Mr Pavey with a desperate little gesture which betrayed the calmness of his voice; 'he hadn't got the mark.'

'What?'

'No. It was a weak, sensual hand, but that was all – except that the Life Line ended when he was about thirty.'

'Then what,' demanded Mr Niven, apprehension and dismay struggling in his voice, 'what, in the name of all that's just, made you assume that he was the murderer?'

'His wrist was scratched, Mr Niven.'

Mr Niven stared at him in the wan glow of the street-lamp. Mr Pavey nodded.

'Yes. A long deep scratch on the wrist, just like the papers said the murderer must have, from her brooch. I saw it when I gave him his change. It was hidden by his cuff, but my eyes are pretty sharp, you know, and I saw it when his sleeve slipped back a little.'

Mr Niven was silent. Both turned, and stared away down the dim little street where the two shapes had receded.

'*The Line of Head*,' murmured Mr Pavey, '*rising on the Mount of Mars and cutting through the Line of Heart*. No, he hadn't got that. But his wrist was scratched, and he came back, like they always do. I'm sure it was him, Mr Niven. And if it is, they'll get him. It's only a case for patience.'

To the writer, still staring into the dreary dark of the street's end, it seemed also a case for pity.

The Hoofer and the Lady

She really was a lady, and only eighteen. She lived with the only unforgivable type of aunt: the type that throws a detestable philosophy of life at a young mind until it is compelled, in self-defence, to wrap itself in layers of silence and apparent stupidity. Mighty like a rose, I agree; and Alicia looked like one, too. She was one of those large, white, still girls, with a great deal of pale golden hair and eyes too large for human nature's daily food; and she ate less than nothing, because her mother had been inclined to fatten, if left alone, and Alicia, with a twenty-six inch waist, was taking no chances.

The aunt was not at all like a rose; she was like the sweet but expensive champagne which is sold in bad clubs and leaves the drinker with a wicked hang-over. She was simply rabid to see Alicia make a good marriage.

She was to be pitied, if you look at the matter impartially, because she was always just getting the house properly furnished and the servants properly trained, and just getting to like a neighbourhood, and just beginning to think that Alicia was really starting to see sense at last; and then, out of the blue and human nature, the fashions in decorations changed and the servants ran amok and all the nice (read 'rich') people left the neighbourhood and Alicia had an attack of ideals, and the aunt had to start all over again.

It was tough. The woman never got a chance really to relax and be herself.

However, she did not flag. A fortnight before Christmas she established Alicia and herself in a little, dull, exquisitely select old hotel tucked away at the back of the Haymarket, and began to scoop in invitations for her irritating niece.

They came easily and in flattering numbers, because the aunt, though nasty, was one of those women who automatically get asked to the choicest parties; her pedigree assured this. Alicia's name appeared with pleasing regularity on Corisande's page in the *Evening Standard* among the names of young girls seen at dances. 'Miss Alicia Paget, wearing a white dress sprinkled with tiny silver stars, was one of the prettiest girls there.' 'Miss Alicia Paget is one of the tallest girls in Society, and is a keen rider to hounds.'

'I wish we hadn't chosen a Deernell dress, Alicia,' said the aunt fretfully. 'His gowns are so distinctive, and people will soon begin to know that dress.'

Certainly Colonel Trumpet knew it. As soon as he entered a ballroom, he looked for the white dress with the silver stars, and as soon as he saw it, and Alicia's still, golden head poised on her long neck rising from its simple neckline, he mooned over to it and stood stiffly at her shoulder and asked her if she would give him the pleasure of a dance.

Alicia, egged (it is a coarse word, but will suffice) on by the aunt, usually accepted. She could not be said to dislike Colonel Trumpet so much as not to notice he was there. He was forty odd, older than the rocks on which he sat; and who was interested in old men? Not Alicia. Girls who are foolishly romantic fall in love with middle-aged men as part of a routine, but girls like Alicia, who are burningly, secretly, silently romantic, seek youth.

Alicia did not seek it at the Pallorpheum, but it was there that she found it. Among the aunt's faults was a painful anxiety to keep young, and she followed the follies of the day so far as she might without getting herself talked about. When there were treasure-hunts, she hunted. When it was amusing to go and see 'Maria Marten; or The Murder in the Red Barn,' at the Elephant and Castle, she went there too (hating it, but game as a cock sparrow). And when these pastimes, like those of Babylon and Tyre, also had their day and were not, and were replaced by a rage for going to see Non-stop Variety, thither, bored but gallant, went Alicia's aunt.

She even went a step further, and held a party for a gang of silly people whom she had collected about Alicia, with the object of going on to the Pallorpheum later in the evening.

Everybody said this was quite marvellous, because they did so adore jugglers and tumblers and red-nosed vulgar comedians, and as for the chorus . . . had any of you ever tried to do even the simplest chorus steps?

Colonel Trumpet said, 'Could he come too,' and the aunt said, 'Of course, that would be delightful.'

'Poor old weasel, I expect it makes him pretty wistful,' said one of the young men to Alicia, as they drove to the Pallorpheum in his car (Alicia having avoided, more by instinct than by desire, a ride in the Colonel's car).

'Why should it?'

'Oh, because I expect he remembers the naughty 'nineties and all that. Pretty grim to see Nervo and Knox rioting over the very spot where Cora Pearl used to swoon about in yards of grubby lace, what?'

'Who was Cora Pearl, anyway?'

'Oh, a siren,' said the young man vaguely, wondering why it did not seem indelicate to mention the name of any famous living lady who was free with her favours, yet seemed in bad taste to talk about a dead one.

'Is this it?' asked Alicia, looking up at the winking red, gold, and green lights.

'This is it.'

Well, the aunt got them all into their stalls, and Colonel Trumpet got himself next to Alicia, so he was happy, and this made the aunt happy, too. Poor woman! – give her a crumb, only a crumb, and she perked up at once.

Everybody would have felt it a duty to laugh loudly, even if they had not been amused; but they soon really were amused, and the Colonel sat and listened for Alicia's pretty, low laugh. She was the only girl he knew who had not got a scream for a laugh when they were handing out the laughs Up Above. No wonder the poor old man wanted to marry her!

And then, following quite simply and naturally on an unkind song about the darker side of marriage given by a Mr Stan Derby, came a speciality dancing act. 'The Three Varconis,' it was called. Onto the stage dashed a tall, dark man in tails, and two tiny, fair creatures in tights.

'Hoofers,' they call them in America. That means dancers; people who live by their hoofs and earn their bread and jam by the speed and grace with which they can move those same hoofs. Most people's feet, compressed all day in shoes and never shown to the grass, are far more like hoofs than the feet of most hoofers.

These hoofers were not extra-good. They were good, of course, because they would not have been on the vast stage of the Pallorpheum if they had not been, but they were no better than hundreds of other hoofers, here and in America.

But there was something about the young man . . . The aunt, the gang of silly people, even Colonel Trumpet sitting in silence beside the silent Alicia, had to hand it to the young man for that something. Grace? Personality? Charm? All three, perhaps, varnished over with the thick bloom, the mist, which only youth can give.

He had a low, slurred American voice, hoarse with exchanging back-chat with the rest of the Pallorpheum gang. He had hair across which the light lay in a blue-black bar, and a sweet, quick smile.

Right across yards of air, blue with smoke and quivering with reflected light, he found time and space to smile at Alicia.

'Angel!' thought Alicia, smiling back. 'Oh, I wonder if either of those two little creatures are his wife – is, I mean.'

Tap, tap, tap went his light feet across the dusty boards, in the pauses of the orchestra's music. He seemed to have no weight. He walked on his hands as easily as on his feet, and did wonderful, careless things with his hat and cane. And even when he was upside down, he still smiled his quick, sweet smile.

When he went off, on his hands and bent over like a croquet-hoop, Alicia felt a delicious pang. Oh, there he was again, waving at the audience, and twisting his legs in the most amusing way. Oh, a dear, funny, beautifully *fit* young man. Alicia had fallen in love.

'Chap has to keep in good condition to do that kind of thing,' said Colonel Trumpet. 'No drink.'

Alicia did not hear him.

When it was time to go, Alicia shocked everybody by mulishly wanting to stay and see the show all over again. Nobody else wanted to, and she was not allowed to, of course, but her aunt, being kind to her in public, smiled and told the dear, funny child that she should come again next week, if she really liked it so much.

'Next week, hell!' thought Alicia, who had been forced, in self-defence, to cultivate a secret vocabulary as well as a secret philosophy of life. 'I'm coming to-morrow night.'

She did, telling the aunt that she was going to the pictures with a respectable female companion. Even Alicia did not quite dare to go to the Pallorpheum by herself, and sit surrounded by large, inquisitive men with cigars, so she took Dorothy van den Lyn with her, and told her to shut up, and just eat the chocolates and not interrupt, because she, Alicia, wanted to watch someone.

Dorothy, who was terrified of the large, silent Alicia, did as she was told. Alicia had secured two front-row stalls, and this time the young man smiled at her three times. He recognized her!

'Alicia,' said Dorothy, daring much in respectability's name, 'he smiled at you. Do you know him?'

'Not yet,' said Alicia.

'There,' said Dorothy, looking over her shoulder at the fifth row of the stalls, 'is Colonel Trumpet.'

'Silly old thing,' said Alicia. 'Now do pipe down, Dolly, because it's his turn again in half an hour, and I want to think about him in between.'

They sat through to the end of the show, and left under some comments from the programme-sellers. Someone was heard to observe that they hoped them two had had their money's worth. Dorothy writhed with shame, and told Alicia that she had sat through it once but would not do it again.

'Yes, you will,' said Alicia. 'I'm coming again tomorrow night, and so are you.'

And she did, and Dorothy did, and so did Colonel Trumpet.

This went on until the end of the week. The love-maddened Alicia (to borrow a fragrant and useful head-line from the American Press) also ventured there during the afternoon by herself, but in the evenings she always took Dorothy, and the aunt worried herself black in the face, declining the most luscious invitations for Alicia, and pestering her with questions about her evening excursions.

'I've told you,' said Alicia patiently. 'I go to the movies.'

'It isn't natural,' said the aunt, 'to go three times a week. I tell you I won't have it, Alicia. I am allowing you a certain amount of licence, because I think you will very soon have a piece of news for me, won't you?'

'I shouldn't think so,' said Alicia.

'. . . but at the end of the week you must stop this nonsense. I can't think what's come over you.'

And she went upstairs to coo to Colonel Trumpet over the telephone, and assure him girls were often a little nervous at Alicia's age. It would wear off, she was sure. Girls often took these odd fancies. Alicia was spending her evenings at the cinema.

The Colonel, who was by now as well known to the attendants at the Pallorpheum as were Alicia and Dorothy, did not give Alicia away.

When the end of the week came, and Alicia realized with a shock that next week the programme was changed and that she would see her dear love no more, she became desperate and did a most imprudent thing.

She wrote a shy, cold little note burning with secret love, and entrusted it (she sent it by the wretched Dorothy, who was, by now, on the edge of collapse and fathoms deep in frightful lies) to the stage-doorkeeper.

'For Mr Varconi, Miss?' said the stage-doorkeeper, giving Dorothy a keen, respectful look which went to her poor little heart. So, just so, did Batson, their very own butler, look at her when she told him to tell young men on the telephone that she was out when she was in. Very remiss, but then Batson was one of those butlers who had dandled all the younger members of the family.

'Please,' faltered Dorothy.

'I'll see he gets it, Miss,' said the stage-doorkeeper, looking more than ever like Batson.

So it happened, on that December evening when all the may trees in the London parks were silhouetted like little black lace umbrellas against the starry sky of winter, Joe Dunks (that was Mr Varconi's real name) came out of the stage-door to find a big car waiting for him, and sitting in it a big, snow-pale, frightened young lady.

He was very tired after the show. It was his first job in

London, and he had not been making big money for so long that he had got in with a hard-drinking crowd that went along to parties after the show; and he liked to go home peacefully to bed. He thought this young lady was a nuisance, but he was used to fobbing off ritzy dames in Chicago and on Broadway who sometimes gave him the come-hither, and he had reduced his technique to an art. But, oh! how he wished he was peacefully in bed.

He came up to the car, and put his head in at the window.

The snow maiden inside gave a huge start.

'Howdy?' said Mr Dunks. 'You Miss Paget? I think it's swell of you to want to meet me. Real friendly. Not like most of the British. Freeze you a mile off. You interested in our show?'

'I . . . I think it's lovely,' said Miss Paget faintly. 'Are . . . are the steps difficult to learn?'

'Sure. But not to me and the girls and other hoofers. We're used to it, see. Easy as falling off a box, after the years we been at it.'

'I . . . I was wondering,' she said diffidently (for Mr Dunks, at close quarters, was a little too perfumed and a little blue-chinned and a little American, bless his heart.) 'I was wondering if you would care for a lift home?'

'Sure thing. Mighty nice of you,' said Mr Dunks, with real gratitude, and he hopped into the car, and Alicia told the chauffeur to drive through the Park to South Kensington, whence Mr Dunks assured her he could get home.

'Are . . . are your partners . . . have they gone home too?'

'Gone to supper with a coupla boy friends,' said he briefly.

When once they were in the Park, driving rather slowly along its deserted avenues under the bare, black trees, glamour returned to Mr Dunks. Poor Alicia, still wondering painfully why she had done anything so silly, stole a look at him, and decided that he was, after all, very nice.

'You must think me very strange . . . very unconventional,' she said impulsively, 'asking you to meet me like this. But I did so admire your dancing, and I wondered what it would be like to meet . . .'

You cannot say to a man 'I fell in love with your smile.'

'Oh, sure. Sure. I think you're swell,' said Mr Dunks, who was nearly asleep. 'You're a great kid.' And he put out his hand, and easily patted Alicia's.

Alicia sat very still. She had not thought that Mr Dunks (whom she still thought of, and always would, as Mr Varconi) would pat her hand. She had once thought that perhaps he might try to kiss her, but had immediately closed her mind sternly to the thought. And she had not thought what he would be like to talk to, nor what she would say to him when she met him. In fact, she behaved like most of us do when in love; she never thought of her beloved as a human being at all, but only as an image upon which to drape dreams.

Mr Dunks withdrew his hand.

'Guess you go to a lotta ritzy parties?' he said, politely making conversation.

'Oh, yes – lots. There always are a lot at Christmas, you know. I think Christmas is such a nice time, don't you?'

This showed just how young Alicia was. The shadow of bulging stockings seemed to fill the car.

'Sure,' said Mr Dunks.

Poor Mr Dunks was nearly asleep, but just for a second, as Alicia's clear young voice solemnly announced that Christmas was such a nice time, he opened his blue eyes quite wide and looked at her. He never in his life had seen anyone so fresh, so innocent, so earnest. He felt he must do something about it at once, and not what most men would have done, either. He knew just what was the matter with her, and why.

He sat upright, and put his hand over hers again. For the second time Alicia sat very still.

'Sister,' he said ('I like that,' thought Alicia, with a little surprised, pleased feeling), 'will you do something to please me?'

Alicia wanted to reply 'Sure I will,' but curbed herself and replied correctly, 'Of course.'

'Well, will you just tell your shuvver to take you home? Right now. Because I'm not so sleepy I might not say something I'd be sorry for, if you don't. You're a swell kid. Now you go right off home, will you? and tuck yourself into bed. I'll give you my ad-dress at home, and then won't I be pleased if you'll write to me one day soon and tell me you're going to marry some great guy! Now, is that all right with you?'

'Of course,' said Alicia, remembering she was a lady and must not show when she was conscious she had been told where she got off. 'I'm very pleased to have met you, Mr Varconi.'

'And that goes for me, too,' said Mr Dunks, fervently.

Then he took the liberty of leaning forward and asking the chauffeur to stop.

The chauffeur (goodness knows what he thought about it all, but, then, he was not paid to think) opened the door for him, and he got out, and stood, hat in hand, smiling in at the still, silent Alicia.

'Well, thanks for the buggy-ride, Miss Paget. I'm sorry I'm a bit off my stroke to-night; non-stop sure does take it out of you. Here's my home ad-dress. Perhaps you'll come along to our dressing-room some time, if you're down Streatham way (that's the place we're going to next week) and meet the girls. They'd love to know you. So long!'

'Good-bye,' said Alicia.

She sat still, watching him crossing the road to the taxi-rank outside the station. He stopped a cab, gave a direction to the driver, and got in. She could almost feel the sigh of relief with which he collapsed on to the seat.

'Where to, Madam?' asked the chauffeur, thinking this was the rummiest go he was likely to see to-night.

'I'll tell you in a minute,' sighed Alicia.

As she sat there, smiling and sighing and thinking what a silly, lonely girl she was, and how beautifully, as beautifully as any Society hostess, Mr Dunks had handled the embarrassing situation, another car drew up beside her own.

It was the car of Colonel Trumpet.

Colonel Trumpet got out of it, and came stiffly towards her.

'Miss Paget? Thought it was. Lovely night, isn't it? Been to the Pallorpheum?'

'Yes,' sighed Alicia. 'I'm just getting over something. It's nearly gone.'

The Colonel waited in silence.

'Gone?' he asked presently.

'Almost . . .'

'Gone?' he asked again, three minutes later.

'I . . . really . . . think . . . it has,' said Alicia, laughing her pretty, low laugh.

'Mind if I light a cigar?' said the Colonel.

He leaned against the closed door of Alicia's car, staring between the trunks of the trees to the glittering streets outside the Park and their skimming traffic.

'Gives a man a great attraction, that lightness on his feet. Like a Harlequin. I remember when I used to step-dance—'

'YOU?' cried Alicia, bending forward and turning huge amazed eyes on him.

'Certainly. It's a good while ago, now, but I used to do a lot of it at one time. Regimental concerts and that . . . silly week-end parties, too, before the war. Can't do it now, of course.'

He hesitated.

'At least, it's years.'

But he moved out on to the wintry grass under the motionless black may trees and began to dance. Slow, uncertain were the movements at first, but they quickened, and at last the Colonel was darting here and there, lightly as a boy.

'It's really no use, on grass,' he called to the petrified Alicia, 'you want boards, of course. But this is how I used to do it.'

77

And away he flew, in and out of the black shadows, his coat-tails flying and his topper at a dandy's angle.

'Colonel Trumpet,' called Alicia, her voice lost between anxiety and delighted laughter, 'Colonel Trumpet, you'll get a shocking cold. The grass is wet . . .'

He did not hear her.

'Have a gasper?' asked the Colonel's chauffeur of Alicia's chauffeur.

'Ar – I don't mind if I do.'

Sisters

The three women stopped talking when Elaine Garfield came into the village shop.

'Good morning, Mrs Trewer,' she said brightly, 'isn't it a *lovely* day!'

''Morning, Miss Garfield. Yes, it's nice to-day.'

'It *smells* so divine everywhere!' She looked from one heavy face to the other, her eyes wide open and a little moist. 'Quite different from the smell of April, isn't it? I suppose it's the hay . . . anyway, it's the real summer smell at last!' She laughed, glancing down at a paper she held as though just remembering it. 'Now, what do I want? You know what a scatterbrain I am, don't you, Mrs Trewer! I must have my precious list . . . and usually I lose it! Now let me see . . . candles, and an ounce of red wool and two ounces of blue, and some yellow raffia and two three-halfpenny stamps . . .'

Her high-pitched excitable voice went on with the list, and while Mrs Trewer moved slowly about getting the goods together, the two other women steadily stared at Miss Garfield, their expressions touched faintly by contempt.

She was tall and slight and dressed in a blue frock of hand-woven material with a belt and necklace of hammered metal, and sandals over woollen stockings. Her hair was plaited in coils round her ears and long wisps stuck out at the back of her neck under a girlish straw hat. Her face was small, with a little pathetic mouth and large, bright, slightly protuberant blue-grey eyes, whose expression was strikingly sweet, like that of a sensitive yet happy child. She was about forty years old.

As she went on reading out her list with little laughing asides to Mrs Trewer, the two women went on with their conversation in lowered voices.

'What's she done with it, then?'

'Left it with some woman in Hatfield.'

'Fancy. Leavin' the poor little thing.'

'That's what I said. I said to Mil, I said, well, if it was my grandchild I wouldn't leave it with no woman in Hatfield, even if it was a – you-know – I said.'

'What she say then?'

'Says she ain't got room for it down her place, an' she don't want it round the place, neether. She's got enough to do with Stan the way he is, she says. It's sickly, too. Has to have some special kind o' milk. Mil says it fair upset her the first time she went to see it, the way it cried. Sort of exhausted, she said. Not natcheral. Ivy goes down ter see it every Saturday.'

'What's she pay for it, then?'

'Five shillin's a week.'

'Fancy! Seems a lot, don't it?'

'I dunno where Ivy gets it. She's out o' work again.'

'Fancy.'

'Yes. Down at Mil's. She was waitin' in some café in Hatfield, but the work was too 'ard, she said. *Work was too 'ard!* So Milady stays away a few days and gets the sack.'

'What'll she do now, then?'

'Mil says she don't know. Ivy takes on something awful about the kid, Mil says, she was screamin' all over the place last night, sayin' she was goin' to do herself in. Mil says she was afraid they'd hear her up the bungalows.'

'T-t-t-t.'

'Mil says she's afraid Ivy might do something, too. Well, you know yourself she always was a nervy sort o' girl. That big fat sort often is. Mil says she's always 'owling. Fair makes you miserable to be in the place with 'er. Mil says—'

Here both became suddenly aware that Miss Garfield was standing beside them, looking down at them from her tall height with a flush in her thin cheeks.

'You mustn't mind — I didn't mean to listen, but I couldn't help overhearing what you were saying,' she said rapidly. 'About that poor girl, I mean. Ivy. Weren't you saying that she — she's got into trouble?'

They stared stupidly, then one nodded. 'That's right. Ivy Bank. Her mother's a nice woman. I've known Ivy since she was a kiddie.'

'You see,' Miss Garfield went on, speaking still more quickly, her hands clenched, 'I simply can't *bear* to think of people being unhappy. I *cannot* bear it,' she repeated passionately, staring away at the trees and the winding blue river that could be seen beyond the shop door. 'It spoils everything for me, and everything's black and horrible until I can help a little. I should so like to help this girl.' She paused, smiling winningly at their blank staring faces, then

81

went on with a touch of dignity, 'I should be so grateful if you would give me her address. Will you, please?'

She paused, trembling, and a muscle at the side of her mouth twitched helplessly. The two women stared at her, then at one another. But Mrs Trewer, leaning over the counter, said firmly—

'Now, you don't want to go worrying yourself about Ivy Bank, Miss Garfield. It's very kind of you, I'm sure' (she spoke kindly yet severely, as though to a child) 'but you can take it from me (and I'm a good lot older than you, miss, if you'll excuse the liberty) that there's nothing *nobody* can do about a girl like that. She's just naturally a bad, loose, immoral girl, Ivy is, and always has been—'

'She may not be bad, Mrs Trewer,' Elaine interrupted, her eyes brimming with tears; 'she may only be . . . very loving, and perhaps she was lonely . . .'

(An indescribable expression appeared upon the faces of the listeners at this.)

'. . . and you remember,' Elaine went on resolutely, looking from one pair of hostile eyes to the other, 'that the – the best and bravest Person who ever lived said *"Whoso is without sin amongst you . . ."* you know . . .'

(General embarrassment. To-day was Monday, not Sunday.)

'. . . so please,' Elaine ended pleadingly, 'do tell me where she lives.'

A pause. At last one of the two women said civilly, trying not to look at Elaine's twitching muscle:

'She lives down Church Cottages. Anybody'll tell you down there.'

'Thank you. Thank you *very* much.' And then Elaine

impulsively put out her hand, saying, 'Please. No . . . really. I'd like to, if you don't mind. Just to show that you don't think I'm being silly.'

They did think she was, and their expressions showed it, for the village was given to discussions in its leisure about whether Miss Garfield was wrong in the head or not. However, each gave her a slack freckled hand to shake, for they did not dislike her. Great Warby found Elaine Garfield a bit barmy, but all right. Her friendliness, her impulsive kindness, had taken twenty years to conquer the villagers, but now it had done so; and though they laughed at her, they liked her.

She turned to the counter again, and Mrs Trewer's disapproving face.

'Are those my goods and chattels, Mrs Trewer? And one and fourpence change . . . thanks most awfully. That's everything, then . . . candles, wool, raffia, floor polish . . . yes, everything. Well, good morning, thank you, Mrs Trewer. Good morning,' to the two impassive faces.

She went out quickly with her light youthful step and the three fell upon their feast of gossip.

Elaine went across a meadow and up the hill to her house. It really was a house, not a cottage; a plain square brick building that had been a farm-house some thirty years ago, but no one had worked the land around it since the childless old farmer died, and the cornfields and oatfields had run to coarse pasture in a few years. The pigsties were six feet in nettles when Elaine first saw the place and in the vegetable and flower gardens there was the strangely disturbing sight of blossom and root going back to their wild nature.

Elaine had slowly recaptured Bryant's for civilization. It had taken her twenty years, but now the house was a picture. 'Miss Garfield, your garden's a perfect picture; you've got green fingers, miss, that's easy to see.' Green fingers was the country name for time, patience and love working together. Elaine did all the work of the garden and most of the housework, but Mrs Trewer's sister, Mrs Briggs, came in three days a week to do 'the rough'; the lamps, the hearthstoning of the red bricks in the scullery, the flag-stones in the kitchen. There was no bathroom, telephone, gas, electric light, or indoor sanitation. Elaine cooked on an oilstove. Except for this and one or two other concessions to progress, the house looked much as it must have done in the late seventeenth century when it was built.

Only the healthy stir of life was lacking. It was an old maid's house. The loudest sound heard there throughout many a long day was the noise of the well-rope running down, or the barking of Miller, Elaine's dog. The smell of pinks floated in the rooms in summer, and the scent of burning apple-wood in winter, and the same square patches of light from the windows lay on the floors that had lain there two hundred years ago.

Elaine talked affectionately to Miller, who was dozing on the kitchen floor, while she put her parcels away. She was going down to Church Cottages to see Ivy Bank before lunch. She had no clear idea what she would do when she got there, for she had not yet emerged from the feeling of passionate pity for the girl that had swept her as she stood in the shop. She only knew that she must help, and quickly.

'Walky?' she said to Miller, standing at the door. He opened one eye, sighed, and shut it again, so she went off alone.

Now, what can I do? she thought, as she hurried down the hill again. I shan't have any money until the first of the month, but I can tell her I'll give her some for the baby when I've got some, and I might talk to Mrs Cuthbertson (the Vicar's wife) about her – only I expect she wouldn't like that, poor girl, and probably Mrs C. knows all about her already. The whole village does, I expect. That must be horrible for her – people whispering and sneering and some of them feeling sorry for her – all her private feelings being talked about . . .

As she went down the hill one of her coils of hair shook loose and she impatiently pinned it up as she went, staring down at the village in its miniature valley with the peace and pleasure that the view always gave her. Great Warby was not a beauty-spot, but it had the charm of an unspoiled English landscape where people have lived for a thousand years and every foot of earth has its human history. Elaine loved the place; she could not think of any other part of the earth as home, and she hoped to die and be buried there.

Church Cottages were down at the far end of the village, in the slovenliest but prettiest part. They made Elaine (who always saw things as people) think of dirty little scowling old women with hair of silvery thatch and eyebrows of crimson roses. A little girl told her where the Banks lived, and she went up the garden path to the open front-door.

A middle-aged woman stood at a table in the tiny

over-furnished room, opening a tin of pineapple. She looked up as Elaine came to the door, with a defensive, suspicious expression.

'Oh . . . good morning,' began Elaine. 'Are you Mrs Bank?'

'Yes.' She stopped her work, but kept her hands on the tin while she stared in alarm. 'What is it? Who did you want to see – miss?'

'It's quite all right; please don't – I am afraid you will think this is very rude of me, but I don't mean it to be, so you mustn't mind,' Elaine dashed on. 'It was just that I happened to hear—'

'Is it about Iv – about my daughter?'

'Yes! Yes, that's it! If I could just speak to her for a moment – if she's in?'

'She's upstairs.' Mrs Bank went red. She put down the tin, pulled forward a chair, and wiped the seat with her apron. 'Won't you come in and sit down, miss?'

'Oh . . . thank you.' Elaine still stood awkwardly in the doorway. 'The – the fact is, Mrs Bank, I was wondering if your daughter had ever done any housework. Because I'm in need of somebody to help me – my house is called Bryant's, it's up on Shardler Hill, perhaps you know it? – and I thought perhaps your daughter—'

She had not meant to say this. It just came to her, as though it were the right, and only, thing to say; and even while she was speaking she knew that the one way that she could help the wretched girl was to take her into her own home, and show the little world of Great Warby that 'nice' people, represented by Miss Garfield of Bryant's, did not look on her as an outcast.

Mrs Bank was looking at her doubtfully.

'I don't know as Iveen (we call her Iveen) 'ud like that, miss. She's always had to keep her hands nice, you see, 'cos of her waiting work. She's not in a post just now though,' going red again, and a bitter, furious look passing over her face, 'and perhaps if there isn't much rough—'

'Oh no, not much, and I live very simply. Just the cooking and two beds—'

'Live in, do you mean, miss?'

'Yes, I thought so. I mean, it would be better, wouldn't it?'

'It 'ud do Iveen all the good in the world to get with nice people,' Mrs Bank suddenly burst out in a low tone, glancing at the staircase. 'The fact is, miss, she's had a bit of trouble – well, there's a little one, and that's telling you straight out,' wiping her eyes on her apron, 'and I haven't always been as strict with her as I ought to have done, she being the only girl and four brothers, she was spoilt-like, and she got with some woman in Hatfield that ought to be killed, that's what she ought to be, wicked, if ever a woman was . . . But if you won't mind her having been a bad girl, miss—'

'I don't mind, Mrs Bank. I – I don't think of her as a bad girl, either,' answered Elaine, with her strikingly sweet smile. 'If you will let her come to me, and if she wants to come, I should be very glad to have her.'

While they were talking she had been aware of heavy movements overhead, and suddenly a voice began to sing in crude imitation of the women who croon on the air—

'Your heart and mine,
They belong together
Just like April weather—'

'There she is now,' exclaimed Mrs Bank. 'She's coming down!' She began busily working on the tin again, as though she had not heard what Elaine said, while heavy steps came down the stairs.

'Visitors!' exclaimed Iveen, pausing at the entrance as though amazed. 'Why, I know you, don't I? It's Miss Garfield from Bryant's, isn't it? I've often seen you about.'

She was a big girl, with dyed yellow hair hanging untidily on her shoulders in a Garbo-bob, a pale face with large features, and pale blue eyes that watched her own movements in a mirror on the opposite wall while she spoke. Her nails and face were badly painted and she was not quite clean. She looked defiant and 'cheery,' yet as though she had suffered some awful shock. She was very young; Elaine thought that she could not yet be twenty.

'Yes, Miss Garfield's come to see if you would like to work for her, Iveen,' said her mother nervously. 'Live in, up at Bryant's on the hill.'

'It's wonderful of Miss Garfield to have thought of me,' said Iveen emotionally, watching herself in the mirror. 'You've got a wonderful garden up there, haven't you, Miss Garfield? I'm ever so fond of flowers, I think they're such wonderful, wonderful comforters when you're feeling blue.'

'You could start to-morrow, couldn't you, Iveen?' her mother interrupted sharply. 'How much was you thinking of giving, miss?'

'Oh . . .' stammered Elaine, taken aback. She had not

thought about wages. She lived on fifteen pounds a month, sent to her by the lawyer who had managed her dead parents' affairs, and her life was so frugal and quiet that she found this more than enough. The house was her own; she had bought it with some of her father's capital. Her diet was chiefly milk, and vegetables from the garden, but Iveen, who looked as though she had lived for years on tinned salmon and potato crisps, would want a more civilized and expensive menu, as well as wages. Elaine saw all kinds of difficulties, but she did not change her mind.

· 'I don't know much about wages,' she said, looking from one to another. 'Mrs Briggs gets half-a-crown a week for three days. Would – would five shillings do – and all food, of course?'

'I'm afraid Iveen couldn't come for less than seven and six,' put in Mrs Bank firmly, cutting across a mutter from Iveen about 'Oh, I'd come for *nothing*, Miss Garfield—' 'She got twelve and six a week at the Horseshoe Café where she was last, *and* tips.'

'I could manage that, I think,' said Elaine, smiling at the girl, her heart warmed by the generous young offer. 'And I think you might like being there, Ivy. It's quiet, but—'

'Quiet! Iveen won't like that,' interrupted Mrs Bank, laughing abruptly. 'Quiet places drive her dotty, she says. She finds this place "quiet" after Hatfield, so what she'll do up the hill I don't know.'

'Oh, Mum, do shut up! Whatever'll Miss Garfield think? I'm not like some girls, always craving for thrills and excitement. I think it'll make a wonderful change for me. Thank you ever so, Miss Garfield. You won't regret your choice, I know. When would you care for me to come up, Miss Garfield?'

'To-morrow morning?' suggested Elaine, wondering with a faint feeling of dismay if she would find Iveen's voice so disagreeable when she had to listen to it all day, or if she would get used to it. 'At nine o'clock?'

'Rightee-o, then, Miss Garfield. I'll be there. Nine o'clock sharp to-morrow morning, and thanks ever so. Can you find your way out?' as Elaine stepped through the door. 'Oh, fine. Rightee-o, then, and thanks ever so.'

Elaine walked slowly home. Every now and then a waft of rich rose-smell blew over her, then a dry sweet breath from the hay. It had been a record year for hay, the high-piled masses were already whitening in the strong sunlight. Beautiful, beautiful world! yet so sad. If only I can take away the awful look from that child's face, thought Elaine, it will be worth any little sacrifice of my own peace.

That evening she went for a walk in the maze of lonely little lanes behind Bryant's, for she felt too strangely disturbed in mind to settle to any one of the three or four hobbies with which she filled her life, working at them as hard as most people do at a profession that makes money. Her raffia work and wild-flower pictures, embroidery and music, suddenly seemed meaningless. To-morrow, after twenty years of solitude, she would take another human being into her life, and the prospect frightened her. For she could not treat Iveen with the pleasant friendly distant-ness with which ladies treat servants. She must give her love. *The greatest of these is charity* . . . if I don't give her that, I might as well not have her at all.

How selfish I am! Surely I can put up with her poor affected voice and those dreadful red nails for a little while, to try to help her?

Perhaps (she stopped suddenly in the lane, staring at the rising moon) later on I might have the baby, too! I should love that, the little pet. And Ivy would be happier if the baby were there, of course; I expect she misses it dreadfully. I wish I'd said I would have the baby as well. Never mind, I can tell her that to-morrow.

Calmed and made happier by this thought, she turned homewards.

'What's that?' lazily asked Iveen, lying in the arms of a young man behind the hedge.

'Only some old woman.' He pulled apart the meadowsweet to look. 'Oh – your new missus. She's potty, isn't she?'

Iveen laughed, and they lay down again.

Elaine caught the murmur of voices. Lovers, she thought, delicately turning her head away so that they might not think that she was trying to see them. As she pushed open the gate of Bryant's she was smiling faintly, as though from the reflected glow of happiness, but then she sighed.

The next morning she had a strange feeling, as she sat in the dining-room sipping tea and staring out at the garden, that she would never sit like that again. It feels like moving-day, she thought. Everything looks as though I were seeing it for the last time.

How silly. It's only because I'm so nervous.

Exactly at nine o'clock Iveen pushed open the garden gate, waving cheerfully to Elaine, who came down to meet her. She looked much neater than she had yesterday, for her hair was rolled into fat curls and she wore a clean, bright cotton frock, but her thick legs were bare, her sandals broken, and her toenails were painted scarlet. She was certainly a big girl. Elaine, who never thought about her own body and was hardly conscious that people had them, reflected that modern dress was undoubtedly difficult for some types. Later on, she thought, I might try making her a peasant dress, with a tight bodice and a long full skirt . . . well, a fairly tight bodice.

'Morning, Miss Garfield!' said Iveen, putting down her cheap suitcase. 'I do hope I'm not late, am I? To tell you the truth, I had a few words with Mum before I came out,' spreading her skirt and glancing down at her legs, 'she didn't want me to come up here without any stockings. "Aw," I said, "Miss Garfield won't mind, she's a sport."' She laughed ringingly, while her pale-blue eyes stared over Elaine's shoulder into the dining-room. 'Oh – you've had your breakfast! What a shame . . . I could have got that for you. I expect you'd like it in bed some mornings, wouldn't you? Never mind, I can be getting on with the washing up. Oo – er – keep off, will yer!' she shrieked suddenly, as Miller walked stiff-leggedly round the water-butt, his nose pointing inquiringly. 'Sorry to be a fool, Miss Garfield, but I'm funny that way. About dogs, I mean. Never could stand them, even when I was a kiddy. He looks a gentle old thing though,' she added hastily. 'You wouldn't bite anyone, would you?'

Miller, who had been steadily looking at her, moved his tail an eighth of an inch and walked away. He was neither old nor gentle, but Elaine was touched by Iveen's use of the words. The girl was honestly trying to be friendly and grateful; she was meeting Elaine half-way.

'Oh, he won't bite, don't be afraid,' said Elaine. '(I'll show you your room, Ivy, come along.) He keeps himself to himself, you know, but he's not vicious.'

The girl stared suspiciously at the back of Elaine's untidy head as she followed her upstairs. What a barmy thing to say about a dog! Was Miss Garfield trying to be funny? Making out she, Iveen, was that ignorant she didn't know that was what you said about people? And she didn't like being called Ivy, neither, it sounded so common, like a servant. It wasn't half going to be awful here. Her spirits went down with a rush.

But when she saw the pretty bedroom they rushed up again, and she turned to Elaine, crying, 'Oh, isn't it *sweet* – it's sweet, it really is!' in the first natural, youthful tone that Elaine had heard from her.

'I'm glad you like it . . . my dear.'

'Oh, I *do*. Oh, I'm sure I'm going to be wonderfully, wonderfully happy here, Miss Garfield. It's ever so sweet of you to have thought of me – and the roses too, they're my favourite flowers—'

'Later on,' said Elaine timidly, looking out of the window, 'I thought perhaps you might feel happier if – if we had the – your child here, too, my dear.' She had not meant to tell Iveen this so soon, but the girl's pleasure and gratitude had moved her, and there were tears in her eyes.

She heard a sort of gasp behind her, and then there was a dreadful little pause. She did not look round. She was painfully aware that she had said just the wrong thing. Then Iveen said in a shrill artificial voice:

'Oh, yes, that would be wonderful, too. We must discuss

that later, mustn't we. Yes. What a wonderfully sweet face that lady has in that photo, Miss Garfield. Is it your mother?'

Elaine, only longing to get away and get over her shame at her blunder, explained that it was a Mrs Gaskell, a writer who died many years ago, and hurried downstairs, leaving Iveen to unpack.

She went straight out into the garden, which was not overlooked by Iveen's bedroom, and sat down under the pear tree. She felt as tired as though she had been spring-cleaning for a week. And she had not yet told Mrs Briggs that her services would not be wanted any more. She was not looking forward to that interview. Sighing, she leant back and shut her eyes.

Old beast, thought Iveen furiously, putting on her overall in front of the glass and staring at her pale, full face. Dragging that up. As though I'd bring it up here, poor little devil, with everyone jawing about it fit to bust their blasted faces. She'll start spouting religion at me, that's what she'll do, before I can turn round. I know that sort. All right. If she does, I shall just walk out and she can lump it.

It was only half-past nine. To both of them, the morning seemed already to have lasted a very long time.

Elaine spent the morning gardening, going into the house at half-hourly intervals to tell Iveen what work she could get on with next and to say 'Not lonely, Ivy?' with her sweet childish smile. Iveen sang determinedly in her low nasal voice, giving Elaine a bright artificial grin every time she came into the kitchen, but Elaine was sure that she, too, was ill at ease. Certainly the house felt quite different because of her presence; there was blood-stained paper on the table, in which chops had been wrapped, and the air seemed to vibrate with her low brassy singing. Even in the garden Elaine could hear it, as she knelt on the flagged path layering the ancient, silver-blue clumps of carnations. Miller had gone off on some affairs of his own, as he always did when the routine at Bryant's was interrupted, for he was a selfish dog who hated any break in his habits. His departure seemed the last straw to his mistress, though she told herself that it was nonsense to mind.

Lunch was wretchedly awkward. True to her plan, Elaine made the girl lay it for two in the dining-room, and they slowly ate half-raw chops together, exchanging remarks about the weather, the health of Ivy's mother, Miller, and the beauty of Elaine's garden. Elaine found the girl very difficult to talk to because she was so affected; she gushed enthusiasm over Elaine's simplest remarks and tried hard to be 'refined.' Elaine felt sure that her real enthusiasms were not for flowers and sunsets, but she (Elaine) was so unused to talking to strangers in her secluded life that she could not even make a guess at what Iveen's true interests were, and try to talk to her about them. Elaine's own nature was completely without self-consciousness; that was why the villagers found her conversation so embarrassing. She, in her turn, was embarrassed and troubled by self-consciousness in others, and she found Iveen very troubling indeed. After lunch she sat miserably under the pear tree and wondered if all their meals together would be as difficult. If they are, she thought, I don't really think I can bear it . . .

Oh, if *only* it's doing her good being here, I *will* bear it. But I believe she's as uncomfortable as I am.

Desperately she got up and went into the kitchen, where Iveen was messing about with the contents of the table-drawer and wasting plate-powder on the cooking-forks.

'Look what a good little girl I am!' she said brightly, holding up a bent and broken but dazzling fork. 'Just for something to do.' She added less affectedly—

'Gee! It's quiet here, isn't it, Miss Garfield!'

'I was wondering if you would like to run down and spend the rest of the day with your mother, Ivy, just to tell her how you've got on this morning.'

Iveen's face lit up.

'Oh, thanks ever so, Miss Garfield. I expect they're wondering how we're getting on up here, all on our little lonesomes. But what about your tea, Miss Garfield? There, I nearly forgot! Shall I just pop on the kettle before I go? Where do you have it? In the dining-room? Or what say I put it out all cosy for you in that cute little summer-house down the garden?'

'Oh, thank you, Ivy, that's very kind of you, but I can get it myself, I always do. Don't bother. And I – I shan't expect you back until after supper, as it's the first day. About half-past eight – or nine, if you like.'

'Oh, thanks ever so, Miss Garfield. Oh . . . what about your supper? Anything cooked, do you have?'

'Oh – eggs – anything.' Elaine smiled at her, and hurried out of the kitchen, feeling so relieved at the prospect of some hours of solitude that she could only hope her pleasure was not noticeable. She waved to Iveen as the girl hurried down the path a little later, then wandered out into the garden to enjoy the silence.

Half an hour later the front gate was pushed open and

Miller walked stiffly in, still looking offended, but ready to share with Elaine the cup of tea and cake that she had carried out under the pear tree. They ate and drank together in a silence broken by the singing of a thrush, who afterwards flew down on to the lawn and finished their crumbs. Oh, dear, I do wish I wasn't dreading her coming back! thought Elaine, inhaling the delicious air of the late afternoon and enjoying the peace and silence that had returned to the house. It's even worse than I was afraid it would be. I suppose I've got so used to living alone with Miller (gently scratching under his lifted chin) that all kinds of little things get on my nerves that an ordinary person wouldn't notice.

I must be patient. It's as bad for her as it is for me; I'm sure she finds it very dull up here, poor child. And after all, it's only the first day.

Just before ten o'clock Iveen returned, bright-eyed and giggling and inclined to tease Miller, who took not a shred of notice of her, and the household then went up to bed.

The next day was nearly as bad, and darkened for Elaine by a dignified call from Mrs Briggs, lasting an hour. Elaine, in a fit of cowardice the night before, had written to Mrs Briggs telling her that her services would not be wanted any more, at least for the present, instead of going down to see her and explaining. Mrs Briggs now came in person to answer the letter. Mrs Briggs asked only one question: why had a bad girl been given her job? Wasn't Miss Garfield, after twelve years, satisfied with Mrs Briggs? Was it the time Mrs Briggs broke that little cup with the leaves on it what belonged to Miss Garfield's mother? Mrs Briggs had said at the time how downright sorry she was about that little cup. *Why* was it? Why did Miss Garfield want that bad girl in the house instead of her, Mrs Briggs?

Fortunately, the interview took place after Iveen had gone off on her afternoon visit to her mother, and Elaine was able to explain freely that she wanted to give the girl a chance. 'You see, Mrs Briggs,' she almost pleaded, 'if people see that she's up here with me, earning her living like everyone else, they won't look down on her so much, and that will give her back her self-respect.'

But Mrs Briggs, settling her flowered Sunday hat on her head as she got up to go, only sniffed and said that Ivy Bank had never had no self-respect and she only hoped that Miss Garfield, who had a very kind heart as everybody in the village knew, wouldn't be sorry she ever took her in. Mrs Briggs would be very glad to come back as soon as Miss Garfield wanted her (came to her senses, said her tone). With this Elaine had to be content.

As the week went on, Elaine found the situation becoming easier. She suspected that her mother must have been giving Iveen a talking-to, for the girl was plainly trying to please Elaine by the way she worked, and her manner was quieter and more respectful. As a result, she did not get so painfully on Elaine's nerves; Elaine even found herself amused and entertained by some of Iveen's stories about the café where she had worked in Hatfield, for she told them in a droll, vivacious way that was strikingly different from her 'sweet, refined girl' manner. It flitted dimly across Elaine's innocent mind that this must be the way Iveen talked to men, and that men liked it. She had been wondering what they saw in Iveen: the girl was so lumpy and unattractive, poor thing! Yet Mrs Briggs had hinted darkly at strings of admirers. A gay manner, of course, always went down well with men.

Elaine was much encouraged, too, by a piece of gossip she overheard one day in the village from behind a hedge where clothes were being hung out to dry.

'So Ivy Bank's up at Bryant's now,' said the first voice.

'Yes. Might do her a bit o' good to get into a good place with a lady like Miss Garfield. Her mother's pleased about it, too. O' course, she ain't—'

Elaine had hurried on, as ever delicately anxious not to eavesdrop, and had thus missed what she had presumed would be an unkind remark about Iveen, but which was in fact an unflattering comment upon her own soft-headedness. For the village, though agreeing that it *might* do Iveen good to work for a lady like Miss Garfield, had not yet changed its mind about her character. Great Warby did not have changes of heart in a hurry. It was just waiting to see what would happen.

But Elaine, convinced that the village was following her lead, thought that Iveen's good character was already half restored, and she felt that her sacrifice of peace and solitude was well worth the result.

But when Iveen had been there a fortnight there came a very bad day indeed.

Rain fell occasionally from dawn, in weak showers that did not cool the stifling air, and sent a thick dull mist muffling down over the fields. Elaine made an attempt to get on with her usual occupations, but weather like this always disturbed and unsettled her, and all she had the strength to do was to sit in the dim drawing-room for the greater part of the day with a book on her knees, staring out at the dull dripping garden. After lunch Iveen snappishly asked if she might go out as usual, and went down the path with her fat curls looking unnaturally yellow under a torn umbrella and her bare legs already spattered with mud. Elaine was not so pleased as usual to see her go, for the day was so devitalizing that she had been unconsciously glad of Iveen's youthful, exuberant presence in the house; it made everything seem less exhausted. It suddenly occurred to her, as she watched the sturdy figure hurrying down the path, that if Iveen were to leave now she would miss her. It shows that one can get used to anything, thought Elaine, amused, but also a little pleased. I wonder if she feels the same, poor child. She picked up her book, and passed the time between reading and dozing until it was five o'clock.

At a quarter-past five, just as Elaine was getting up to make herself some tea, Iveen suddenly came in, looking sullen and wretched, and shut herself into the kitchen without a word. Oh, dear, I wonder what's wrong? Elaine stared in dismay at the closed door, but decided that it would be wiser to leave the girl alone. She seemed to remember the women in the shop saying that Iveen went to Hatfield every Saturday to see the baby, and perhaps something had happened there to upset her. She's been crying, thought Elaine agitatedly, crumbling biscuit for Miller and putting some down in her cupped hand for the dog to thrust a hot, bored nose into. I do hope the baby isn't ill.

The clouds were breaking and a golden misty sunset was pouring light into the garden. The raindrops on the brilliant green trees glittered wildly and all the birds were singing at the tops of their voices.

'Tea's ready,' said Iveen suddenly, putting her head round the drawing-room door, then going quickly back into the kitchen. Elaine went into the dining-room and drank some tea; she was too upset to eat. The kitchen door was shut.

While she was sitting over her second cup, letting it cool while she stared out of the window, Iveen came in, sulky and quiet, and began to clear away.

'It's lovely now, isn't it?' said Elaine timidly. 'Are you going out again, Ivy?'

The girl shook her head, her lower lip trembling.

'Oh . . . what a pity. And your afternoon was spoilt, I'm afraid.'

Iveen gave a noisy sob.

'My dear! What's the matter? Here—' taking the girl's thick arm and drawing her gently down beside her on the little sofa. 'Sit down here. Now do tell me what's the matter. Don't you like being here, is that it?'

Iveen, now crying loudly, shook her head and blubbered into her hands like a child.

'What is it, then? Do tell me, Ivy, I only want to help you.'

Iveen only cried louder with an hysterical violence, as though she meant to give way completely to her feelings, and all Elaine could make out was 'Some lady I used to know – some lady—' Her own tears, never very far away, came as she tried to comfort the girl.

'Don't, don't, Ivy – look, you're making me cry, too. Don't, there's a good girl; you'll make yourself ill. Something happened this afternoon to upset you, is that it?'

Iveen nodded, blowing her nose on a piece of torn rag.

'Was it – about the baby?' asked Elaine, swallowing the

lump in her throat, and Iveen suddenly looked up, her face quite frighteningly hideous from crying, its every detail shown in the glaring sunset light.

'Some lady I used to know,' she began chokingly, 'Miss Morris down the Sunday school where I used to go, she saw me up the High Street this afternoon with the kid, and she didn't half tick me off. Went on at me as though I'd done I don't know what. Sayin' I was wicked and I'd go to hell and Jesus wouldn't love me and all that and how I'd end up in the gutter and the poor little kid too. That got me down, Miss Garfield,' beginning to cry again, 'sayin' that about the kid.'

Elaine nodded, tears running down. The cruelty of good people!

'She hadn't got no right to interfere!' burst out Iveen fiercely. 'What's it got to do with her, an old maid like that, not knowing anything about anything? Mother's bad enough, without a lot more old cats starting off. I mind my own business and I'll thank other people to mind theirs.'

Suddenly her face screwed up again and she cried brokenly, her hard-boiledness completely swept away. Elaine watched her, trembling and crying silently and wiping her own eyes with a plain fragrant little handkerchief. She longed to comfort her, yet there seemed to be nothing that she could say, she was so unused to comforting people. It was many years since she had sat beside someone who was crying. Oh, if I could only say something to make her feel better!

Iveen muttered, staring down at the grubby rag she was twisting:

'Made me feel so low-down, as though I was dirt. Goin' on as though I was the only girl as had ever gone wrong—'

'Oh, but you *aren't*, Ivy!' cried Elaine uncontrollably, bending forward and taking her hand. 'Of course you aren't. Hundreds of girls have done what you did – for love.'

She hesitated, but only for a second, then went on, looking straight at Iveen—

'I did, Ivy.'

'*You* did?' staring at her stupidly.

'Yes, I did. I'll tell you all about it – if it will make you feel better to know that someone else . . . It was during the war. I was just your age, only twenty, and I was at an art school in London, living with my cousin; my parents lived in the north. I was so young – and very pretty, too (it doesn't matter my saying that now, because it's so long ago), and we were a lot of wild, silly, happy young people all together, in spite of the horrible war. I met him at a party in a friend's studio. He had only a week's leave. I think he knew he would never come back, because he would never let me talk about the war or his going back to it – he said he just wanted us to be happy while we could. We – we loved each other at once. It seemed as if,' she drew a deep sobbing breath, 'we had always known each other and been away from each other for a long time and met again. We were so happy. We went away to a lovely little cottage in a peaceful little place he knew about, and stayed there for the rest of his leave, and forgot all about the war and that he had to go back so terribly soon.'

She clenched her thin hands, staring out at the garden, the muscle at the side of her mouth twitching convulsively. The golden light was dying away.

'We were so happy. I hadn't thought it was possible to be so happy. It was like living in heaven, every day was so wonderful, even the ordinary things. It was he who first made me see that the little ordinary everyday things can be wonderful . . . We cooked on a funny old stove that wouldn't burn properly, and there was a little stray white dog that came to live with us and came down to the village every day with us to shop. Even the weather was beautiful. And then,' she drew the awful sobbing breath again, 'he had to go away.'

There was a long silence.

'We were going to be married,' she said at last, more quietly, 'but of course he never came back.'

Iveen was crying again, but very softly. The after-glow in the room had faded into twilight.

'So you see,' said Elaine at last, turning slowly and looking at the young, unhappy face that she could barely see, 'you must never, never feel that you're a bad girl who's done something wrong. Love – real love – is the only thing that matters. And you've got the child, too . . . How I wish I had had a child! But I didn't . . . I didn't. But I understand how you feel' (she smiled faintly). 'In a way, you see, we're sisters.'

She pressed Iveen's hand, but the girl said nothing. At last Elaine said gently, 'Do you feel a little better now?' and she looked up.

'Yes, thanks ever so, Miss Garfield. I'm ever so sorry about – what you said, you know; it's ever so sad. Quite a romance. Quite young, was he?'

'Twenty-three.'

'Well . . . it's ever so sad, I think. Doesn't do to let things get you down, does it? Fancy you—' she broke off in a little confusion, then said louder, 'I'd better be getting the tea-things cleared away, hadn't I? It's nearly dark.'

Elaine, feeling curiously weak and disturbed, went upstairs to change her dress before supper. As she looked at her tear-ravaged, drawn face in the mirror, she tried not to think that she had profaned Guy's memory by giving their secret, after twenty years, to another human being. Vigorously she pushed the thought away. He had been the kindest, warmest, most tender-hearted person she had ever known, and if it could comfort some wretched creature to know their story, he would have wanted it to be told. The telling of it meant that the living of it had not been altogether selfish, shut away in the twilight of one woman's memory.

Iveen did not go down to see her mother that evening, but sat in the kitchen reading (or, rather, staring at the pictures in) a cinemagazine; and Elaine went early to bed with a book.

The next day was Sunday, cool and peaceful. To Elaine there seemed to be a new, quietly happy feeling between herself and Iveen; sometimes they smiled at each other as they went about the house. Iveen seemed to have got over her storm of yesterday, and to be much calmer and happier. What a wonderful power human warmth and sympathy has, thought Elaine, spending the afternoon gardening after a morning at church; I'm glad I told her.

After tea she sat down to write to an elderly cousin in London, her only living relative.

'Please, Miss Garfield, can I run down to Mum's for a bit?' asked Iveen, at the drawing-room door.

'Yes, of course, Ivy. I thought you'd gone long ago,' said Elaine, looking up with a kind smile.

'Oh no, Miss Garfield, I've been clearing up a bit, the kitchen was in a fine old mess what with the rain yesterday and you walking in and out with your gardening,' retorted Iveen, but her tone was so unself-conscious and completely without offensiveness that Elaine's heart warmed. She laughed.

'You'll get used to that. Ivy,' she added impulsively, 'you do like being here, don't you? I mean, you're happy here, and you'd like to stay?'

'Oh *yes*, Miss Garfield!' cried Iveen ardently, her airs and graces all gone, real affection shining on her coarse pale face. 'I like it ever so, I was only saying to Mum the other night.'

'Well, I'm very glad, my dear. Run along, now, or your mother will be wondering where you are.'

The letter was a long one, as Elaine's to her cousin always were, and after it was finished she became absorbed in some embroidery. When at last she looked up wearily, her eyes aching from the dazzle of brilliant colours on the canvas, she was surprised to see that the time was half-past ten. The house was utterly quiet. Miller slept in his basket and the clock ticked loudly. Elaine was a little startled; Ivy was never as late as this! But she sensibly concluded that there was something special going on down at the cottage and that Ivy had stayed later than usual to take part in it. Nevertheless, when she went up to bed at eleven o'clock she was becoming seriously alarmed, and she lay awake for some time listening. But when at last she fell asleep, Iveen had not come in.

The next morning about half-past eight, as Elaine was sitting white-faced and nervous over her breakfast, the garden gate clicked, and she looked up to see Mrs Bank hurrying up the path, in overall and hat, her lips pressed tightly together. Elaine got up and ran out to meet her.

'Oh, Mrs Bank – what is it? Is Ivy ill?'

Mrs Bank jerked her head over her shoulder.

'No, she's not ill. She's down home. I kep' her with me last night, that's all. I jus' come up to tell you she ain't coming back.'

'Not coming back?' Elaine sat down suddenly on the bench outside the door, staring up at the other woman.

'Why not?'

'Well—' Mrs Bank was very embarrassed and twisted her hands nervously in her overall while she spoke, 'I think she's better off at home with me. Her mother's the best one to look after a girl who's done what Ivy's done, and that's the truth, Miss Garfield.'

'But doesn't she want to come back? What's the *matter*, Mrs Bank? Everything was all right yesterday . . . she told me only last night that she wanted to stay here.'

'Never mind what she wants,' said Mrs Bank sharply. 'I've been talkin' to her and I've made her see what's right. She was very upset, Ivy was, because you've been kind to her – which you have, I will say that. But she's better off with me. That's all.'

'But *Mrs Bank*,' said Elaine desperately, 'surely I have a *right* to know why you've taken your daughter away from a place where she was happy?'

'Well, miss, if you will make me say it, it's what you told her the other night, then. If you must have it plain,

I don't think you're the sort, miss – madam – that ought to look after a girl like Ivy. You don't seem to know the difference of what's right and what's wrong. Tellin' her there wasn't no harm in what she done, and how you'd done the same thing, and all . . . I wouldn't believe it when she told me, that I wouldn't. "Miss Garfield's a lady," I said, "and ladies don't do that sort of thing, not like our class," I said. But she says you told her right out, miss.' She paused, very distressed, a question in her tone.

'Yes, I did,' said Elaine faintly, staring down at the ground. 'I did tell her.'

'And it's true, then?'

Elaine nodded.

'Then I think you ought to be ashamed of yourself, that's what I think,' burst out Mrs Bank, going very red and lifting her head to stare at Elaine, 'when you know what sort of a girl Ivy is . . . telling her you wish you'd had a child and all that stuff. It's downright wicked, and foolish, too. I'm very sorry for you, miss – madam – if your young fellow was killed in the war, but I can't let my girl stay with a person that thinks in the way you do. It wouldn't be right. So I'll say good morning.'

She turned, and walked quickly and stiffly away. Elaine got up and went blindly into the house and sat down at the kitchen table. In the silence, Miller sighed deeply and dropped his chin on her knee.

In the end, it was not the contempt of the village but its incredulous, half-amused sympathy that broke Elaine's courage. Within a month of her interview with Mrs Bank, a *To Let* board stood in the garden of Bryant's, and the house was empty.

The Walled Garden

'Good-bye, dear, I'll try to be back for dinner but, of course, I can't promise. If I'm not, make my apologies, won't you?'

Dr Alfred Wilson took his wife's face between his hands and tenderly kissed it. The sound of a child singing quietly to itself came into the spare room from the nursery next door, and through the open window a shabby perambulator, with a white net over it, could be seen on the lawn. The peaceful noises of a country town about its morning business sounded outside.

The doctor ran downstairs.

Susie Wilson leant out of the window and assured herself that Baby was all right, then she went back to making up the spare bed, whistling as she did so. In a few hours, she thought, Mike and Noel will be here!

She had not seen them for more than a year, and then only during a hurried lunch in town. Before she married, when she had been earning a living as a not-unusually gifted fashion artist in London, the three had shared a flat and enjoyed a gay, untidy life whose casualness was, in their eyes and those of their friends, more than excused by the passionate concern which all three felt about the misfortunes of people whose lives were even less orderly than their own.

'Mike and Noel'll look after her for a bit, just until she finds something!' was the common saying in their set when anyone lost a husband or a job.

But when Susie married a country doctor and went to live in his native town, she had naturally dropped out of the set; and when the baby came, a year later, she found herself so absorbed by domesticity that she had no time even to write to her old friends. Now there was a second baby, asleep out there on the lawn, but Susie's husband had insisted upon installing a capable nurse, and at last Susie had time to look about her and please herself. One of her first acts had been to write to Mike and Noel and ask them down for a week-end.

The rest of the day was her usual busy one. She shopped, arranged the meals for five grown-ups (her husband's unmarried brother, Ted, lived with them and acted as the doctor's partner) and two children; mended, looked after the children while Nannie took her afternoon off, and even managed to find time for a little gardening.

By five o'clock she was driving to the station under the pink evening sky, between the hedges covered with little bright green leaves, wearing a new suit and feeling completely happy. The house waited for the guests, with flowers in their bedroom, and a fire in the drawing-room 'because the evenings are still chilly.' The children were left in the charge of Winifred, Susie's 'general.'

The train was in. And there, standing by the big battered

suitcase that Susie remembered so well from foreign holidays in the old days, were Mike and Noel, looking as queer,
as untidy, as distinguished as ever, bless them!

But horrors! Who was that with them? Not Helga?

Yes, it was Helga. No one else would have worn black
corduroy trousers, a striped sweater, and climbing boots
with ski-ing socks. No one else had hair exactly the colour
of marmalade, which blew so Garboishly in the wind.

Susie's heart went down into her shoes.

'Noel! Mike! Here I am!' she called, waving gaily. They
turned and ran towards her, Noel lugging the suitcase and
Mike waving his long arms and shouting 'Hullo, darling!'

But Helga stayed by the bookstall, looking timid and
sad.

That means she's either out of a job again or someone's
just let her down, thought Susie, as she kissed Noel's cool,
unpainted cheek and then Mike's unshaven one. *What did
they want to bring her for?*

'It's heavenly to see you again!'

'However long is it? It must be a year!'

Noel took Susie's arm and pressed it lovingly and led her
up to the tall girl standing sadly by the car:

'Darling, you remember Helga, don't you? I knew you
would love to see her again, she's staying with us and she
doesn't like being alone just now. You can fit her in somewhere now you're a Lady of the Manor, can't you?'

'Of course — lovely — I'm so glad you did. How are
you, Helga? It's awfully nice to see you again. Quite like
the old days,' said Susie warmly, smiling all over her round,
pale little face and shaking Helga's hand after a quick

decision not to kiss her rather unsavoury painted cheek because of Baby and Kitty.

'I can go back, you know, if there isn't room,' said Helga abruptly, in the deep voice that Susie too well remembered. How often, far, far into the night, had their flat reverberated to that voice, telling them it could no longer endure the sufferings inflicted by the He of the moment!

'Of course not, there's plenty of room,' she answered hastily, as they all settled themselves in the car, 'and I love having you. The country air will do you good.'

'Yes, I look pretty foul, don't I? I'm quite aware of it. Country life suits *you*, anyway; I shouldn't have known you.'

Susie gave a smile – it is to be feared of the kind known as sickly. At the back of her mind a furious re-planning was going on.

Now Helga and Noel would have to share the spare room.

And Mike would have to sleep on the couch in the drawing-room.

But there was no more bedding!

Oh, well, he would have to cover himself with coats and the rug from the car.

But all the heavy coats had just come back from the cleaners and been put away for the summer.

Besides, Winifred always 'did' the drawing-room first in the mornings.

And Mike *had* to sleep late in the mornings or he was nervy and touchy all day.

Of course, in the old days she would have thought joyously: 'Oh, we'll squeeze in somehow.'

But it was not the old days now.

'Charming!' pronounced Mike, as the car stopped in front of the doctor's house. It was a tall, thin house of red brick, with white window frames and fanlight. Four steps, worn by the feet of generations of patients who had been coming to 'see Doctor Wilson' for a hundred years, led up to the front door, which was now open, and framed a group consisting of Winifred, Baby and Kitty, Susie's daughter, who came down the steps to meet them, one step at a time (while Winifred called anxiously, 'Not so quick, Kitty!').

Mike carried the suitcase upstairs (for both the doctors were out on their rounds), dumped it on the spare-room floor, took a pipe from his pocket, and asked if he might go into the garden and get the taste of London out of his lungs?

'Of course. Do. I hope you'll like our garden,' said Susie, smiling at him as he went slowly down the stairs.

'Why? Is there any reason why I shouldn't?' He looked back at her, smiling affectionately, yet with the touch of criticism, of discontent, that marred his approach to everything. He wanted perfection, and had never become resigned to doing without it.

'Oh, no. Only it's got a wall all round it and some people find it a bit shut-in.'

'H'm,' said Mike, and went slowly across the hall and out through narrow old french windows.

A long lawn and flower-beds were enclosed on three sides by a high wall of red brick, and against the wall fruit trees – apricots, pears, apples, plums – were spread. They were just coming into blossom, and the leaves and flowers made a continuous pattern all round the three sides of the garden against the wall. The lawn was thick and soft and old. Overhead was the evening sky. No houses over-looked the walled garden. There was the wall, the pattern of fruit trees, the lawn, the quiet sky, and that was all.

It was very quiet. Noises came from the High Street, but the wall seemed to muffle them; they were far away, and sounded beautiful and peaceful, like music.

I wonder if Susie knows anyone who could give Helga a job, thought Mike, slowly pacing up and down and making a half-circle, each time he came to it, to avoid a child's wheelbarrow overturned on the grass. Poor child. Something will have to be done about her.

'Oh, Susie, it's peaceful here!' sighed Helga, falling across the spare-room bed. 'You're a very, very lucky woman. What's your man like? Is he a good lover, and do you adore him?'

Winifred had just entered the room with some hot water for the ladies-who-were-staying to wash themselves for dinner, and she caught the full force of this remark. She quickly glided out of the room with the tips of her ears a roasting scarlet, and Susie felt exactly as if someone had dropped a trayful of crockery. She smiled vaguely and said nothing.

'What's up?' Helga glanced from her hostess's disturbed face to Noel's, amused and a little disapproving. 'What have I done now? Oh, god, the domestic! Isn't she used to unbuttoned speech? I'm terribly sorry, Susie, but you've come over very county, haven't you?'

'People are still easily shocked in the country, you know,' explained Noel, with a frown and shake of her head while Susie's back was turned.

'I'll be more careful, I will really. I'm awfully sorry, darling.' Helga went across to Susie and gave her a rather tobacco-ey but sincere kiss. 'The fact is I'm a swine these days, but I have had enough to make me. I've been living with Tony for nearly a year.'

Susie made a sympathetic noise. She was wondering where Nannie had got to, and thinking it was time Winifred was getting on with the chickens for dinner.

'And three weeks ago we had the hell of a row—'

Susie put the chickens to the back of her mind and settled down to listen.

While Mike was lying under the pear tree near the house, smoking and staring up at the sky, a short young man with red hair and a cheerful expression came across the lawn, saying pleasantly:

'How do you do? My name's Ted Wilson. I'm Susie's brother-in-law. Lovely evening, isn't it?' He sat down beside Mike on the grass. 'Do you know this part of the country at all?'

Mike replied civilly, but with sinking spirits. He found the young man's conventional opening irritating; and though he honestly tried to keep the conversation to trivialities, it somehow developed into an argument. Mike's voice went up and Ted's ears got red, and upstairs in the spare-room Susie sat on the bed, listening with one ear to Helga's tale of woe and with the other to the alarmingly loud tones coming from the garden, and wondering wildly what had become of Nannie. It was nearly half-past six, and Kitty was supposed to be bathed at six o'clock.

Helga abruptly finished her story, got up, and strolled into the nursery, where Winifred was 'minding' Baby and Kitty with her thoughts on the chickens which she should have been preparing. She glanced up and smiled bashfully at Helga.

'Do let me stay here with them, I adore kids,' said Helga, looking devouringly at the two small rounded forms with their peach-like skins and liquid eyes. 'Absolute little loves, aren't they?'

'Oh yes, miss, and so good too! Well, if you really don't mind it would be ever so kind of you, miss, because Nannie's that late, I can't think what's happened to her, and I've got me chickens to see to.'

'I'd adore it. I promise I'll take care of them. You run along.'

So Winifred gladly ran along, and when Susie and Noel came into the nursery ten minutes later they were surprised by the spectacle of Helga lying on the floor with Kitty bouncing gently up and down on her thin flat stomach, while Baby lay on his side watching; grave, but plainly entertained.

'It's awfully good of you to bother with them, Helga. Don't let them tire you,' said Susie.

'This isn't the sort of thing that tires me. I adore kids, don't I, Noel?'

'Of course she does,' said Noel gently, looking down at the beautiful but worn face framed by golden hair spread out on the nursery floor.

'Why don't you try for a job looking after children?'

suggested Susie kindly. 'You ought to be good at it. Kitty, how would you like Auntie Helga for your Nannie?'

There was laughter over this exquisitely funny notion, and for the next few minutes the nursery was very noisy while Helga rushed round and round with Kitty on her back and Baby crowed with excitement as he bounced up and down on Noel's knee. Susie looked on, smiling benevolently.

But a sudden stop was put to these antics by the entrance of a slim young woman in a printed frock under a dark coat, looking flushed and defiant.

'I know I'm late, Mrs Wilson,' snapped Nannie. 'I'm sorry. The fact is, my friend and I got talking, and I didn't notice the time. But you seem to be getting on all right.'

There was a guilty silence.

'Kitty'll be nice and excited, I'll never get her to sleep to-night. I'll just get my things off and get her into her bath. A nice mess you've made, Kitty! Look at your nursery! It'll take poor Nannie half the evening to clear up the pickle.'

And Nannie whisked off to her room to change her clothes, leaving the three amateurs very dashed by the arrival of the professional.

'What a—!' yawned Helga, slowly swinging Kitty round and round. 'Is she always like that?'

'Oh, no, usually she's very good-tempered,' said Susie, flustered (*oh, heavens, would Nannie give notice?*). 'She was only upset because she was late, and she doesn't like the children to see many visitors, she says it's too exciting for them.'

'But she shouldn't have spoken to Kitty like that; the

child looked really wounded,' said Noel earnestly. 'It's so important to keep them in an atmosphere of harmony and peace. She looks like a sadist to me, Susie, with those thin lips. You ought to sack her and have someone who truly *loves* the children.'

'I'm sure Nannie's really very fond of them,' said Susie – more firmly than she would have thought it possible for her to speak to Noel. 'Well' (as Nannie came back, crossly buttoning her apron), 'shall we go into the garden?'

In the garden, Mike was telling Ted that Susie had changed.

'Five years ago she was – well, sweet is the only word; she was like newly ironed linen, or honey. And now she's nothing but the Complete Married Woman.'

'Is that such a bad thing to be?' inquired Ted, wishing the women would come down so that the drinks could be had.

'Sense of humour gone. Individuality gone. All swallowed up by the children and the stifling shut-in-ness of marriage,' went on Mike.

'Oh, I say!'

'Children,' pursued Mike, 'are little cannibals who eat their parents' individuality. That's why I won't agree to Noel's having any.'

'I see,' murmured Ted. He saw something pretty good coming towards him across the lawn; something with a head of golden hair and big sad dark eyes. The eyes met his own, steadily. Oh, boy! thought Ted, what have I done to deserve this?

Dr Alfred came out to them later, smoking one of the little black cigars which he had specially imported for him from South America, and Mike felt vaguely affronted because he was not plump, slow-witted, rosy and prejudiced, as a 'typical' country doctor should be. His thin, dark face and dry voice seemed suited to a more urban setting.

The evening passed without unpleasant incident, but by ten o'clock both hosts and guests were aware of a strain. Mike, Noel and Helga talked about the delicious food they had eaten in out-of-the-way places in Europe, and the tragic or amusing types they had met abroad. The brothers and Susie listened politely, laughed and exclaimed and envied, but towards the end of the evening Susie became rather silent.

Only a little while – such a little while ago, but it seemed like twenty years – she had wandered with Mike and Noel through those beautiful, romantic places; footloose, poor and gay.

Of course, she was perfectly happy. She would not go back to her old life. But as she listened to the talk of her friends, her heart began to ache with longing for those far-off places.

Under cover of the conversation Helga's eyes were busy with Ted's; by the time the drinks came in at ten it seemed the most natural thing in the world when Ted murmured that he would love to drive her down to the river to-morrow morning to look at the kingcups.

The revelries ended with the drinks, for country air had made the Londoners sleepy, and everyone went to bed.

'Ted seems to have fallen for Helga, doesn't he? He was making heavy passes at her all the evening,' said Susie to Alfred when they were alone.

'He does at everyone. She won't take him seriously, will she?'

'Oh Alf, I hope not! She's so affectionate!'

'That's what you all call it, do you?'

Susie smiled gently. Poor Helga! Eight years ago, when she was twenty, her parents had gone lightheartedly off to America and abandoned her. She had two pounds ten a week, left to her by a pitying aunt, and on this she lived. Emotionally she lived upon her friends, who said that she was not fitted to stand up to life. She was always ringing people up and saying hoarsely: 'Is that you, Eleanor? My god, I'm sunk; can you come round?' and round Eleanor would have to go, no matter what her engagements for that day might be.

'Poor Helga!' said Susie, but she giggled; after the strain of the evening it was a relief to giggle with Alfred.

'Charm, but no stamina,' said Alfred drowsily.

After Baby had finished his breakfast next morning, there was a terrible piece of news: Nannie announced that she would leave at the end of the week. She would give no reason; she would only mutter something about 'too quiet here,' and whisk about the nursery with her apron flying, tidying up and slamming things into cupboards.

Susie was too disturbed to keep this blow to herself. She went out to the garden where some of the others were sitting under the old pear tree and announced, in a tone that she tried to make light and amused:

'Awful news! Nannie's leaving.'

'Not our fault, I hope?' asked Mike rather disagreeably (must this already intolerably smug atmosphere have domestic upheavals added to it?) while Alf took his little black cigar out of his mouth and stared at his wife in dismay.

'Of course not, don't be silly. It's just that she's sick of country life or something – I can't get her to say what's the matter. Anyway, she's going.'

'But Susie!' Noel sat up, with her eyes shining. 'What a piece of luck! You won't have all the sweat of looking for a new one. There's one on the premises, all ready for you!'

Susie stared at her, and Alf, a horrible light breaking upon him, took out his little cigar and parted his lips to speak. But Noel went on gaily:

'Helga, of course! She adores the kids and she'd give her eyes for a job like this. Oh Susie, it would be *perfect*! And there's another thing, too—'

She turned to Alf, who was watching his wife's troubled face.

'Your brother! He's quite obviously in love with her. If she stays here to look after the children she and Ted will get to know each other, and it might be the solution of all poor Helga's troubles. A home, a husband, children, security . . .' Noel's kind brown eyes shone at the picture.

'Oh I say, Noel,' began Mike rather uneasily, glancing from the stricken face of his hostess to the appalled face of his host. 'I hardly think Helga is Ted's cup of tea, is she? She's a – a good deal more experienced to begin with—'

'That's just what I was thinking,' interrupted Alf, giving him a grateful glance and replacing the cigar.

'But that's exactly what Helga needs, a simple, decent type without complexes!' cried Noel. 'Ted would iron out

all the creases in her miserable little mind and cure her of
being so – so easily attached to men.'

'But Noel,' said Susie at last (she had gone pale). 'I'm
afraid it's simply out of the question.'

'Why?' demanded Noel. 'You've known her for years.
You know how affectionate she is and what a rotten time
she's had. You can see how the kids adore her. Why *shouldn't*
she be their Nannie?'

Noel's face had taken on the exalted, obstinate look that
Susie knew and dreaded. That was how she used to look
in the old days, when she was pleading with Susie to turn
out of her bed and give half a week's salary to some friend
who was without either.

After an embarrassed silence she muttered something
about Helga 'finding it awfully quiet down here.'

But Noel shook her head, crowned with its red-brown
braids.

'It's no use, Susie,' she said steadily, sitting with her hands
linked round her knees and staring up at her friend's
distressed face, while the two men listened in silence. 'You
know, in your secret heart, that you ought to give this job
to Helga. It may be her last chance.'

'She's always having last chances!' cried Susie, beginning
to get angry. 'She's been hanging on to you and everybody
else for years, and why should I be dragged—'

She checked herself, ashamed, and searched in her bag
with shaking hands for a cigarette.

'Exactly,' said Noel, not taking her eyes from her face.
'Why should you be dragged into it? You're comfortable,
you've got everything – husband, home, children, you've
even got a position. You—'

'But that's just the point!' said Susie, trembling, 'I've got other people to think about now. Alfred and the children – it isn't like the old days—'

'It certainly isn't. You used to be a generous person.' Noel's voice was not quite under control and suddenly she looked away from her friend's face.

There was an uncomfortable pause. Then Susie said: 'I'm awfully sorry, Noel.'

Noel did not answer. Her head was bent and she was digging a little stick into the soft grass.

'You see—' Susie stumbled on, 'you admit yourself that I've got a position. And if you're Somebody, however small, in a country town—'

'My god!' said Mike, softly but audibly, staring up into the branches of the pear tree.

'—I know it doesn't matter what people think about one in London, but it does matter in the country,' Susie ended. She had gone red.

'And what do people think about you?' demanded Noel, driving her little stick into the ground and looking up at last.

'Well, they know I'm a doctor's wife and they know Alf's family have been doctors here for nearly a hundred years and they expect me to behave sensibly, like everybody else does!' burst out Susie, 'and if I had Helga to look after the children they'd simply think I'd gone mad.'

'What does that matter, if you knew you were doing what *you* thought was right?'

'But, Noel, I *shouldn't* be! I don't think Helga's the right person to look after Kitty and Baby. I don't think she's—'

'Well, what? You don't think she's what? Go on,' said Noel in a hard tone.

'Well – wholesome,' said Susie at last in a low reluctant voice.

There was a very unpleasant pause. It was broken by another voice:

'May I speak to you for a moment, please, Mrs Wilson?'

It was Nannie, looking grim and inscrutable in a clean apron, who had come unobserved across the lawn to the pear tree.

'Yes, Nannie, of course. What is it?'

'It's Kitty, Mrs Wilson. She's got three spots I'd just like you to look at, if you will, please.'

'Oh, Nannie! Of course!'

And Susie at once followed the intimidating figure towards the house.

'What sort of spots? Where are they?' Susie said imploringly as they walked along quickly side by side.

Something was happening to Nannie's face. It was losing its hard, defiant expression and becoming troubled, almost embarrassed.

'Well, the fact is, Mrs Wilson, Kitty hasn't any spots, she's quite all right, bless her' (Nannie's voice gave a peculiar quaver, then righted itself). 'The fact is, I had to speak to you at once, so I just said that about Kitty's spots.' Nannie gulped. 'I'm sorry.'

Susie waited.

'Mrs Wilson, I just heard from Winifred that that young lady in the trousers is coming here in my place to look after the children. Is that right?'

Susie opened her mouth to cry: 'Good heavens, no!' Then she shut it, and opened it again to say:

'Well, Nannie, as a matter of fact, we were just discussing it. She seems very fond of the children—'

'If you would reconsider my notice, Mrs Wilson, I should be very pleased,' said Nannie, the quaver reappearing. 'The fact is I had some bad news about a friend yesterday and it upset me. But I'm really fond of the children, you know that, Mrs Wilson, and the fact is,' suddenly speaking faster, 'I don't like to think of my two little ducks being looked after by that young lady in the trousers. I'm sorry I said that about Kitty's spots, Mrs Wilson. Perhaps you won't reconsider my decision after my saying that, but I'd be very glad if I could – could stay, Mrs Wilson.'

'Oh Nannie, I'd love you to stay!' breathed Susie.

'Thank you very much, Mrs Wilson.' Nannie took out her handkerchief, stared at it fiercely, and put it back in her pocket. 'Well, I'll go and get on now. There's always plenty to do with two of them.'

She gave Susie a quick nod and walked smartly away towards the house.

Susie went on to the kitchen garden and lingered there for a few minutes, pulling gooseberry leaves to pieces while she tried to compose her feelings. She now had a cast-iron excuse for not giving Helga the job, but that would make things no easier with Mike and Noel. Suddenly she found herself wishing to heaven that they had never come!

In ten minutes she rejoined the group under the pear tree.

'It's all right, the spots are only heat bumps,' she said,

smiling falsely at the three glum faces. 'And I think Nannie's going to stay, after all. So that—'

'Did you ask her to stay?' interrupted Noel.

'No, I didn't. She offered to. She's changed her mind,' retorted Susie.

'Why?'

'Well, really, Noel darling, it isn't awfully interesting, is it? She's had a change of heart, I suppose.'

'Or else you told her that Helga was after her job.'

'I did *not* tell her, Noel! She guessed – if you must know.'

'Well, no doubt it's a let-out for you—' Noel was beginning coldly, when Alf exclaimed, 'Hullo, here's Ted!' and they all turned to see him coming towards them. He was red in the face and looked annoyed and embarrassed.

'Oh, hullo!' he said. 'I've just come back for Helga's rucksack.'

'Whatever does she want it for?' exclaimed Noel. 'Is she going off somewhere? I thought you were going to picnic?'

'Oh, well, the fact is, we met some people I know slightly down by the river, the Price-Olivers, and they've got a chap staying with them that Helga seems to know.'

'What's his name?' demanded Mike and Noel, in one breath and alarmed voices.

'She called him Tony.'

'Tony Lisle!' wailed Noel. 'Oh *no!* Mike, she mustn't! Just as we'd got her away from him! He's *such* a bad influence for her! Is she going off with him?' Noel scrambled to her feet.

'Looks like it. They seemed very pleased to see each other.'

'Oh, we *must* stop them! Where are they?'

'Waiting down by the bridge in his car.'

'But what about the Price-Olivers? Didn't they think it awfully queer?'

'They didn't say much. They seemed used to him.'

'You'll drive us down, won't you?' Noel said this over her shoulder as she hurried down the garden with the skirt of her bright cotton dirndl flying picturesquely about her. 'We've *got* to save her!'

But when they arrived at the bridge they found that Tony and Helga had decided not to wait for the rucksack. Only the Price-Olivers were there, picnicking rather hysterically among the kingcups with the air of people who have been suddenly relieved of a burden.

'I never thought I should have been glad to see the back of Mike and Noel,' said Susie sadly, late that night. She and Alf were standing by their bedroom window, indulging in a little gossip before retiring to rest.

'They'll never feel the same about me again,' she sighed, dragging the brush slowly through the curtain of hair hanging down over her face.

'Does that matter very much?'

He put his arm round her, and she laid down the hairbrush and rested her head comfortably on his shoulder.

'Of course it does. They were my best friends in the old days.'

'It's what usually happens to friendships when people marry.'

'It oughtn't to.'

'Perhaps not, but it does.'

'I feel so bad about it.' Susie picked up the brush and went on brushing. 'Poor Helga. I've got so much! And it seems so horribly selfish—'

'You needn't feel bad about it. You can't live like a married person and a bachelor as well.'

'How do you mean?'

'Well—' He leant both hands on the window-sill and stared down into the garden, dimly lit by the summer moon. 'Mike and Noel are still living a bachelor life. They're married, but they've no children, and no responsibilities and so they can change their plans at a second's notice and give all the time they want to the work they like doing, or pop off abroad whenever they like.'

'I'd love to go abroad again,' she said dreamily.

'I suggested it in April, but you wouldn't leave Baby, you may remember.'

'Of course not! How could I? I was forgetting.'

'There you are, you see. It's no use. You've chosen to be a married person. You mustn't expect to lead the life of a bachelor.'

'But it seems so awfully selfish not to try and help people. Mike and Noel were so hurt.'

'You've chosen the people you're responsible for – me and Kitty and Baby and Ted—'

'And Winifred and the practice!'

'Exactly. You can't go helping every lame dog you meet; that's the bachelor's job. A marriage—' his sleepy eyes, wandering over the familiar garden, noticed the deep shadow cast on the moonlit lawn by the old wall '—a marriage has got to have a wall round it, like the garden. Inside the wall everything's safe. It's got to be, so that the fruit can grow—'

'And the children.'

'And the children – exactly.'

After a little pause, during which her eyes rested on the trees rustling softly against the tender sky, she said doubtfully:

'But surely *all* marriages aren't like a walled garden?'

'All proper marriages are,' answered her husband.

A Charming Man

'Georgie, run down to the Library before they close, and change this book. Daddy says he's read it.'

'What book? Oh – *A Wanderer in the Andes* – I'm in the middle of it. Can't we hang on to it till I've finished it? It's swell. I could take it back to-morrow evening.'

'Daddy wants a new one, dear. Run along, now; here you are. Be quick, or they'll be shut.'

George slouched into the little hall, and took his hat from the hallstand. His unattractive, suspicious young face looked back at him resentfully from the narrow mirror as he settled his new hat on his head.

He spent a minute or two seriously adjusting the angle of the hat until it satisfied him. His school cap hung discarded on the highest peg of the stand, not to be used again until term began.

His mother had unconsciously been listening for the slam of the front door, and when after four minutes it did not come, her soft fretful voice floated into the hall.

'Whatever are you doing, George? Do hurry up.'

The front door slammed, louder than she had expected.

'Oh!' sighed Mrs Ward. 'Thoughtless boy!'

And she passed her hand nervously over the back of

her faded fair hair, her glance straying vaguely through the window into the evening light.

Daddy was playing tennis with some people at the tennis club. He would not be home till nine or later. His supper – 'my nightcap,' as he playfully called it – waited for him on one end of the table, carefully set out with a fragile lace cloth, fresh flowers and speckless glass and silver.

Mrs Ward sighed faintly and picked up a half-mended sock. She switched on the wireless and settled back in her chair to mend and listen and let her thoughts flow vaguely and resentfully over her life as she lived it from hour to hour.

George stopped near Silver's End tube station to catch a tram. The clock on the War Memorial said ten to seven, and he looked at it and scowled. He would scarcely be back before half-past, and he was meeting Delia, his girl, outside that same Memorial at half-past.

He comforted himself with the thought that she would be late. Delia was always late.

'Well, Georgie, and how are you? How's your mother? And your dear father? I've just been watching him playing tennis – a perfect picture, I thought. Where are you off to?'

He turned, with a sinking heart, to confront the sunken eager face and withered prettiness of little Miss Ashe, an acquaintance of his mother's.

George dragged off his hat sheepishly, wishing that he could hit all the people who called him Georgie.

'I'm very well, thank you, Miss Ashe,' he muttered. 'I'm just going down to the Library to change a book for father.

He's very well, thanks. So's mother. Er – how – er – are you keeping – pretty fit?'

Miss Ashe put her helpless little hand, in a darned glove, to her lips and coughed delicately.

'Trying weather,' she explained. 'But so nice to see everything looking so fresh and green, isn't it? Remember me to your father, Georgie. Tell him we're looking to him to make the show next week a *great* success. Such a charming man – a perfect gentleman, and with lovely manners. An example to your generation, my dear. Good-bye. I mustn't keep you. Good-bye.'

George's unformed mouth curled in a sneer as he watched her hurrying away, but he was sorry for her, too.

In the tram on his way to the Library he met two more people who asked after his father, both with that smile of interest and pleasure that George had seen on people's faces ever since he could remember, when his father was mentioned.

As he got out of the tram he saw a placard outside the Library announcing that the Silver's End Players would shortly present 'Ariel: A Fantasy,' written and produced by Hugh J. Ward, at the Assembly Hall, for three nights only.

'He's done a lot, in three years,' thought George vaguely, lounging up the steps of the Library. 'Everybody knows him, and likes him. Wish I had some of his personality. Not that I'd get a look in, if I had. There's only room for one like father in the family. He's a wonderful chap. No wonder he gets people so. Only—'

He suppressed a disloyal thought before it was born.

His eyes wandered warily round the Library as he went in, hoping there would be no one in the room whom he knew, and when he saw that all the people in the room were strangers to him, he sighed with relief, and crossed the room to the counter to return his book.

George, at sixteen, was as friendly as a young hedgehog, and about as approachable. He hated talking to people; tennis-parties, parties of all types, were torture to him. He did not even like listening to other people talking. He liked best of all to indulge in long, muddled day-dreams, in which he was the hero, and to boast at length to Delia about his accomplishments, his conquests and his ambitions.

And Delia, who had a perfect little face, round and blank as a peppermint cream, would breathe 'Oh, George, did you really?' and hear not a word.

He looked regretfully at *A Wanderer in the Andes* as he passed it back to the assistant. He had been enjoying it, but if his father wanted a new book, there was nothing more to be said.

Suddenly he drew into his shell, every hair on his head stiff with aversion and dislike.

A woman was smiling at him as she slowly crossed the room to the door with two books under her arm.

George smiled, or produced a grimace which served as a smile, and muttered 'Good evening, Mrs Millard.'

She paused, lingering near him in a cloud of perfume. Her eyes had once been the most beautiful features in a beautiful face, but now they were thickly and unskilfully painted, like her cheeks and the generous curves of her mouth.

He hated her – her rich, unusual clothes, which she wore badly, her dark hair cut in the shingle of twenty years ago, her vivid face and battered charm.

He thought she was going to speak to him, but she did not. She hesitated, murmured a few words, and moved away, smiling vaguely.

One or two people exchanged smiling glances as Kitty Millard swayed out of the library.

George, always secretly and furiously on the side of the under-dog, suddenly longed to defend her.

'She's married, she's got a big house, and money,' he thought angrily. 'Father likes her. He's sorry for her; he said so. It's only . . . She's all wrong, that's all, living here. She ought to live somewhere else. We're too – oh, I don't know what we are. I suppose we're too pleased with our own way of doing things. Just because she's rich, and gives noisy parties, and knows lots of men . . . I don't see that that's so awful. There's no real harm in her. But I don't want to talk to her, or have anything to do with her, that's all.'

He chose a new book, and forgot Kitty Millard.

And when the news broke next morning that she had been found dead in bed, with an empty bottle under the pillow, Silver's End echoed George's verdict.

There had been no real harm in her, but they just had not wanted to have anything to do with her.

And now no one would ever again be offered the opportunity.

'Shockingly sordid, this business of poor Kitty Millard,' said Hugh Ward, rustling the local paper at breakfast next Sunday. 'Wretched creature. Bad for the neighbourhood, too. Tragic muddle she seems to have made of her life.'

His thick cap of silvering hair caught the sunlight as he lifted his head to glance at his own reflection in the sideboard mirror. It was so pleasant, so familiar to him for the past forty-eight years, that he almost smiled at it.

Mrs Ward gave a sniff.

Her husband looked over the paper with raised eyebrows.

'Charity, Ella my dear, charity,' he said softly, a whimsical smile on his lips. 'She was our friend, remember. Not a very intimate one, perhaps, but still, a friend. I liked her,' he added simply. 'She was kind, and that's a lot in this bitter old world. And they say Millard was a brute to her.'

The breakfast cups were rattled defensively.

'Paint and powder,' muttered Mrs Ward.

Hugh laughed indulgently.

'Woman's vanity, my dear Ella. Poor Kitty! Why shouldn't she put up her poor little barrier of defiance in the face of old age? I respect her for it. She made a gallant fight.'

'What beats me,' said Mrs Ward, 'is how they found out all those things about her past − about that man she was engaged to who was killed in the war, and all that about her bad nerves and all the rest of it. "A friend of the dead woman," it says here' (and she pointed to the front page), 'gives the following impression of her character. Nice sort of a "friend," I must say! Why, it makes her out to be much worse than she really was, I'm sure. It reads like a pack of lies, to me.'

Hugh's eyelids flickered, but he said nothing.

'It was a mean thing to do, whoever did it.'

Again her husband made no reply, and slowly Mrs Ward became aware, by the aloof pose of his head, and his silence, that she had said something that displeased him.

She tried anxiously to think what it could have been, while she began a nervous, one-sided conversation with George.

For the next three days George became used to hearing speculations as to who had supplied the character sketch of the dead Kitty.

No one seemed to know anything about it, but everyone to whom he listened agreed that they had no idea Kitty was as bad as that.

'It makes her like somebody out of a book' was the general verdict. 'Fancy knowing a woman all those years and never seeing she was like that!'

And some of the women, the less prosperous and complacent ones, added softly 'Poor thing!' But most of them agreed that Silver's End was well rid of Kitty Millard.

George only heard one expression of opinion on the mystery from his father. 'Somebody has an eye for character,' observed Hugh Ward, when the article was pointed out to him, 'and there's a definite touch of style about the thing. I don't think it does Kitty's memory any harm. It's a piece of pure art – above good and evil – when a woman's character is presented as accurately as it is here. I wouldn't worry about it, if I were you.'

But George worried in silence.

He was no knight-errant. The memory of a dead woman whom he had rather disliked than otherwise was nothing to him. He scarcely thought of Kitty during his idle, self-absorbed day. But he felt, with a curious mixture of snobbery and shame, that anything would be better than that the authorship of the article should be brought home to the person he suspected.

His love for his father was not love as most sons and fathers experience it. He had a youthful hero-worship for his father's charm and popularity, but his admiration was threatened, as he grew older, by doubt and a shade of contempt. His father's easy, charming condescension to himself became galling where it had once been welcomed with shy pleasure.

He knew nothing of his father as a man. Hugh Ward relentlessly kept George as a rather dull, but lovable, foil to himself; a whimsical offshoot from his own mercurial personality.

George resented being used as an amusing background; he resented being smilingly called 'my amiable heir' in public, and being gently tolerated in private.

Yet his father's popularity in Silver's End gave him, as the son, a pleasant prestige.

He was terrified of anything happening to destroy the easy, popular idol which had dominated his horizon since he was old enough to think and feel.

And when he thought of his father's half-laughing, half-wistful ambitions towards authorship; those fragile, polished little verses signed 'H.J.W.' which had appeared in local papers; those dignified letters to the Press; that half-finished novel; the frequent, 'By Jove! There's a short story in that!' and 'Ariel: a Fantasy' – George was sure.

One Sunday afternoon some weeks later, two or three people came to the Wards to discuss some points arising out of the play which was to be given next week.

They had tea in the garden, in the spring sunlight. There were two elderly men present, acquaintances of Hugh Ward and what is called 'prominent local personalities'; a shy girl in her late twenties who was in love with Hugh but did not know it, two or three young men, and two middle-aged married women, one an earnest church-worker and the other a bridge-fiend who made her own bridge-coatees and wore them with an air. Mrs Ward poured out tea.

George slouched in a deck chair, feeding the fox-terrier with cake crumbs and watching his father.

As usual, Hugh pleasantly dominated the assembly. The adoring eyes of the women and the absorbed eyes of the men watched him as he easily outlined schemes, disposed of hitches and hypnotized everyone into an amiable mood. He was one of those people, decided George, watching with his lower lip unbecomingly protruding, that made you feel pleased with yourself.

That was why people liked him so much.

And then, like a whiff of the unusual scent she used to wear, like the sweet, unhealthy smell of a rich marshflower, the name of Kitty Millard crept into the conversation.

'It's a pity —' said the church-worker hesitatingly, and then hurried on: 'We shan't be able to have that Chinese robe for the King in the second act, Mr Ward. It was just what we wanted!'

'Why not?'

Hugh saw his mistake too late. George, watching, saw his eyelids flicker, as they had done at tea a few days ago when his wife had said that the character sketch of Kitty seemed like a pack of lies.

'Oh – h – h! Mr Ward!'

The church-worker's demure, pleasant voice was shocked.

'It belonged to poor – to Mrs Millard, you know. She promised to let us have it; seemed to want us to, in fact. I was talking to her about it only the day before she . . .'

Hugh moved in his chair and silently, with a smile at his wife, passed his cup for more tea.

'I dare say we can hire something as good,' he said equably. 'The Chinese robe is out of the question, of course. I'll drop in to Bennett's to-morrow and see what they've got for hire.'

'Poor Kitty,' said the bridge-fiend comfortably. 'She always was generous. That was one of her best points. Even that precious "friend" of hers who slandered her in the paper admitted that.'

And then – inevitably—

'I wonder who it was? Somebody who wanted a bit of easy money, I suppose.'

Her sharp little eyes rested musingly on Hugh's face.

'Truth, like murder, will out, dear lady,' he smiled.

She shrugged her shoulders.

'Truth, yes . . . but that wasn't the truth. Poor Kitty – who wouldn't have hurt a fly, even in her worst tantrums! No. That article seemed to me as though it was written by somebody who fancied themselves as a writer.'

She laughed shrilly.

'Somebody like you, Mr Ward – a literary genius.'

Afterwards, George knew that she had meant nothing more than a heavy pleasantry. There was no hint of suspicion in the words. But the sight of his father's face, blank, with lowered lids, as he carefully stubbed his cigarette in his saucer, frightened him.

George parted his dry lips and spoke:—

'You're all wrong,' he said abruptly, in his uneven, breaking voice, 'I wrote it. I wanted some money, and I wrote it. I – told everything I knew about Mrs Millard.'

He drew a deep breath and blundered on—

'I – I knew her pretty well, you see, and I – I just thought – I wanted some money, you see—'

His voice trailed wretchedly away into the shocked silence. With shaking hands he fumbled for his cheap case and lit a cigarette.

But the silence was broken by another voice – the calm, pleasant voice of Hugh Ward, but now so filled with a savage note that it was scarcely recognizable.

'My amiable heir is lying,' he said, slowly. 'He could not have supplied that sketch of Kitty Millard, because it needed an artist to describe her as she was – an artist, and an older man. The sketch was a work of art – the only completely successful work of art in a mediocre artist's career. I wrote it – I wrote it, and I will not sit here and hear the only decent bit of writing I've ever done claimed by a young cub who doesn't know the first thing about writing.

'I don't care whether it was kind to Kitty, or not, and I'm not ashamed of it. It was true; it was Kitty as I saw her, and that's all that matters to me.'

And rising a little unsteadily from his chair, he stalked, through the stunned silence, back to the house.

Golden Vanity

Deltenham, the country town to which colonels and admirals retire on their pensions, stands in a bowl whose sides are green hills. When a visitor gets out of the train at Deltenham he notices at once the difference in the air: it is fresh and cold, and so it should be, blowing down as it does from those flat summits padded with ancient turf.

The town cannot be said to have fallen asleep in 1760, when most of it was built, because, even then, it was not fully awake. To-day, its life flows tranquilly through wide streets, past pale square Anne and Georgian houses, and pastry-cooks' shops, where the ageing daughters of very old generals sit eating éclairs from silver forks, quietly dying into the background of England's history.

On the green hills above the town the strings of race-horses go out to gallop through the dew, and once a year the streets are full of unfamiliar cars and faces, and the hotel proprietors put beds out into the corridors to accommodate the bookmakers who overflow the town on the four days of the meeting when the Deltenham Silver Cup is run.

But during the rest of the year Deltenham sits tranquilly on the green skirt of the map of England, growing ancient gracefully as a well-bred town should.

The sharp air of the hills should not encourage dreams. But in the spring, when the Silver Cup is run, the air softens, and then people who are dreamy by nature get worse still.

'. . . worse and worse,' said Miss Hilda Bremmer, stirring her eleven o'clock cup of chocolate so vigorously that if she had not been a gentlewoman the spoon would have tinkled against the sides of the cup. 'Somebody ought to speak to her about it. I wonder the library keeps her on. The girl seems half-witted. This morning, for instance, I went in to change a book for father. (He likes his book changed twice a week, you know.) I was taking back *From the Cape to Khartoum on Foot* and I wanted *With a Camera in the Alps.* Imagine my astonishment (and I know I spoke particularly clearly when I asked for the book, because Mrs Archer was at my elbow, and I have never forgotten that remark of hers at Mrs Vereker's Book Tea three years ago, about father preferring *light* literature, and I wanted to prove to her that his reading is serious), imagine my astonishment, I say, when Miss Jameson hands me *Where Angels Fear* by Geoffrey Whithorne. Quite inexcusable carelessness, I thought. And I had already been kept waiting quite ten minutes. It's not the first time it has happened, either. This is the *third* time Miss Jameson has handed me a book by this creature Whithorne when I have asked for something quite different. *Most* odd, I call it. I must say I spoke sharply to her. Very sharply. She turned the colour of a beetroot, and I thought she was going to cry.'

Miss Bremmer paused, and drank chocolate. Her withered face beneath her unfashionable hat was so full of spite that, could she have seen it in a mirror, it might have shocked her.

'Did you keep the book?' Miss Ada Sands glanced inquisitively and with a stealthy interest at the two books lying on the table beside Miss Bremmer's shabby handbag and gloves.

'Oh . . . well . . . I did not get it for father; of course, I sent Miss Jameson back for the right one, immediately. But as I wanted another book for myself (I finished Amy Marriot's *A Lifetime's Sacrifice* last night; such a pretty tale), I thought I might as well take one by this man Whithorne . . . as it happened to be there. After all, Ada, one should not *condemn* without having *seen for one's self.* I am no Puritan, I hope. A woman who has lived in the East, as I have, must be prepared to "see life steadily and see it whole." I felt' (and Miss Bremmer smiled down her large nose) 'that I ought to give Mr Whithorne a trial.'

'I wish I might read it,' said Miss Sands, looking covetously at *Where Angels Fear*. 'They say he's *very* outspoken. But it would be no use, even if I were to get it out. Mother would be sure to discover it. She keeps the *strictest* eye on what I read. I sometimes think it is a little unfair.'

As Miss Sands would be fifty-two next month, it did seem a little unfair. But to Miss Bremmer who was over sixty, it seemed natural enough. Younger women who were unmarried must be kept in innocence. When they were over sixty, and the possibility of their being married was remote, rules might be relaxed a little.

'I will tell you what I think about it, Ada, when I have read it,' said Miss Bremmer graciously. 'To a woman of my experience, it will probably seem mild enough. But I tremble, I literally *tremble*, when I think what the effect of such books might be on a morbid, odd kind of girl like Monica Jameson.'

'So queer . . . her liking to live alone,' mused Miss Sands.

'She is queer altogether. Not healthy. Not normal. Not *merry*, as a girl should be. As you were, Ada – as I was,' retorted Miss Bremmer.

And having finished her chocolate, and stood in some impatience while Miss Sands gulped down her own, Miss Bremmer gathered up *Where Angels Fear, With a Camera in the Alps*, her gloves, bag, and umbrella, and swept out of the shop, followed by Miss Sands.

The two ladies made their way homewards through disagreeably crowded streets.

The adjective is theirs, and perhaps one per cent of the population of Deltenham would have agreed with it. But the rest of the town admired large men in loud checks and curly bowlers, small bandy men with sad, simian faces, glossy, haughty horses looking out from their blanket hoods like members of the Ku Klux Klan. The rest of the population revelled in that air of immense knowingness and of money and whisky flowing like water which descends upon a smallish town on race days. Three-quarters of Deltenham did not bet, but the whole town loved the smell of a race.

This was the first of the four days of the meeting. Deltenham has one of the prettiest courses in England, and it was looking its springtime best; the favourite had been meek as a dove for a week, and had apparently forgotten that he was reported to suffer from a temperament; the hotels were crammed, and fresh crowds poured into the town by every train. All was set for four days' perfect racing.

Monica Jameson went out to lunch at half-past twelve, picking her way through the crowded streets. She slipped her fists deep into the pockets of her old grey tweed coat and drifted along in the sunshine – a tall girl with one of those heavenly English faces that never mature, despite years and wrinkles, which are as fair-skinned, as maddening and remote, at sixty as they were at sixteen. Heaven help the man who marries such a face and expects a definite philosophy of life, or passion, to come out of it. Nothing ever does, except the sweetest platitudes and school-girlish words of tenderness.

Monica was thinking about a book and a horse.

She liked horses; nervous, haughty, swift creatures. She missed her riding so much that she did not dare to think about it. Instead of riding, she read.

The name of the favourite for to-morrow's race, the most important of the four days' events, was Golden Vanity. That was the horse.

And to-morrow Geoffrey Whithorne's new novel would be published; and it, too, was called *Golden Vanity*. That was the book.

No one could have guessed, from looking at Monica's shabby, typically English figure, that she was thinking about a picture in a square silver frame which stood on her dressing-table at home. Not only are such thoughts difficult to read in a young woman's face, but few young women would have been so foolish, so morbid, so unnatural, so un-merry, as to treasure a photograph cut from a two-year-old copy of *Books and Authors*, beneath which was inscribed 'Geoffrey Whithorne, author of *Where Angels Fear*, a best-seller of this spring.'

And only another dreamer, like Miss Jameson herself, would have understood how she, at twenty-six, was still so much of a schoolgirl, so lonely, so turned in upon herself for companionship and entertainment, that she imagined herself in love with the photograph of a man, and did not consciously wish for a living lover.

The English climate retards physical development. Life in English country towns, though delightful, is curiously unreal, and encourages day-dreaming. Lastly, the daughter of a dead gentleman (who broke his neck riding to hounds and left a trail of debts behind him as strong as the scent of a fox), who works in a local shop, is not regarded with favour by the mammas of local sons. Especially when her eyes are large, grey, and cool as the sky on an April afternoon.

All these facts conspired against Monica Jameson, and the result was to make her imagine herself in love with Geoffrey Whithorne.

Her room in a house on the outskirts of the town overlooked the river Dell; she could have dropped pennies (if she had had any to spare) into a bushy willow just under her window, and on moonlit nights in spring she often stood looking down on the buds and long spiderlike twigs, inhaling the delicious, damp water-smell and dreaming. She had lived here since she was eighteen, resisting, with the obstinacy so often bestowed on over-gentle people, the attempts of firm aunts to make her go and live with them.

So, after a time, the aunts gave up trying to make her. (Unlike bulldogs, aunts do drop off, if systematically discouraged.)

The novels of Geoffrey Whithorne came into her lonely, unreal life like shooting stars.

His method was to choose as heroine some ordinary young woman ('*Just* like me,' thought all the Monicas all over Great Britain and America) and glorify her.

He did not glorify her with money, or beauty suddenly acquired at the hands of the beauty specialists. He glorified her by pointing out that she was, in reality, an unawakened goddess; mysterious, filled with amazing potentialities, living her own rich feminine life. And if Mr Whithorne had to concede to public taste by marrying his goddess off to someone on page 300, he did not do it until he had thoroughly convinced his reader that the someone was a very lucky chap to get her.

It will not surprise the astute reader of fiction to learn that Mr Whithorne's income increased with each successive novel. He was soon able to afford the most effective kind of publicity: the hush–hush method.

No one ever saw Mr Geoffrey Whithorne dining quietly in his favourite corner of the Oakleaf Restaurant. No one saw photographs of Mr Geoffrey Whithorne going round the links at the Glenswallows Hotel with Lady This or the Honourable Shirley That. Monica Jameson had been lucky to get her photograph of Geoffrey Whithorne when she did: none had been taken since that one appeared in *Books and Authors*, two years ago.

'Mr Whithorne,' said the highbrow critics, when they did condescend to notice his books, 'has done it again,

and even better.' And one of them had once added that
Mr Whithorne had succeeded in convincing the ordinary
woman from China to Peru, that she was a goddess: and
therefore deserved the thanks of women all over the
world.

But Monica, after thinking the matter over very seriously and intelligently, had decided that Geoffrey
Whithorne's novels did not make *her* feel like a mysterious
goddess. Not at all. It was just that he had such a power
of saying exactly what she had always felt about things,
but could not put into words.

That was why she loved his books; and dreamed over
his dark face and that one poetic lock of hair, which lay
dramatically across his black thatch.

That was why she was looking forward with excitement
so intense as to be painful to his next book.

It would arrive to-morrow; her own copy, for which
she had sent seven shillings and sixpence to Messrs.
Entwhistle and Braddock, Geoffrey Whithorne's publishers.
She had sent it two months ago, on the day when she had
seen that Mr Geoffrey Whithorne's new novel, *Golden
Vanity*, would be published in the spring.

Perhaps . . . perhaps it would be about a girl living in
a small, dull country town; a girl who loved poetry, and
had no one to whom she could talk to about it; a girl
who read the lives of great men and women, sitting alone
in her little room overlooking the river. And one spring
a young playwright came to stay in the town, while he
worked on a new drama . . .

'Miss Jameson! I say . . . Monica!'

Monica turned impatiently. When roused abruptly from

one of her waking dreams she was, like other drug-takers, usually rather cross.

But when she saw who it was who spoke to her, she smiled politely and said 'Hullo, Bobby.'

Bobby Vereker. Agent to Lord Vanhomrigh. Diana Vereker's brother. Monica and Diana had been at school together, but when Monica had left at seventeen, and gone into the library as little muck-and-bottle-washer, Diana had gone on to a finishing school in Austria ('and finish her, it did, so far as I'm concerned,' said her only brother ruefully, a week after her return).

'Oh, Bobby, I'm sorry. I didn't realize it was you. How are you? How's Di?'

For though the school acquaintanceship between herself and Diana had long ago faded to an exchange of shy and chilly smiles, Bobby firmly encouraged it.

It gave him a correct excuse to speak to Monica, and sometimes to take her out. And an excuse he must have, because he was so painfully, so hopelessly in love with her, and this in face of her own indifference and his family's disapproval.

His face, to his perpetual fury, was round and plump, and it refused to grow thin and interesting, but if Monica had had eyes to see, she would have beheld Love sitting enthroned on Bobby's pink cheeks and glorifying even his small red moustache.

'Oh, Di's flourishing. You'd heard she's engaged, of course? Chap in the Highland Light Infantry, stationed in India somewhere. Can't be married for two years. Rotten luck. They seem very wrapped up, and all that. Fact is,' he blurted out, coming to the point with a rush, 'I wondered if you'd come racing with me to-morrow, Monica. Do . . . You'd like it, I'm sure. It's months since we've been anywhere together. I thought you'd forgotten my existence.'

And he laughed, a fatuous sound. (For it is a distressing fact that Love usually makes his victims appear silliest just when they long to appear most attractive.)

Monica's small, dreaming face wore a considering look, but that was only out of kindness to Bobby, whose presence and whose suggestion embarrassed her. Her mind was made up.

Go racing? To-morrow afternoon? With Bobby Vereker? But to-morrow afternoon was Thursday, and the library closed at one o'clock and she was going to spend the afternoon sitting at the open window in the sunlight, with the green light from the willow leaves thrown up into her face, reading *Golden Vanity*.

Bobby guessed the answer before she spoke, and his face fell. This made the muscles round his eyes relax, and his ridiculous monocle fell against a button on his coat with a musical little tinkle.

'I'm so sorry, Bobby,' said Monica, 'but I'm afraid I can't. You see, on Thursday afternoon I always write my letters, and do my mending, and get all the little odd jobs finished that I've no time for during the rest of the week. And you know I'm a very methodical person, don't you? I never break my routine.'

Even as a white lie, it was not a good one. Bobby knew that Monica was far from being methodical. As for mending . . . had he not, on more than one occasion, been amused and touched to see half an inch of rosy heel gleaming through a hole in Monica's grey stocking?

He was not deceived for one second. She did not want to go with him. Goodness only knew what her real reason was (impossible to guess; she was the queerest girl), but it was clear that she did not want to.

Naked misery came into his eyes. He knew that he had no chance at all with this funny, dreamy creature, all large eyes and long legs and shabby clothes. But he felt that, if she would *only* give a chap a chance, he could perhaps make her happy; even make her love him. At the thought, his heart seemed to contract with pain. He wanted to take care of her, and make her laugh at silly shared jokes.

Monica saw the eyeglass fall, but being a very selfish young woman she did not observe the naked misery.

'Oh, I say. Too bad ... Still, I quite see your point. Mustn't interfere with the old routine, what? Still, if you do change your mind, Monica, give me a ring. I'll be at home until two. Good-bye.'

He turned away so abruptly that Monica was a little hurt. That was not like little Bobby, to be casual. Perhaps he was sorry he had asked her? She knew that he offered her his invitations in face of his family's disapproval, and that could not be pleasant for him. She was sorry, in her turn, if she had offended him. She never wanted to hurt or offend anyone. She only wanted to dream.

The next morning, when all the bookmakers were slowly cramming into themselves mounds of grilled ham and fried eggs, and the shining horses were pushing round their heads to watch the grooms polishing their rumps, and a thousand decent Deltenham breakfast tables were anxiously discussing the weather, Monica came down to breakfast in the boarding-house where she lived, and found the long-desired parcel waiting for her in the hall.

She did not open it then and there. She carried it off to work, to peep into at her leisure. Doubtless she would have been more sensible to leave it safely in her bedroom, but she could not bear to do this. If she did not find a chance to glance at it during the morning she would at least know that it was safe, near at hand, in her private drawer at the library.

She walked to work through the wide pale streets, under the budding lime trees and planes, between whose branches the hills could be seen, with huge April cloud shadows drifting over them.

The local buses were plastered with notices telling strangers to the town that they could be taken to the course and back for sixpence. (Residents knew it was quicker and less expensive to walk.) Charabancs thundered past on the road leading up to the hills, and after them slid smart, closed cars full of women in superb tweeds and tiny dark bérets with diamond clips, and lean Nordic-looking men who carried field glasses slung over their shoulders, and never opened their mouths.

So, with all the world going to the races, the library was almost deserted that morning.

In three hours Monica and Miss Duff, the other assistant, served only old Colonel Bremmer with *Up the Nile with an Outboard* ('Can't stand this twaddle about taking snaps in the Alps. Feller's a fool. M'daughter got it for me. Fool of a woman. Worst of leaving these things to women. All fools. M'daughter's the worst of the lot.') and poor Miss

Dancey, who asked for a book about Church vestments and their history.

The two girls sat in the large room, with the shadows of the plane branches dancing over the shelf labelled 'Recent Fiction.'

Monica successfully concealed from Miss Duff the fact that *Golden Vanity* lay on her lap. She pretended that she was reading Miss Gladys Cooper's autobiography, and agreed that it was too bad *Golden Vanity* came out on a Thursday, and would probably arrive in Deltenham after the library was shut, and would not be get-at-able until to-morrow.

And then, after Monica had made each sleepy, casual exchange of remarks with Miss Duff, her eyes would return to the book lying open on her lap, and once more she would plunge, deep, deep into the gay and tenderly ironical story of a girl who was a waitress in a Hollywood café, and pined to be a star.

She was plain, she was shy, she was Monica . . . Edna and Louella . . . she was all the shy plain girls in England and America. There was no doubt that Mr Whithorne, as they say, knew his stuff. And Monica adored his heroine . . . and him.

She was reading so avidly that Miss Duff's final remark, made at half-past twelve, while Miss Duff was adjusting her blue cap on her fair hair, reached her through a mist.

'Well, I'm off,' said Miss Duff. 'Shouldn't think Mr Turner would mind, would you, Miss Jameson? After all, you're here, aren't you, and I'm going racing this afternoon. Mustn't miss the start. I'm getting my boy to put me five bob on Golden Vanity.'

'Yes, do go, I'm here,' murmured Monica, lifting dazed eyes for a second from the pages of the book. In fact, she was not there at all; she was in the studio of the Inter-Pan-National Film Company at Hollywood, watching the little waitress make a mess of her first and last chance of a 'test.'

Miss Duff went.

The library sank into sunny silence. The pleasant murmur of a holiday crowd floated through the open windows, with the fresh smell of new grass and buds. The clock chimed a quarter to one in the old church opposite the library.

It was not unusual for Monica to lose herself in a book. She was now as lost as though she had strayed into an unfamiliar wood. Her lower lip protruded ever so slightly, and her breathing grew a little heavy, in ludicrous and charming caricature of those absorbed old gentlemen who attend concerts of classical music. Deeper, deeper, lost as a sleeper is lost in heavy dreams, she read on and on.

The lady who came into the library at one o'clock had to repeat her remark before Monica looked up, startled, staring at her with the eyes of a dazed angel.

'What . . .? What is it . . .? Oh . . . I beg your pardon . . .'

'I said,' remarked the lady, 'that Geoffrey Whithorne ought to be flattered. Isn't that his new book?'

'I . . . oh . . . yes. Yes. *Golden Vanity*. Really, I'm so sorry. Dreadful of me,' said Monica, putting aside the book, and standing up, and looking penitently down from her tall young height at the lady, who was small. 'Did . . . do you want a book?'

'Well . . .' and here she glanced cautiously over her
shoulder with a deprecating smile, as though she did not
wish to be overheard, at another person who was wandering
round the shelves at the further end of the room. 'As a
matter of fact, I'm only down here for the races to-day,
and I just wanted to see if the new Whithorne was in. I
see it is. You've got it very quickly.'

'Well, as a matter of fact,' said Monica, wishing that
the lady, if she did not want a book, would go away and
let her return to her own, 'it's mine. It came this morning,
to my home address. I am afraid that we shan't have the
libarary copies in until to-morrow now, as to-day's
Thursday. But any of the big London shops would have
them, of course . . . if you are going back to town
to-night?'

'So you get your copy in advance, do you?' mused the
lady, who, most annoyingly, showed no sign of going. 'Do
you do that with all his books? Are you a great admirer
of this man Whithorne?'

'Oh, *yes,*' said Monica, so roused from her reserve by
the stimulus of *Golden Vanity* that she spoke candidly as a
child. 'I *love* his books.'

'Like his style, do you?'

'Well . . .' she hesitated, 'it isn't so much the *style* as the
characters, especially the heroines. He makes everybody
so *real*, somehow, and yet they're much more interesting
than people in real life. He must be a *wonderfully* sensitive,
intelligent man, I should think. He understands women
marvellously,' concluded Monica solemnly.

The lady moaned.

'And I suppose,' she pursued, 'that you're very interested

in Mr Whithorne from a personal point of view. Wonder what he's like, and if he's married, and all that?'

'I know,' said Monica, with dignity, 'what he's like. I've . . . I've seen a photograph of him, in *Books and Authors*.'

The lady, who seemed eccentric, gave another little moan, and then startled Monica by calling, 'Geoff! Come here! Here's another of them!'

Someone at the far end of the room gave a whistle; an amused, dismayed, musical whistle.

Then round a stand of books walked Geoffrey Whithorne.

He stood looking admiringly at Monica's white, startled face. And oh, the horror of it! He was fat. Fat. *Fat.*

The horrid word leaped to Monica's lips before she could suppress it. Afterwards, she was not even sure that she had not, in the confusion of the moment, murmured it aloud. The shock was dreadful. She thought how she had murmured 'Darling' to this man's photograph. And here he was . . . Fat.

The lady was saying pleasantly:

'I'm so flattered by your kind remarks about Geoffrey Whithorne's books that I'm going to let you into a secret, but before I tell you I want your word of honour, please, that what I tell you will not be repeated. I believe that, by now, what I am going to tell you is fairly well known in London, but I am not anxious for it to spread further.'

'Of course,' murmured Monica. 'I won't tell.'

But she was not quite sure what she was saying, even as she spoke. She felt dazed. (And where, oh, where was that dramatic lock of silver hair? Gone . . . and the thatch it had once adorned was thin, and suspiciously, painfully black . . .)

'Well,' said the lady briskly. 'Sit tight. I'm Geoffrey Whithorne.'

'Oh!'

'Yes. You see, *Where Angels Fear* was written more as a joke than anything else: I mean, I wanted to write a book as though I were a man who understood women, and I succeeded amazingly. No one was more surprised than I was when it became a best-seller. Then, of course, people began bothering me for photographs, and I thought it would nip a promising career in the bud if I admitted to being a woman. I'd already pinched my cousin's name (we invented the Whithorne), so I saw no reason, at the time, why I shouldn't pinch his features as well.

'So (very foolishly, I admit), we sent a photograph of Geoff to *Books and Authors*. Of course, we only did it once. We realized immediately how reprehensible it was of us. That's why you never see a photograph of me nowadays. That's why I never appear in public except as Miss Alice Little. I get fifty letters a week from girls wanting photographs of Geoffrey Whithorne . . . not bad is it, in these days of competition from cinema stars? There must be more lonely young women in England and America than it's nice to think about. Eh?'

Miss Alice Little looked sharply at Miss Monica Jameson's crimson face.

'Yes,' said Miss Jameson, faintly.

'I wonder if *you* ever wrote?' pursued the little lady.

'Well,' and Monica, despite much shame and distress, began slowly to smile, 'no, I didn't. You see, I *had* a photograph of Geoffrey Whithorne!'

The lady smiled, and the plump (it is a better word,

everybody agrees) gentleman began to smile. The atmosphere perceptibly lightened. Then they all laughed.

'She'll be all right. Young man in the offing,' thought Miss Little. Then she said:

'Like me to sign it?'

'Oh, *please*,' said Monica prettily. 'After all, it doesn't make any difference to the *stories*, does it? They're still lovely.'

'Well, you're the sort of reader for *me*!' said Geoffrey Whithorne, and she signed her name with a flourish.

Monica, looking at her dowdy hat as she bent over the desk, felt as though a tooth had been pulled out of her soul! There was a sense of loss. Absurd, of course, but English misses, with large grey eyes and slim legs, are often like this.

'Good-bye,' said Geoffrey Whithorne, glancing at the clock, which now said 1.15. 'We must fly; we're meeting some friends at the course for lunch. Now you *will* keep this to yourself, Miss – er . . . won't you? As a personal favour to Geoffrey Whithorne?'

And she suddenly turned upon Monica the blaze of a hundred candle-power smile which lit her personality as though someone had turned on flood-lights. Seeing that smile, it was possible to realize that she wrote best-sellers.

'Of *course*,' breathed Monica almost reverently. 'I shall regard it as an honour to have been told.'

The lady and her cousin then went out, with mutual murmurs and pleasantries.

Monica was alone.

She felt extremely depressed. She was so lonely that she wanted to put her head down on the desk, and cry like a little girl. Possibly it was the reaction from the excitement of reading (for Monica was a nervous person. Too nervous, as Miss Hilda Bremmer was never tired of remarking). Possibly it was just because one of her dreams, which were her life, had gone.

The hands of the clock said twenty-five minutes past one.

And suddenly, quite naturally, as if in response to an encouraging whisper from the fresh spring smells which were wafted in through the window . . . Monica hooked her finger in the dial of the telephone.

As she swung its black face over to DEL 17, her own face grew less serious. She even began to smile faintly. 'I'll ask him to put five shillings on Golden Vanity for me . . . for luck,' she thought.

And her smile widened.

And when her lips shaped the words, 'Is that you, Bobby?' she was smiling outright; and he, at the other end of the line, heard the smile in her voice, and was so surprised and delighted that he opened his mouth wide. His monocle fell from his eye, striking against a button on his waistcoat with a musical tinkle.

Poor, Poor Black Sheep

Mr Basil Merryn and Miss Pompey Taverner were dining together by the river on a summer evening. The last sunlight had gone from the tops of the elm trees and the first midges were rising from the gliding water as the liqueurs were reached, and by that time they both felt as if it was only a few days since they had last dined in each other's company. But the sobering truth was that it was ten years.

He had been banished to a job in Brazil by his exasperated family after a sensational divorce case in which he had played a part; and she had lingered on, the last of a set of Bright Young People who had amused and shocked London in the hectic 'twenties, watching one delightful idiot after another marry and settle down to found a family. The papers had stopped putting 'Pompey' in inverted commas; they even occasionally used her baptismal name of Annette.

He and she had run across one another that morning in Bond-street. At first he had not recognized in the beautifully dressed woman of thirty-odd the amusingly ugly girl of ten years ago, but then she had drawled: 'Why, hul*lo*, Baa-Baa!' and he knew her at once, and they stood there, laughing and shaking hands, a tall woman, and a tall man with the lean good looks sponsored by the more expensive tailoring firms in their advertisements.

'My dear! We all thought you were *rotting* in a Mexican *jail* or something!'

'I only got back a few days ago.' He hesitated. 'My father died. Didn't you know?'

'Of course – I'm so sorry,' she said quickly. 'I suppose you'll *stay*, now you are back?'

'I think so. There are all kinds of things to see to about the estate, of course. I say, it's marvellous to see you again.' They had turned together down the expensive street and were strolling along smiling at one another while their friendly eyes took in the little changes that ten years had made. 'Are you doing anything to-night? Do dine with me, if you're free.'

'Adore to,' she said.

He remembered that this had always been her pet phrase, and that she always made it sound like an absurd dying gurgle at the back of her throat. His restless grey eyes approvingly took in the too-slim lines of her body, for he was very tired of looking at fat South American women and all the girls in London seemed surprisingly plump. It must be these Milk Bars.

'Is that little place near Henley still in existence? Would you like to go there?'

'Adore to.'

So it was arranged: and they smiled lingeringly as they parted, both looking forward to a delightful evening.

They had so much to talk about that the time flew by, as they sat on the terrace overlooking the river. How was the Louse? inquired the Black Sheep. Married, answered Pompey, with three children. And Noel? Married. And Barbara? Married, but not so good; a divorce was in the offing. And Judy? Oh, married, with two children.

'Everybody' he observed 'seems to have children.'

'My dear, *indeed* they have, and so *regularly*, too, like Jane's Fighting Ships or something,' said Pompey, cheerfully, draining her brandy glass and looking at him. He was better-looking than ever. He had silver hairs over his temples (if those *were* his temples?) and fetching wrinkles round his eyes. Ten years ago Noel and Barbara and Judy had all fancied the Black Sheep. But they had all got over it, and were now more or less happily married. Only she and the Black Sheep were left of the old crowd. And he was still a lady-catcher; four women at tables near them were talking rather loudly and dropping things or sitting very quiet, trying to catch his eye. He had the stamp of a man successful with women, and that attracts other women (some other women).

'And now *you* tell one,' she said. 'What are you going to *do* with your life, so to speak?'

'Sell the furniture and sack the staff at the White House. Buy some horses and settle down there and hunt.'

'You won't *live* there all the year *round*?'

'Service flat in town for the season, country in the winter. Marvellous!'

'Marvellous!' she echoed, while her large amused hazel eyes dwelt affectionately on his face. 'I take it you won't blur the prospect with a spot of *work*?'

'I'll see. What dogs are worn just now? I might breed them, if I could find a partner with ideas.'

'Or you might run the White House as a roadhouse?'

'I might,' he said smiling.

She said nothing for a moment, dreamily watching two aeroplanes going over at a great height, pure silver in the light that had already left the earth. He's going to marry and settle down, she thought with a little pain in her heart. Of course, she still had a marvellous time; people and parties and fun; but she did sometimes feel that things weren't like they *used* to be. Almost *everybody* worked nowadays, and everybody seemed so *worthy*, always breathing heavily down your *neck* and having little talks with you for your good; not only *uncles* and aunts but even the *young*; and people were always *leaping* off to the most blood-curdling lectures and classes and things *just* when you wanted to make up a party. And looking at you as if you were a *sweeper* or something because you tried to live a *normal* life . . .

She sighed and hugged herself into her fur cape.

'Too amusing, your going to live at Hillmellow,' she said. 'All the girls down there have been brought up to simply *blench* at the mere sound of your *name!*'

'No, have they really?' and he began to laugh, looking at her over the top of his brandy glass. But he was thinking complacently: *And therefore they think about me all the more, if I know anything about girls.*

'Is there a good crop down there this year?' he went on. (Pompey had been born near Hillmellow, too.) 'I can just remember Nesta Browne-James. Fair hair, very serious. Rather like Alice in Wonderland.'

'She still is. And Gay Morning—'

'What a cramping name!' commented Mr Merryn.

'*Isn't* it. But she's divine to look at. Hermione Meadowes is lovely, too. She dances a good deal. But . . .'

Here Pompey seemed to check herself in mid-sentence as if she had thought better of something she had been going to say; and just at that moment her fur cape slipped to the floor. And while he was grovelling for it under the table and she was looking down laughing at his broad shoulders and bent head (was there a hint of thinness in the dark hair? She found that touching) he forgot to ask her what she had been going to say.

'Isn't there rather a shattering *gale* getting up?' she demanded plaintively as he put the cape round her shoulders, and she glanced out across the river where little ripples were starting under the slaps of a rising breeze. 'Shall we *go*?'

'Of course. Would you like to go on and dance at the Black Spot?'

'Adore it.' She was putting some more purple paint on her large shapely mouth. 'You've learned all the best places to go, Baa–Baa, even if you *have* been languishing for years in that jail.'

'One soon gets back into things.'

He followed her down the terrace, thinking how pleasant it was to be home in England among the half-shades in climate and the half-shades in the social structure; thinking that she was not a pretty woman but that *belle laide* seemed exactly to describe her; thinking with agreeable anticipation of Hillmellow, where the girls had been brought up to think of him as a romantic and dangerous figure. He could see the joke in that, of course – but it was nevertheless a useful reputation to have.

The houses in Hillmellow were built of golden-grey stone and the country round about was full of strong, fast, cunning foxes. Here lived people who had known his grandparents; here lingered the stupid, intolerant, splendid spirit of nineteenth-century England. Here a man who was tired of wandering could settle down on his family estates and marry one of the charming young girls who were ready to adore him. It was a fair prospect and Mr Merryn's spirits rose to greet it.

I suppose I ought to have warned him about those girls, reflected Pompey, lying awake in her small smart flat a few hours later, *but I couldn't bear him to think I was a jealous cat. Anyway, he'll soon find out for himself, poor Black Sheep. Oh dear, it was fun stepping out with him. Of course I'm not his cup of tea at all, which is a pity, for I always did fancy the Black Sheep. As though life weren't squalid enough these days without me getting a crush on the Black Sheep. Oh well, no cross, no crown, as Nannie used to say to us when we were small.*

She sighed, and immediately fell asleep.

A spell of fine weather greeted Mr Merryn's return to Hillmellow, and everybody rushed into the country for the week-ends and gave luncheon, sherry, and dinner parties to which he, as a wealthy, well-bred and well-discussed old acquaintance, was asked.

It happened that he was in what he realistically thought of as 'my nostalgic mood' when he walked into Mrs Browne-James's drawing-room at cocktail-time. This meant a vague, by no means unpleasant sadness. He put it down to the exquisite weather and the charm of this countryside which he had known as a boy. And suddenly, the mood was summed up in a girl standing at the far end of the room.

She was listening, with her blue eyes fixed gravely on his face, to a tall young man whose fair hair fell over his brow. Cheerful and idiotic words seemed to be pouring from the young man's lips but his eyes were those of a lost heart; they implored the girl's eyes; they were miserable and adoring behind the thick lenses of his glasses. The girl wore a blue dress and immediately behind her was a large vase filled with lupins and delphiniums.

'Is that—?' softly inquired the Black Sheep of Mrs Browne-James when they had been talking together in a confidential murmur for some moments like the old acquaintances they were. And he just moved his head in the direction of the girl standing beside the tower of blue flowers.

Mrs Browne-James, who had her worries as every mother must, was pleased by his tone and his look.

'Yes, that's Nesta,' she said, also glancing towards her daughter. But the Black Sheep said nothing for a moment. Then he looked at Mrs Browne-James, and he gave a little, ever such a little, smile.

'How clever of you to recognize her!' said Mrs Browne-James. 'It must be ten years . . . Do come and talk to her, she'll be so thrilled to see you again, she's always heard so much about you, of course.'

If Nesta was thrilled there were no signs. She gave him a cool little hand and one look, so charged with innocence and goodness that he felt quite embarrassed for a second, and said, smiling:

'I'm afraid I don't remember you at all. I was always away at school when you used to stay with us. But I've always heard about you, of course.'

'Nice things, I hope?' murmured the Black Sheep, his famous technique forgotten, his nostalgia for youth and innocence deepening to actual pain as he stared down into her eyes.

But she did not reply. She only went on looking at him, gravely. Not too gravely to please the Black Sheep, who at once diagnosed her reaction as the familiar I-can-make-a-better-man-of-you one.

'I say, you're going to live at the White House, aren't you?' cried the fair young man desperately, as if afraid the conversation was going to drift away and leave him.

'Yes.'

'Pretty country round there. I'm staying at Hollylands,' continued the young man, wretchedly.

'Are you?' Mr Merryn did not look at him but addressed Nesta.

'Does the big carp still live in the lily pond?'

She nodded, smiling faintly. *A heavenly brightness* – the words came suddenly into the Black Sheep's head, as if from a half-forgotten hymn heard in his boyhood on some summer evening in the village church.

'Won't you come and show him to me?'

'*Nesta,*' said the young man suddenly, and stood quite still, staring at her.

'In a minute.' She nodded to the Black Sheep exactly as if promising something to a child; then turned to the fair young man. 'I can't possibly tell you now, Cuthbert, but I'll ask about it . . . you know . . . and tell you as soon as I can.'

'All right. Good-bye.' He swallowed, smiled at her painfully, and moved away into the crowd.

'Now we'll go and look at the carp, if you like,' said
Nesta kindly.

'If *you* like,' he murmured, following her through the
chattering, smoking, laughing groups towards french
windows that opened on the garden.

'Oh yes. As a matter of fact I'm very glad to get this
chance of talking to you alone,' she answered.

He was still incredulously taking this in when they
stepped out of the hot room into the freshness of the
garden.

'There's something I very much want to say to you,'
she ended.

Perhaps she's written a novel and wants my candid
criticism . . . or she wants to go on the stage and they
won't let her . . . or perhaps it's that ghastly young
cub wanting to marry her and she can't make up her
mind . . . after all I suppose I do count as Old Family
Friend . . . I knew her when she was ten. Perfect wrists,
lovely ankles. Those curls make her look like a baby
angel.

'Do sit down.' Nesta sat on the stone embankment of
the carp pond and the Black Sheep sat down beside her
– carefully, because the embankment was mossed and his
trousers were light. He offered her his cigarette case, but
she shook her head.

'Thank you, but I don't smoke any more now.'

'Lucky girl. An expensive and unhygienic habit,' said he
– too cheerfully, because he was actually nervous.

But he knew so well what her next words would be!

You must think it awfully queer of me, saying there was something I specially wanted to say to you.

Girls in Brazil, girls in Paris, girls in Edinburgh and New York and Rome, had all said something of the kind to him in their different tongues and ways. Girls were much the same all over the world.

His nervousness vanished. Amused, confident, he waited for her to speak.

'You've led a very rotten useless life, haven't you,' said Nesta clearly. It was not a question, it was a statement. 'Haven't you ever wanted to be different?'

'I beg your pardon?'

'You must know what I mean. Don't pretend.' Her tone was impatient. 'Haven't you ever wanted to be changed?'

'Changed?'

'Have a change of heart. Be good. Stop being selfish and lazy and third-rate. Aren't you sick of it all? How old are you?'

He could only stare at her with his mouth open.

'You must be getting on for forty, aren't you? I don't mean to be rude but you *look* about forty and there's no point in pretending about things when it's so vitally important. What will you be like when you're seventy?'

Still he could only stare at her. Never, never, during ten triumphant years in Brazil and New York, Paris and Rome and Edinburgh . . .

'I wish you would promise me to think it over,' she said earnestly, leaning towards him with her small face pink with kindness and zeal. 'I expect you'll think it impertinent of me, as I'm so much younger than you are—'

'Oh, not at all,' at last muttered the stunned Black Sheep.

'But you see Mums has talked such a lot about you that I quite feel I know you.'

'Do you?' he said faintly.

'I wish you'd believe what I say. I *know*, you see. From personal experience. Why, before I was Changed I was simply awful. One mass of sensuality.'

'W-were you?'

'Oh yes. I thought about nothing but clothes and young men and pleasure. And smoking and drinking.'

She leaned towards him again.

'Will you promise me something?'

'What is it?' backing a little.

'Will you come to one of our meetings and Share with us. Just get up in front of everybody and tell quite simply all the rotten things you've ever done? You can't imagine what a relief it is and how much better you feel afterwards.'

But the Black Sheep was on his feet and moving towards the house.

'Oh I say' – and he made no attempt to control the horror in his voice – 'I'm afraid that's absolutely out of the question. My generation isn't any use at that sort of thing, you know. I say, I'm awfully sorry but I'm afraid I must be charging off, I've an appointment at eight.'

She followed him, looking regretful but not surprised.

'You're frightened and embarrassed, of course,' she said. 'Most older people are, at first. That, and light-mindedness, are the two biggest things we have to fight. Older people are incurably light-minded.'

'Yes, I'm afraid they are,' said the Black Sheep, whose voice was now under control. He suddenly thought of

Pompey. He could not see her sharing her sins with a roomful of enthusiastic amateurs.

They walked back to the house in silence, between the tiny hedges of dark box. By the french windows they paused and he looked down curiously into her face.

'Tell me something,' he said.

'Of course I will,' she answered at once, lifting her eyes to him with that lovely look that made him think of church on summer evenings.

'It does make you happy, doesn't it, all this?'

'Utterly happy.' Her face had the serenity and mystery of a child's face, the look that has usually gone by the child's twelfth year. 'Can't you see it does?'

'Yes,' said the Black Sheep. 'I can indeed. And you're a darling. And thank you for trying to – er – change me. I'm only so very sorry that it wasn't – quite – my cup of tea. Good-bye.'

'Good-bye,' said Nesta, regretful but not fundamentally ruffled.

But when Mr Merryn was out of sight of the house he stopped the car, wiped his forehead, and went into *The Ploughman* for a drink.

Hardly had he recovered from this interview when he was out riding one morning before breakfast. One of the minor pleasures of being on horseback is the view one gets of the flowers growing along the tops of hedges, such as honeysuckle. Mr Merryn was no flower-fancier, but he did happen to notice the honeysuckle on this particular ride because it was just the colour of a girl's skin; a girl who had ridden past him at the crossroads into the woods. She had dark eyes and wore correct hacking clothes even to a hat.

His nostalgic fancies had changed their tenor since his encounter with Nesta Browne-James; and he now thought of his wife as someone taller and more sporting, a Diana of the Uplands surrounded by dogs and capable of managing a lively horse, a spirited and passionate girl with whom he could play games and have stimulating quarrels. So when he turned a curve in the woodland ride and saw the dark-eyed rider, looking cross and preparing to dismount, his heart stirred pleasantly. Her hat was lying almost under his horse's hoofs.

'Do let me get it for you!'

'Oh, thank you. It was that bough—' she pointed to a low-growing oak branch. 'Such a nuisance. I'm so sorry.'

She watched him while he dismounted and rescued the hat, and as he came up to her she said—

'Aren't you Basil Merryn? I believe you know my brother Ronald. I'm Hermione Meadowes.'

'I am. Ronald and I were at school together. But I used to know you, too —' he had remounted and they were walking their horses down the ride '— I can remember you perfectly at eight years old.'

'I had a band on my teeth.' She did not say it provocatively but rather meditatively, as one who pores soberly over an album of family photographs for some boring reason.

'I wouldn't remember that,' said the Black Sheep gallantly, but feeling a faintly fusty atmosphere as of the Empire and hansom cabs and By-jingo-if-we-do rising on the morning air. My technique is getting utterly dated, he thought depressedly. It's their fault, though. I *cannot* get this new line. We used to think everything was funny, even things that weren't. But this new girl thinks nothing is funny, even things that are.

'You used to stay with the Browne-Jameses.'

'I did.'

'But you've been abroad for a long time, haven't you?'

'Yes, nearly ten years.'

'Weren't you in Brazil last year?'

'Yes.'

Her head was beautifully poised on her long neck and crowned by two plaits of dark hair, but so far she had not once looked at him as if she really saw him. Still, she was at least *pretending* to be interested in his adventures.

'I thought you had been; Ronald thought so too. I'm so awfully glad to have met you, because . . .'

That nightmare feeling of it-has-all-happened-before – began to creep over the Black Sheep. He did not even make polite murmurs, he only stared at her, glassily.

'. . . I wondered if you might be able to help me.'

'Anything,' he said, straightening his shoulders.

'You see, I'm at the School of World Dietetics in town and I've got to do a paper for next term on the effect of a practically meatless diet on primitive and industrialized peoples. If you could just give me a typical diet-sheet for a typical Indian—'

'I'd be delighted to, but I'm afraid I don't really know much about it—'

'But don't you know anyone out there? Anyone you could write to? I only want a few facts. I can draw my conclusions from those, easily.'

'I do know one or two men out there, of course, but—'

'Well, you could easily write to them and explain what I want, couldn't you? Surely they must know what the Indians eat?'

'Oh yes, and what they drink, too,' said the Black Sheep frivolously.

She looked at him reprovingly.

'It is *extraordinarily* difficult to get the average person to take the science of dietetics seriously,' she said severely. 'After all, it is one of the most important studies in the world, *and* one of the most interesting. Haven't you ever realized that a person's whole make up is conditioned by the type of food they eat?'

'I'm afraid I hadn't. You tell me,' said the Black Sheep, calculating that they were about three-quarters of an hour from home if they walked the horses all the way.

She did not want to trot, so they did walk the horses, and the Black Sheep listened for three-quarters of an hour to her fresh young voice telling him about malnutrition, starch, the fatty acid type, carbohydrates, energizers, proteins, vitamins, calories and calcium. When she stopped at the gate of her own home she said:

'Good-bye. You *will* come in at cocktail-time one evening soon and see Ronnie, won't you? I'm so glad I met you. That information will be awfully useful. You will remember to write, won't you? Promise!'

She bent over her horse's neck and gave him her hand, with a charming smile.

'You're just down here until the School re-opens, I suppose?' he asked.

'Yes. This will be my last holiday for some time. When I've got my certificate I'm going to get a job in the clinic the school is opening in the East End, to advise women about buying and cooking.'

'Marvellous,' said the Black Sheep, looking up curiously into her young, glowing face.

'Yes. It's lovely to be doing the work you like, isn't it? Good-bye!'

He held the gate open for her and watched her ride down the shady avenue until she had disappeared.

Then he let his exhausted face-muscles sag into an expression of utter weariness, and rode slowly home.

That evening he went out to dinner with some old acquaintances who lived just outside the town, and while drinking a before-dinner sherry in the drawing-room he got into conversation with a pink and earnest young man. After some exchanges about the Test Match, the Black Sheep said cautiously:

'I say, can you give me a bit of information?'

'I'll try,' said the pink-faced one.

The Black Sheep lowered his voice still more.

'Who's the girl in grey?' he asked, barely moving his lips.

'That's Gay Morning,' said the pink-faced one, in a slightly less friendly voice.

'Oh,' said the Black Sheep, gazing (no longer anticipatorily but wistfully) at the small slender girl in a dress of grey chiffon with jasmine in her curly red hair.

'Would you like to meet her?' said the pink-faced one. 'As a matter of fact, we're practically engaged.'

'I'd love to, but later on. Don't let's interrupt her now; she looks so interested in what she's saying.'

The girl in grey was talking, with eloquent gestures of her little hands.

'She's very Left,' said the lover proudly, gazing at her. 'She's being trained for ballet, but she won't do it professionally; she's going to put her creative talent utterly at the service of the Party.'

'And how will you like that?' inquired the Black Sheep.

'Oh, it won't affect me at all. Why should it? We've decided not to attempt to shape each other's life-patterns.'

Neither man spoke for a moment. Then – 'I think I'll have another sherry,' said the Black Sheep.

'But, my poor sweet,' said Miss Pompey Taverner, laughing so much that she could hardly get her words down the telephone, 'how *dire* for you! Of course I ought to have had the moral *courage* to warn you that *all* the girls are like that nowadays, *too* earnest and worthy! Times have *changed*, my pet, that's what.'

'And you and I haven't, I suppose?' came the voice of the Black Sheep (sounding older, for some reason, over the telephone).

'But I don't *mean* to, Baa-Baa! After all if one is *naturally* incurably light-minded I mean one *is*, isn't one? And heaven knows *somebody* has to be, nowadays.'

'I suppose so. And anyway . . . there are two of us, aren't there, Pompey?'

'I hope so, my sweet.'

A little pause.

'May I come up to town this evening and take you dancing?'

'*Adore* it,' answered Miss Pompey Taverner.

More Than Kind

Lillian Wardell brought the car neatly into the station yard, parked it against the kerb, shut off the engine and leant back with a long, tremulous sigh. She pulled off her gloves and noticed with annoyance that her hands were shaking.

'Lillian, can we go in and wait for Mother?'

The children were leaning eagerly over the back seat; the boy already had the door half-open and the girl's face had the self-conscious, excited expression which it only wore when Sophie came on a visit.

'Of course.' Lillian settled her hat, bent down, and passed a duster over the tips of her shoes.

'Aren't you coming?'

'In a minute. Run along, but there's heaps of time. We're early.'

The girl lingered for a second, looking shyly at her stepmother. She knew as well as if Lillian had told her that the older woman was miserable and needed comforting.

'Run along, darling.'

She tore off to join her brother, and Lillian got out of the car and discovered that her legs were shaking as well. She glanced at her reflection in the mirror as she went through the booking-office to the platform, and tried to relax the muscles of her face, and assume an amused, welcoming expression.

But it was useless. Sophie, who read people as easily as she read books, always knew when another woman felt gauche and uninteresting in contrast with her own piquant beauty. She knew that Lillian was nervous and at a disadvantage, and she would enjoy the situation. She was full of mischief, was Sophie; she saw the wicked, amusing angle before she saw any other, and gave the famous gurgling laugh which men found so fetching.

The train was late. The children prowled round the slot-machines and the bookstall, while Lillian sat on the seat in an easy, relaxed position and wished that she were dead.

She was the second wife of Ian Wardell, a successful publisher of 'advanced' works of fiction and sociology, and the fascinating Sophie, whom she was here to meet, was his first wife, divorced by him two years ago.

Lillian, the only daughter of a quiet professional man, had charmed Ian Wardell by her gentleness and sincerity as much as by her candid fair beauty. He lost no time in falling in love with her, and deciding that there was now a strong reason why he should divorce Sophie, who had always been difficult and had now become impossible.

The divorce and Ian's re-marriage had gone through without a hitch; and Lillian found herself wife at twenty-seven to a man who had been the husband of another woman for ten years, and moving in a circle as unlike her own sober girlhood one as it was possible to imagine.

Ian's friends had no religion. Their politics were faintly pink and their pacifism a bright scarlet. They considered

that the world was in a deplorable state, but trusted that
scientific planning would one day tidy it up, and they were
so busy discussing so many angles of so many questions
that they had time only for the simplest moral code.

They called it Being Kind.

Being Kind meant that no one was condemned nor
banished from the 'set' whatever he or she did. Divorced
husbands dined with their ex-wives and new partners,
former lovers accompanied one another to all-in wrestling
matches, the children of a legal marriage stayed with the
illegitimate fruit of a pre-marital experience of either parent
and got on admirably together. The set lived with some
social elegance but without moral barriers of any kind.

It had taken Lillian months to become used to this
atmosphere; and although she tried in her serious affectionate way to accept Ian's views on Being Kind and
Civilized, she was often uneasily conscious that her outlook
was what Ian called bourgeois.

It became secretly very bourgeois on the occasions when
Sophie, his ex-wife, came to stay at the Wardells' home in
Kent to see the children.

There was no reason, said Ian, why Sophie should not
come to stay with them. She and he had parted as friends
who had simply agreed that they could no longer make
a life together. It was more natural (said Ian) for the children to see their mother in their father's home than for
them to meet her at an hotel in London. They might
develop complexes.

Lillian listened to his views and honestly believed that
he was right. Her own heart was kind and her nature was
tolerant; she did not take pleasure in condemning people's

behaviour. She was in favour of forgiving and forgetting, and she quite saw that it would be pleasanter and less embarrassing for Sophie and the children if they met as mother and children in Ian's house.

But when Sophie actually came, Lillian found herself wondering if after all, Ian were right.

Each visit, for various reasons, had been worse than the last.

I *must* have charity, thought Lillian, sitting on the platform seat and trying hard. Sophie had just parted from the man for whom she had left Ian, and would presumably be in need of charity.

The train came round the bend and drew into the station. Lillian stood up, refraining from nervously straightening her jacket, and the children skimmed up and down the length of the carriages, looking for their mother.

'There she is!'

'Mother!'

The girl flew to hug the slender woman in a scarlet suit who stepped from the train, laughing, waving to Lillian, holding out a hand to the boy, who hung back shyly.

'Darlings! Marvellous to see you again. Belinda, how you've grown! You're going to be a beauty and put your mother in the shade . . . and what a naughty little hat you've got! Lillian, how dare you buy my daughter come-hither hats at the age of fourteen? John, come and kiss me. But you've grown up! I left you a little boy, and you've grown up.'

'It's the long trousers,' smiled Lillian, wondering why her own hat, which was as smart as Sophie's, did not look it. 'They make such a difference.'

'Mother, you look *lovely*,' burst forth Belinda.

'Darling, I feel a wreck. I've been having the most awful time. Jack . . . do they know about Jack, Lillian? About his going away, I mean? I've had such an awful time, I've been so miserable, I can't sleep. I'm so used to having him in the room, you know.'

Lillian nodded stiffly, conscious that two porters, the station-master, and Mrs Peacey of Elmdean, were listening to these revelations with a bourgeois but lively interest.

The girl stared solemnly up at her mother's big hazel eyes that were full of tears.

'Mother, why did he leave you? He must be a beast.'

'All sorts of reasons, my poppet; I'll tell you some of them later. Come along, now, we're keeping Lillian waiting,' her brilliant smile made a stranger of Lillian, 'and I'm longing to see Daddy.'

Lillian slipped into the driver's seat and John climbed in beside her. He had been eager to see his mother, but had suddenly become embarrassed. Her beauty, the brilliant colour of her suit, and her bell-like voice uttering emotional remarks all made him feel shy and antagonistic towards her. He was in his first term at a big school and was avidly absorbing its creed, Thou Shalt Not be Conspicuous.

Sophie, who was always intensely conscious of what people were feeling about her, was trying to make him jealous by sitting very close to Belinda in the back seat and murmuring to her an account of Captain Jack Sands' desertion. Belinda listened with parted lips and her shining eyes gazing in awe at her mother's face. This story was more exciting than any novel, because its heroine was her own lovely mother.

At the back of her mind was a slightly ashamed feeling of pity for Daddy. Surely he must mind Mother loving Captain Sands so much? But then Daddy had Lillian now, so of course, he must play fair and let Mother have Captain Sands.

It was very puzzling.

But it was exciting, too. Belinda looked forward for months to Sophie's visits, not so much because she loved her mother and missed her painfully as because Sophie's mere presence in the house could make everything exciting; and Belinda, who was her mother's daughter, loved excitement.

The car stopped in front of the Wardells' home, which wore its summer dress of pink hanging geraniums, sun-blinds striped with the same gay colour, and basket chairs in the well-kept garden.

'Darling house,' murmured Sophie. 'I shall never love any house as much as I love this one. Oh, Lillian, you've had the lime pruned! My favourite tree! How could you!'

Lillian expressed regret and wished for the thousandth time that Ian had been able to afford to move into a new house with his new wife. But he, like Sophie, professed attachment to the house in Kent and made the excuse that he could not support the expense and fatigue of an unnec-essary move.

Lillian, glancing at the upper windows, observed the corner of a white frilled curtain slipping back into position. That would be young Miss Treadgar, Belinda's holiday companion, trying to get a peep at the ex-Mrs Ian Wardell.

For weeks Belinda had been telling Miss Treadgar, who also had an appetite for excitement, that Mother was coming to stay. Miss Treadgar did not say so, but she thought this a queer and shocking notion. She wrote as much to her sister in Maidstone, and promised to write again as soon as the ex-Mrs Wardell arrived. She was living with a man to whom she was not married, too; in short, she seemed a pretty hot number. Miss Treadgar dropped the corner of the curtain well satisfied by her first glimpse of the ex-Mrs Wardell. She had That Look. You can always tell.

'Annie!' Sophie's full tones recalled the parlour-maid, who happened to be loitering over some imaginary task in the hall as the party entered, and was now slipping away. 'How are you? How's Frank? and when are you getting married?'

Sophie had discovered Annie's romance on her last visit, and now kept the girl for a minute, pink with embarrassment and pleasure, while she rallied her about Frank.

Lillian caught a glimpse of the face of Cook slowly disappearing behind the half-open door to the kitchen quarters. Cook, who was new, had also heard about Mrs Sophie and wanted to see what she looked like.

If Sophie were an ordinary guest, thought Lillian bitterly as she went upstairs, there would be none of this disgusting excitement. It's only because she's Ian's ex-wife. They can't understand her being here. I suppose they're narrow and bourgeois . . . Ian would say so, anyway.

But since she is here she must be made welcome and it's up to me to do it. After all, she's always been spoiled, she's like a child. She hasn't had a chance to grow into an adult; people won't let her.

She saw Sophie installed in her room and went down to answer the telephone. It was Ian, wanting to know if Sophie had arrived safely. There was no point in being Kind unless you did it thoroughly.

Then she went slowly up to the nursery, where her own baby daughter was shuttling backwards and forwards across the floor, crowing with excitement over this new accomplishment, which she liked better than any of her other pastimes. Miss Treadgar looked up from her sewing with a smile that was a shade too eager and sympathetic, and Lillian arranged with her to take Belinda and Baby for a walk after lunch. She herself would spend the afternoon on the lawn under the cedar tree with Sophie, listening sympathetically to the story of Jack.

She had so made up her mind to this programme that she was really startled when Sophie announced that she thought she would go for a walk with Miss Treadgar, Belinda and Baby instead.

Sophie, on being introduced to Miss Treadgar, perceived that here was someone who saw her in a romantic and slightly lurid light, and at once decided that Miss Treadgar must be told the truth. If Miss Treadgar got a wrong impression of the affair she might pervert Belinda. *Get her on Lillian's side* was how Sophie put the danger to herself, for she was one who thought naturally in tug-of-war terms. It was absolutely essential that Belinda should not go over to Lillian's side.

Miss Treadgar therefore spent a most instructive afternoon listening to why Sophie had left Ian and why Ian had married Lillian and why Jack had left Sophie and why Belinda was Sophie's own sort but John was not. Miss

Treadgar decided to write six pages to her sister instead of the usual three.

At a quarter to seven Ian returned from London, a little drawn and tired from his day's work, a little on edge and trying to pretend that he was not, and very determined to be Kind to Sophie.

He did not love Sophie any more. She had proved herself in the ten years of their marriage to be cruel, vain, and an exhibitionist; she had only never proved to be lacking in charm.

The sight of her, sitting under the dark shade of the cedar tree in a dress the colour of Parma violets and chatting to Lillian, had exactly the same effect upon his nervous system as a very strong cocktail. He loved her no more, but the sensation of excitement, double-dealing, danger and the importance of the immediate moment which she brought into his peaceful home was stimulating. He suddenly felt less tired, more alert, as he crossed the lawn to the two women, telling himself that Sophie always upset things and one had to be damned careful in dealing with her, but that it was after all necessary to behave like a civilized being . . . and she was the children's mother.

Lillian did not look up at him with love and comradeship in her eyes, as she used to do in the early days of Sophie's visits.

The story had got round to Lillian (the set was fond of passing on good stories) that Sophie had spoken of 'Lillian's never-mind-old-boy-we'll-fight-it-out-together look!' and now Lillian had learned to control her eyes.

'Hullo, my Ex,' said Sophie impudently, holding out her hand, 'how are you?'

'Very well. And you?'

'I'm all right . . . except that I've been deserted,' she smiled, while large tears gathered on her eyelashes and glittered there in the evening light. 'I've just been telling Lillian all about it.'

'Well, now you can tell me about it, all over again.'

He sat down heavily in a basket chair, conscious of mingled boredom and shame. He knew so well what Sophie would say about Captain Sands: he felt that Sophie's presence here was not fair to Lillian. But he was conscious also of that quickening in the atmosphere that was like the exciting moment before the curtain goes up at a play.

In the house, where Miss Treadgar was helping Belinda to change her frock for dinner, and Baby was being put to bed, everyone was talking or thinking about Sophie. By now Annie had learned from Miss Treadgar, and had passed on the news to Cook, that Captain Sands and the ex-Mrs Wardell had parted. Cook expressed the opinion that Mrs Sophie had come down here to Try and Get Mr Wardell Back; and Annie thought that Captain Sands must be a Brute. The shadowy image of Captain Sands, in dashing polo kit, seemed to twirl a heartless moustache over Baby's very bathtub. It was all most exciting, though no one, if asked, could have explained why.

When Belinda was dressed she went to the nursery to see how her goldfishes were and found John sulking in the window seat.

'John,' said Belinda solemnly, standing in front of the long mirror (the nursery was also used as a sewing-room), 'I'm going to have a beautiful figure, Mother says.'

'Then you'll jolly well have to hurry up.'

'She says lots of men'll fall in love with me.'

'Silly asses, they'll be.'

'So are you a silly ass.'

'Not half such a silly ass as you are.'

Belinda glanced round at him, and went at once to the point. Reticence was wasted upon her, as it was on Sophie.

'What's up? Don't you like Mother being here?'

'No, I don't.'

'Why not?'

'Never mind why not. You just shut up and leave me alone.'

'*I* like her being here. I think it's exciting.'

She danced out of the room, leaving him slouching in the window seat. He was acutely miserable. The battle in his mind was so violent between his mother's fascination, his embarrassment at what he vaguely felt was wrong in her behaviour, and his sympathy for his father, that he could not bear the thought of going down to dinner, a treat permitted to himself and his sister because of their mother's visit.

'John?'

Lillian put her head round the nursery door.

'Come along, old man. The gong's gone.'

He got up obediently and followed his stepmother downstairs. Had he been old enough to realize what he felt he would have known that her serene and simple personality comforted him; as it was, he went down in the wake of her lace skirts thinking dimly, 'She isn't always bothering you.'

Lillian paused at the dining-room door to disentangle a frill from her heel, and as she glanced into the room she thought that it had lost its elegant yet home-like quality and looked like a room on the stage. The empty chairs, the shining table with its modernist silver and pale flowers, seemed only a setting for Sophie, who stood by the window in her violet dress asking Ian if he remembered something.

They sat down to dinner in an atmosphere charged with excitement. The children felt it, and Belinda showed off and grew noisy, while John sat pale and quiet. Sophie turned all her charm on him, trying to make him talk, asking his opinion, reminding him of incidents that had happened when he was little.

Ian was reminded, too.

'Ian, what became of those Regency chairs we saved up for? You've practically refurnished since my day, of course, but I just wondered . . .'

'God knows.'

'Oh, Ian, you didn't sell them? Don't you remember how you went without cigarettes for a month and I washed and set my hair at home because we felt we'd been so extravagant over them, and then we brought them home in a taxi and I dropped one when I was staggering into the house with it and broke its leg, and how angry you were?'

Annie, handing the stewed celery, was too well trained to allow her expression to change, but her ears had a buttoned-back appearance, especially while Sophie was telling Lillian that she and Ian ought to send John to a really modern school where the instruction in sexual matters was as advanced as it was admirable.

'John does well enough at Bradwick's,' answered Ian

patiently. His dark, thin face, charming but lacking the light of humour, was turned politely towards his former wife.

He's tired, thought Lillian with a swift pang of sympathy. Poor old boy! I wish she'd be quiet.

'You're as conventional as Jack, in some ways,' retorted Sophie, and told them anecdotes about Captain Sands until it was time to repair to the drawing-room.

Lillian could not tell Miss Treadgar that she objected to the light in her bedroom burning until one o'clock in the morning while she and Sophie sat gossiping, creaming their faces, and discussing men and life. Sophie's warm impulsive nature found new friends everywhere; it would be cruel, as well as rude, to imply that Lillian disliked her becoming thick (that was the only word which described the relationship) with Miss Treadgar.

It was plain, on the following day, that Miss Treadgar was On Sophie's Side. Her manner to Lillian seemed to say, *and I thought you were such a nice woman until Sophie told me the truth.*

The house trembled with currents of suppressed excitement and hysteria. Over the kitchen breakfast Annie and Cook were not prevented by an almost total ignorance of the facts from arguing bitterly about the Wardell divorce. It gave you something to argue about when you had seen both the ladies involved.

On Saturday afternoon their parents took John and Belinda, who seemed on bad terms, for a walk in the country.

Lillian went out by herself in the car.

She drove steadily away from the house into the open

country, where the hedges were in freshest new leaf and the orchards, the solitary cherry trees in the woodland glades, were smothered in pink and white flowers. But she felt so wretched that even the beauty of the countryside could not comfort her, and she dreaded the return to her home, with its poisoned atmosphere of excitement and conflict. Her thoughts turned with a feeling of heavenly relief to her baby's farewell kiss; she could still see one round grey eye very near her own and smell the baby's fragrant powder.

When she turned the car in at the short drive in front of her mother's house, the tears were running down her face.

'You need not tell me what's the matter,' observed Mrs Cassell, pouring her out a cup of tea and pushing the greedy nose of the terrier out of her lap. 'That woman's staying with you again.'

'You always talk about poor Sophie as though she were something out of a rescue home, Mother,' said Lillian laughing and crying and trying to sip her tea and fondle the terrier's ears at the same time. 'She's not really bad, you know; it's only just that she loves sensation and she's always been spoilt.'

'Well, you know what I think about it. I've told you every time she's come down here. I think it's disgusting. By every single standard that decent people have put up to protect themselves and other decent people, it's disgusting.'

'Your generation is so . . . severe,' protested Lillian, but she made the remark from duty, not from conviction. She thought longingly how much easier life would have been had she and Ian been able to make a clean cut with Sophie.

'And a good thing, too,' retorted her mother. 'At least we knew where we were. We didn't waste valuable nervous energy in trying to be "kind," as you call it, to people whom it was natural for us to dislike and fear. When a woman behaved as Sophie Wardell has behaved, we treated her as though she were dead.'

'You forget, Mother, that if you judge me by that standard I'm "dead," too . . . Ian fell in love with me before he divorced Sophie.'

'That's different. No, Nicky, no more cake. Go along, now, out in the garden.'

'Besides,' pursued Lillian, 'no one takes that attitude nowadays. Even if I could persuade Ian . . .'

'Ah! so you're coming round to my point of view, are you? in spite of its severity.'

'. . . that it would be better if we didn't see Sophie any more, or have her to stay with us, I couldn't . . . well, I couldn't turn her out of the house, could I?'

'Why not?' inquired her mother quietly.

Lillian sat staring down at her hands. Her mother looked at her keenly, shook her head, moved her chair a little nearer, and began to read her a lecture in favour of the forgotten virtue, Intolerance.

When Lillian came out of the garage just before seven o'clock after putting the car away, she came upon Sophie, Miss Treadgar and Belinda strolling slowly up and down under the cedar tree. The two women talked, nodded emphatically, stared down at the grass under their evening slippers, and Belinda moved between them rapt and silent, gazing first at one face and then at the other.

Miss Treadgar was the first to look up and see Lillian; she started, smiled nervously and waved. Of the three who came slowly towards Lillian across the grass, Sophie was the only one who did not look guilty.

'I've just been talking *seriously* to Angela about putting Belinda on a slimming diet,' explained Sophie. 'She's got the makings of a really marvellous figure, Lillian, and it is *most* important that she shouldn't put on puppy-fat. She says she's perfectly willing to cut out starchy things altogether, if Angela will back her up . . .'

Lillian had known, but had hardly realized, that Miss Treadgar, who now giggled nervously, had been baptized Angela.

'Isn't Belinda a little young to begin slimming?' asked Lillian mildly. This mild tone was the first step in a new campaign, in which Sophie was, for the first time, to be treated not as a friend but as a dangerous enemy.

It was surprising how tranquil she felt since she had admitted to herself and her mother that she hated the sight of Sophie.

'It's *never* too young to begin being a woman,' retorted Sophie oracularly, smiling down at Belinda. 'I want Belinda to be attractive when she's *seventy*, and the sooner she gets into training the better.'

The four walked harmoniously back to the house, Belinda practising a new and peculiar walk which was meant to be grown-up and fascinating.

'Ian,' remarked Lillian, sitting on the edge of her bed just before dinner and slowly buffing her nails. 'I don't wish to sound prejudiced nor to make mountains out of molehills, but I do think that Sophie has a most unfortunate effect on Belinda.'

'She has a most unfortunate effect on all of us,' he retorted grimly, 'but I don't see what we can do about it.'

'Don't you?'

She lifted her head, bound with its plait of fair hair, and looked earnestly across at him where he stood in front of the mirror, frowning over his dress tie.

'Well, we can't refuse to have her in the house, can we?'

'Why not?'

She had stopped polishing her nails and was sitting very upright on the edge of the bed, staring at him with parted lips.

'Don't be absurd,' he said irritably. 'Of course she must come here. We don't want to look fools; nobody intelligent makes those sort of distinctions nowadays. Besides, it would make it so difficult with the children. Do try to be reasonable, Lillian; I know Sophie's difficult. God, I ought to know it; I had ten years of her . . .'

'She won't let me forget that you did . . .'

'. . . but it isn't for ever; she'll have gone by Monday afternoon. Just try to stick it out, will you, there's a dear girl. It's,' he hesitated, then added with that cold, unwilling expression which he wore when he was making a confession which honesty demanded but which his pride disliked giving, 'it's as difficult for me as it is for you, believe me.'

His tone showed her that she had said enough. She resumed the buffing of her nails with a tranquil expression. He was asking her to stand by him; and she would.

But as she went downstairs to dinner with Sophie on

this second evening, she found it difficult to make conversation because of one thought that dominated all the others in her head.

There was no reason why Sophie should ever come to see them again. Because all their circle of acquaintance adopted the new code of extreme tolerance, and lived lives which were conventionally elegant but without moral barriers, that was no reason why the Wardells should do so. A house full of adults was being disturbed, and two children were being exposed to a subtly corrupting influence, only because a group of over-civilized people was afraid of being thought bourgeois and old-fashioned and 'unkind.'

Lillian sat down to dinner feeling as though she had made a most important discovery which had been lying under her nose for the past two years.

The evening was spent in a series of wild charades in which the children joined. Sophie made the willing Belinda pose as a nymph with very little on, and forced the unwilling John to appear as Bacchus with grapes over one ear and a fox fur of Lillian's round his shrinking middle, while she pointed out to Miss Treadgar how embarrassed he was, and how this only *proved* how necessary it was for him to be sent to a school where facts were faced sanely and naturally.

'But *is* it natural for John to wear nothing but grapes and a fox fur?' inquired Lillian, in her new mild, interested voice which Sophie found irritating. 'Is that the usual uniform at Bradwick's, John?'

John gave a sudden guffaw, picturing old Rocky and Stinky Sims and a few others at Bradwick's thus attired.

'I wish we could always dress like this at The Meades,' said Belinda longingly, pirouetting in her blue chiffon. 'It makes me *feel* so nice.'

'That's the normal healthy reaction to it,' approved Sophie. She was great on normal reactions.

Even Lillian, full of her new cold determination to treat Sophie as an enemy, had to admit, as the evening progressed that Ian's ex-wife had such a way of communicating her own excitement to other people that she was a party in herself; and Lillian had to admit against her will that she was enjoying the fun.

Sophie's full vibrant voice seemed to fill the room, her slender body in the piquant yellow dress darted about, making Lillian think of a spiteful little flame striking sparks from the most unlikely people. Even Miss Treadgar gave a spirited impersonation of Grace Darling, rowing across the drawing-room carpet in Baby's Moses-basket and singing a hymn in a giggling treble.

Lillian's determination began to dissolve as the evening drew on. It seemed barbarous and intolerant to treat as an enemy this vivid creature, whose only fault was that she had been given more vitality than most women.

Sophie is a Priestess of Life, thought Lillian, as she went slowly upstairs to bed. You can't blame a priestess if she serves her god. Some of us are wives and some are mothers, but Sophie is like a flame, making us shine with reflected light; and she is no more to be condemned for hurting people than a flame is for burning them.

And with these and other solemn reflections, perhaps a little coloured by her wide reading, Lillian undressed and brushed her hair and climbed gratefully into her cool bed.

In the other bed was Ian, settling himself on the pillows and reaching for a bundle of typescript.

'Aren't you too tired to read, darling?'

'I want to finish this. It's good.'

'Shall you take it, do you think?'

'Oh yes. He's going to be a big figure. Of course there are all kinds of crudities; this is only his second book, but there's the genuine note of authority. I shan't be long, dear. Turn your back if the light worries you.'

He smiled across at her, thinking with gratitude of the peace and comfort with which she filled his life each day; it was as necessary to his existence as bread, and only occasionally did he realize how beautiful it was.

He had not been impressed by Sophie's cadenzas during the evening. He had heard so many of those exciting trills during their ten years together, and knew just what they were worth. The vague excitement with which her presence had fired him on the first evening of her visit was now extinct; he was feeling a little ashamed of it, and glad that she was soon going away.

Lillian obediently turned away from the light, settling comfortably among the pillows and thinking that they really must get two of those reading lamps which could be used without disturbing the one who wanted to go to sleep.

The night was warm and still. The blue curtains at the window, patterned with little silver stars, did not move in the faintest of breezes. Lillian could dimly see through them the dark trees against the moonlit sky, where one real star sparkled, and then she shut her eyes . . .

She was roused by Ian's voice, and sat up, blinking and

bewildered, staring at the wide open bedroom door. Beyond Ian's dressing-gowned figure she could see the Priestess of Life, wearing an exceedingly transparent night-gown. Her charming face was full of the dismay and alarm which had caused her to hurry along to her ex-husband's bedroom without pausing to put on a dressing-gown.

'Oh Lillian,' whispered Sophie, her large bright eyes glancing mischievously round the room and taking in the twin beds, the starry curtains, the pastel portrait of Baby over Lillian's bed. 'There's an enormous bat in my room . . . Ian *must* come and put it out. They simply terrify me, there's something so obscene about them . . . primitive. I'm so sorry to intrude on you like this. I won't keep Ian a minute, but I can't possibly deal with the horror myself. What a charming room you've got! So restful and old-fashioned; it's exactly *you*, Lillian. Doesn't your hair get in your way, all over the place like that? Come along, Ian . . . I'm sure it's eating my biscuits . . . do you remember how I always had to have biscuits by my bed?'

Ian, looking murderous, followed her out of the room without a backward glance.

Lillian sat up in bed, shivering, and reached for her dressing-gown.

She was blushing slowly. An enormous flood of colour and heat seemed to be invading her whole body, with an intolerable sense of outrage.

It's horrible . . . she thought, over and over again, sitting up in bed with her hands locked round her knees and staring out into the darkness and quiet of the passage.

She could hear the story that Sophie would make out of the incident:

'So off I had to go to *their* room, my dear, well, after all, I suppose I can go into a man's room when I shared it with him under the paternal eye of the Church and the Law for ten years . . . separate beds, my dear, at a chaste distance, of course, and a touching portrait of the brat over hers. And she wears her hair all over the place, it really looks like a *growth* or something . . .'

But Ian liked to see her hair loose.

The moments crawled on while she sat there, shivering now and again and staring at the dark passage. No sound came from Sophie's room at the end of it.

She was not 'jealous,' in a vulgar, stupid way, of Ian going to Sophie's room. It was the fact of Ian's former wife intruding upon their married solitude, and making a good naughty story out of her intrusion, that had given the final touch to her wavering courage, and made her decide to turn Sophie out of the house.

Suddenly she swung her legs over the side of the bed, slipped her feet into her slippers, and went quickly down the passage towards Sophie's room.

The door was shut: she could hear no murmur of voices. She turned the handle quickly and walked in.

Sophie was sitting on the bed, staring down at her smouldering cigarette while tears ran down her face. Ian, looking as angry as even Lillian could wish, leaned stiffly against the frame of the open window.

Sophie glanced up casually and sighed. Her expression

was one of misery, but in her eyes there was a tiny sparkle
of malice, half-drowned in tears, but plain for Lillian to
see.

'Oh, come in, Lillian! The bat's gone. Did you wonder
what on earth Ian and I were up to? It's all right; we're
only talking. I suddenly felt that I couldn't exist without
Jack,' her voice shook, 'for another instant, and I simply
had to talk to someone about it.'

Lillian swallowed. She was trembling. Her emotion
showed in her face, and Ian gazed at her curiously; but
Sophie had lowered her head once more and was staring
down at her brown hand with its Persian ring. Lillian
wondered wildly how she should begin. In the modern
world one simply did not say to a woman, 'You are a bad,
dangerous creature, and you will leave my house.'

The silence grew deeper, as a silence does which is full of
unsaid things. Ian moved at last and began uncomfortably.

'Well, since the bat seems . . .'

'I think the bat was only an excuse,' said Lillian in a
loud, nervous voice.

Sophie sat upright, staring.

'Lillian . . .' began Ian.

'Sophie knew that I should very much resent her coming
to our bedroom,' continued Lillian unsteadily, 'and that's
why she came. She enjoys that kind of situation. I suppose
it's because she's mentally ill. No normal woman would
want to come within fifty miles of the room her former
husband was sharing with another woman.'

Sophie sat quite still, staring at her, the light falling
sideways across her high cheekbones and large eyes and
the tilt of her eyelashes.

'It's you who are mentally ill, Lillian,' retorted Sophie quietly. 'What's the matter with you is just plain common jealousy, and you know it as well as I do. Oh, you needn't think that I don't know you hate me being here. You've made it pretty plain,' her eyes filled again, 'you've always hated me.'

'Yes, I do hate you,' said Lillian, 'but I don't hate you because I'm jealous of you. I hate you because you used to be Ian's wife. Even if you were the sort of woman I could like, I should still hate you, and detest your coming to stay here, merely because you used to be Ian's wife.'

Ian stood by the window, looking first at one woman, then at the other.

'You've got a tortuous mind. You twist the simplest feelings until they're complex,' said Sophie, after a silence.

'That isn't true. It's *you* who twist things. You and your friends try to pretend everything's simple and easy and on the surface when really they're all violent and bitter. It isn't *natural* for you to be here, that's why I hate it so.'

'There's no reason why I shouldn't come here and see my children and Ian. Ian and I are good friends,' she glanced at the silent figure by the window, 'and he likes me to come here. We parted good friends. There was never any melodramatic rubbish about parting for ever.'

'I wish to God there had been,' said Lillian.

'I see. I suppose you want me to see the children once a year in a room at an hotel?'

'I think that would be more natural than your coming to see them here, certainly.'

'Well, Ian and I don't; and they're,' she paused, and added slowly, staring at Lillian, 'they're *our children*, remember.'

'I don't get the chance to forget that they are,' said Lillian quietly.

'You used to pretend you liked talking things over before you married Ian, in the old days,' cried Sophie. 'You were so keen on threshing it all out and being fair to me and not having any bitterness and all the rest of that slop.'

Her charming face looked vulgar for a second as the ugly word came out.

'Lillian was very young,' put in Ian, 'and young people have ideals.'

'Well, I don't care for that sort of idealism. It's bogus. Now she turns on me like a fishwife, or like some foul-minded Victorian, just because I come to your bedroom after eleven at night. The thing's farcical.'

She turned away impatiently and stubbed out her cigarette.

'If you must know,' began Lillian again, 'I used to hate those talks we had. They made me *writhe*. I went through with them because I thought they were the right thing to do. I know better now. They were all wrong. It would have been far better if I'd never met you, Sophie, and Ian had kept me in a flat somewhere in London until we could be married. All that talk, talk, talk . . .'

'It's the civilized way of straightening things out, anyway,' retorted Sophie.

'Civilized! When it becomes civilized for a man to have two women by whom he's had children sleeping under one roof, then civilization's corrupt,' said Lillian violently.

Silence.

'Can't you see how horrible it is . . . how unnatural?'

she went on. 'Everyone feels it but you . . . the servants, the governess, everybody.'

'I think it more natural for me to come here as though I were the children's mother and a friend of their father than for me to meet them at some horrible hotel in London. What sort of an idea will they get of me?'

'What sort of an idea will they get of all of us, of the whole grown-up world, when they see you and Ian and me under one roof, and hear you talking about Jack Sands? Where are they going to get any sort of a standard, if we don't set them one? Children need something solid. They can't appreciate the fine shades; they *must* have black and white.'

'They've got to grow up in a civilized world. The sooner they learn that the fine shades exist, and learn to be *kind*,' Sophie's voice reprovingly emphasized the word, 'the better. After all, nothing really *is* black and white. Sooner or later they'll have to learn that tolerance is the only virtue and cruelty the only sin.'

Then Lillian lost her self-control.

'Tolerance . . . kindness!' she cried, throwing up her arms. 'I'm sick to death of the words! I never want to hear them again. Tolerance or no tolerance, you get out of this house to-morrow, and you never come here again while I'm alive. You're *dead*. Do you understand that? You died when Ian divorced you, *and you're going to stay dead.*'

On the last words her voice fell to a frightening whisper, and she thrust her face forward, like a mask of rage, so that it almost touched the alarmed face of Sophie.

Sophie backed from her, with transparent skirts dragging about her feet, and clutched at Ian.

'Ian, she's mad. She ought to be analysed. Don't let her hurt me, Ian. You don't want me to go away, do you? I've so loved being here, with the children, and now Jack's gone I'm so horribly lonely.'

'Far from being mad, I'm afraid Lillian is the only sane person present,' said he mildly, and crossed the room to his wife's side. 'She's perfectly right, Sophie. You can't come here again.'

'She's got you on her side! She'll make you cruel and stupid and narrow, like she is! She'll suck you, and steal your tolerance, you, one of the most intelligent men I know! Oh, Ian, how *can* you be such a fool?'

'It's not easy, but I'm learning. Tolerance has two sides, you know. If Lillian has tolerated your views, you must tolerate hers; and to-morrow morning you must leave.'

Sophie stared at him. She had always disliked his sudden masterful moods, which arose from nowhere and could dispose easily of her own opposition, and now she recognized that he was in one of them. She knew that it would pass, but that the decisions made during it would remain.

'You can't . . .' she began, staring at him.

'I can, and I do.'

'I'll make you look such a fool,' she said wildly, 'you'll be such a laughing stock . . . what do you think the Jamisons and the Arkwrights and Anson will say when they hear you've forbidden me the house?'

'I can easily imagine.'

'It's not like you to be cruel, Ian.'

'No?'

'No, it isn't. It's Lillian . . . it's she who's altered you and made you like this. Stupid, spiteful, provincial . . .'

He moved towards the door.

'There's no point in continuing the discussion, Sophie. I've come round to Lillian's way of thinking and that's all there is to it. We've given the thing a fair trial and it hasn't worked. In future you'll see the children, whenever you want to see them, at an hotel.'

She was weeping, her long hands held in front of her face and her dark head bent.

'Ian, *please!* I haven't done anything . . . I didn't mean to . . . I couldn't help loving Jack . . . I'll be nice to Lillian, truly I will. It's all a muddle . . . we're all tired,' she spoke thickly from between her fingers. 'Let's talk it over tomorrow when we've had some sleep.'

But he shook his head, standing with a hand on the door and one arm round Lillian.

'No. We're never going to talk over anything again, we three. There's been too much talk. That's just the trouble.'

He shut the door.

At half-past two on the following afternoon Mrs Ian Wardell stood at the window of her drawing-room waving good-bye to Baby, just setting off on her afternoon walk with a red-eyed and subdued Miss Treadgar, who was under notice to leave. Her employer's mood favoured clean cuts: and in any case Miss Treadgar had only been engaged for the period of Belinda's holidays.

'Good-bye, darling!'

Baby earnestly waved her fat hand, then turned her attention to a passing pussy as the pram turned the corner.

Lillian turned from the window, and walked across the cool drawing-room to a chair by the fire-place. The frilled

white curtains blew out slowly in a breeze, and three petals
fell from a bowl of roses on the table. The house was deep
in the peace of Sunday afternoon; Ian had gone to play
golf, John was reading in the nursery with a more cheerful
heart than he had had yesterday, Belinda was sulking in
her room; she could be dealt with later.

The train would just about be getting into London.

Lillian sat down, glanced gratefully round the fresh, silent
room, and opened a book.

'Shall I slice the cucumber and get it over?' inquired
Annie of Cook.

'I wish you would; it's a fiddly job.'

'Why do you reckon Mrs S. went off so sudden?'

Cook shrugged her shoulders.

'There's no knowing with her sort. Maybe tantrums; or
p'raps Mrs Wardell put her foot down.'

'And quite right, too,' said Annie, slicing the cucumber
very thin and suddenly deciding that she too was on the
side of convention.

The Friend of Man

On her thirty-first birthday an old friend of Pandora Bland's gave her a picture.

It was a coloured print about sixty years old, issued by the Society for Promoting Christian Knowledge, and intended (the friend pointed out) 'to combine the education of children with their entertainment.' It showed a large, noble, brown dog carrying a basket, against a background of brilliant green rushes and pink flowers.

'The dog,' began the four inches of informative printing beneath, 'is the Friend of Man.'

'And so are you, Pandora, and that's why I've given you this for a birthday present.'

'Well, really!' said Pandora, beginning to laugh, but aware that at the back of her mind there was a sensation of pain. 'How absurd! I don't know what you mean.'

And it was true; she was not quite sure if her friend meant what Pandora feared that she meant. Pandora was not a witty or a sophisticated person, but she was a good listener, kind and well balanced, inexhaustibly sympathetic, yet sensible. These qualities gave her a unique position in a circle of witty, brilliant, discontented people who belonged to the small world of literary London, and whose capacity for falling in love with the wildly wrong person was as deep as Pandora's capacity for giving excellent advice.

'Well . . .' said her friend, 'you're the only person in our lot who's never had an affair with Naylor, aren't you? Or with David? Or with Roger? Or with little Marriot? Or with Michael? And yet you're friends with all of them. I think you're marvellous. I don't know how you do it. I suppose you're just under-sexed.'

And the friend, who was not under-sexed, sighed.

Pandora did not reply, because she was embarrassed. She disliked talking about such subjects unless she was giving advice about them. She poked her coal fire and asked the friend if she would not have some more toast? The friend said 'No'; that she had promised to look in at Lallie's and hear all about it. She stood up, gazing round the quiet room with that wistful expression which is worn by those who have to leave a pleasant peaceful place in order to look in on someone and hear all about it.

'It seems such a shame, Pandora. You were made . . .'

But here she paused, because, judged by the standard of that circle in which she and Pandora moved, she could not honestly say that Pandora was made for love, nor yet for that casual association, that mutual trying-out of pampered personalities, which passed with them for marriage; and which was so easily and so frequently dissolved.

'You ought to have an affair,' she ended lamely.

'You ought to go, or Lallie will be wondering if you're coming at all,' replied Pandora, a shade less calmly than usual.

'But, honestly, Pandora. It isn't normal. You'll develop repressions.'

'Too late. I'm seething with them,' retorted Pandora shortly, and stood up.

When she came slowly back into the firelit room, she crossed to the fireplace and stood for a little while, looking down into the flames, with her foot resting on the copper fender. The picture, in its red frame, lay where her friend had put it, in the seat of the big armchair. At the back of her mind there was the knowledge that she ought to be wondering where to hang it.

But she still stood there, staring into the flames.

Pandora was in love; in the shy, ashamed, rather boyish way in which lonely women fall in love; women whose youth was passed in those post-war years when it was fashionable for women to be either loose or slightly masculine.

Pandora's personality was not masculine, but her dark and beautifully tailored suits, her square signet ring, and her shingled head were a little less feminine than is fashionable nowadays.

She was stamped '1927,' as definitely as a first edition is stamped.

And now (she told herself) she was too old to change, and she did not want to change. But she was extremely lonely; she longed painfully to be married to the man with whom she had fallen in love, after five years of listening to his confidences. She longed to have a child, to leave the important and fashionable library in the West End of London in which she worked, and to spend long days buried in a home, baking cakes instead of listening to other people's wails about their love-affairs.

But when she tried to fit Roger into a home in which

one could be buried, and bake cakes, her honest mind rejected the picture.

Roger, the faun-like, the irresponsible, the eternally young, refused to be fitted. He refused to appear in her imagination as the father of a child. Her painfully honest imagination presented her with a picture of Roger bored by domesticity and distracted by a child. Besides, apart from these disadvantages, he did not love her; and all dreams were neurotic, morbid, a waste of time.

It was a hopeless situation, that was all; a mess. She was in a mess, like Lallie, Michael, Roger, little Marriot, old Uncle Tom Cobleigh and all. She kept her mess to herself, and thereby retained her self-respect, but it was a mess, for all that.

She moved the picture on to the hearthrug without taking her stare off the flames, slipped on to her knees, and crouched there, still thinking.

Suppose she were not herself?

What advice would she have given to a woman of thirty-one who was in love with a divorced man, and who wanted to win his love?

'I should tell myself to make him jealous,' she thought.

But that would be horrible; that would be a blasphemy against their years of friendship.

'All the same,' persisted her thoughts, 'it would probably work. Jealousy would make him notice me in a different way; now he takes me for granted. He just never sees me. I'm just a listening-machine that he can talk to about Norah.'

Norah, that unkind and fascinating woman, was Roger's ex-wife. Roger was still in love with her. His friends said that this was because he had no longer got her, and Pandora tried to believe that this was not true.

Jealousy, thought Pandora . . .

She was painfully restless. The calm, pleasant surface of her life felt as though it was being cracked in every direction by strong forces. Love was running warmly under the ice of her self-control, forcing her to humiliating and desperate decisions. She felt that if she had to spend another year of interesting, congenial work during the days, and sensitive, cultured, intelligent talk in the evenings, she would go mad or die.

It was not enough. She wanted more. She was desperately tired of being the friend of man and listening to men's confidences, and being forgotten when they left her. It was not that she wanted them to fall in love with her; she would have been distressed (so she told herself) if they had. She firmly quelled the beginnings of sentiment such as some of her men friends had shown, because the men who offered them did not move her sufficiently.

She did not want second-best. She wanted the real thing; that real thing which her friends discovered, like the gleeful followers of a treasure-hunt, every eighteen months or so.

And, kneeling there, her quiet face and beautiful eyes disturbed with pain and deep feeling, she had almost decided that any trick would be worth while to get what she wanted, when the door-bell rang.

Roger. He was coming to take her out to supper.

But the man who stood there was not Roger. Roger towered over Pandora; this man's eyes were only a few inches above her own. She thought she had never seen such a red face, such blue eyes, such bad, anyhowish features.

It was a stupid face, too. It opened in the middle, and a voice with an accent said:

'Miss Bland?'

'Yes?' said Pandora, looking inquiring.

The red-faced one then smiled, showing white but irregular teeth, and took off his hat (not before it was time, thought Pandora).

'My name's Carter. You won't know me, but you knew my sister, Grace. She was over here three years ago. I'm over here for a bit, on business, and she said I might as well look you up. I don't know many people in London.'

'Oh . . . of course, I remember Grace. The library was much duller after she left. Do come in, won't you, Mr Carter?'

He hesitated, looking her over in a way which she found unpleasant. She had no use for Empire-builders; they bored her. She had known one or two, and preferred the sensitive, intelligent men of her own set, who knew how to treat a woman as though she were a fellow human being.

Judging by his teeth, his stare, his accent, she trembled to think how Mr Carter would treat a woman.

Crossly, but with a serene and interested face, she took him into her sitting-room, put him into a chair, offered him a cigarette, and of course, he said no, he had his pipe, and would she mind if he smoked that instead? He said, humorously, that he knew ladies did not like the smell of a pipe in the drawing-room, but this kind was all right; it did not smell . . . much.

Pandora asked him how long he was staying here, and where, and what he thought of England, and how was Grace?

Grace was all right. She was married, and had a nipper. *She* hadn't wasted much time, had she?

And Mr Carter laughed slyly.

It was quite frightful, decided Pandora. Most of the women in her set would have found Stanley Carter amusing and stimulating, simply because he was so different from most of the men they knew, but Pandora did not like him at all. She looked at him remotely, as though he were a fish or a beetle. She talked to him pleasantly, and hoped that she made him feel at home, but, oh! how he bored her. What . . . *what* did one talk about to men like this? Imagine being mewed up on a sheep farm, hundreds of miles from anywhere, with a man like this!

For, of course, he was in sheep?

No; he was in wine; and he had come over here to examine opportunities for the further development of the business.

That finished Pandora, who was a wine-snob. A series of awkward silences developed, in which Pandora wished desperately that Roger would come and take her away from this man; and Mr Carter stared at Pandora.

His face betrayed what its owner was feeling, just as a child's face does; and it betrayed wholehearted admiration of Pandora's silky dark shingle, her lips touched with coral and her bright, hazel eyes.

She was not used to seeing this expression in the eyes of her men friends. Once or twice she had seen it, and quelled it, and it had not returned. Some people believe that an attractive woman cannot stop men falling in love with her; but she can. If she really, in her deepest heart, does not want it, neither will they.

Roger was not used to seeing it on the faces of Pandora's men friends, either, and when he arrived half an hour after Mr Carter, he at once treated Mr Carter's admiration of Pandora as a huge joke. He was too well-bred and intelligent to be rude to Mr Carter. His manner was perfect: he asked interesting questions about the wine trade in Mr Carter's continent, and suggested one or two people whom Mr Carter might profitably see in England whose names were not on his list. He said that the *idea* of that continent, just the whole vast *conception* of it, lying there sullenly at the other side of the world, had always appealed to him curiously since he had read Lawrence's *Boy in the Bush* and *Kangaroo*.

Mr Carter said that he had not read either of them. Silences began to fall again. Roger gave Pandora a mischievous look full of malicious understanding. At last:

'Well, Miss Bland and I were going out to get some dinner . . . would you care to join us?'

'It's very kind of you, but, thanks all the same, I think I must be toddling back to my digs. I told them I'd be in for supper. Good-bye. Good-bye, Miss Bland. Very pleased to have met you.'

'You must come to a party some time,' said Pandora, taking him down her narrow hall. 'I have them rather often. They're fun. Do you care for parties?'

It was a silly question to ask of that stocky, red-faced man. She realized that as her words died into the silence. He looked at her, and said with tremendous earnestness and a would-be winning smile:

'I'd care for anything *you* asked me to.'

'Oh, my goodness!' thought Pandora.

'Good-night,' she said charmingly, and waved him down the stairs.

She found Roger sprawling on her divan with his arms behind his head, staring at the ceiling. He slowly turned his head to look at her as she came in, and said in his deep, effective voice: 'My dear, a scalp! An out-and-out conquest! *What* a type! But quite a good fellow, I should think, under all that strong and silent stuff. *Genuine* is the word, I believe. That's how I should sum him up. He fell for you like hot butter, didn't he?'

There was not a shade of anything in his voice but lazy amusement. Some strong feeling seemed to rush into Pandora's heart, and break. She decided to abandon her scruples. She could bear this no more. And Mr Carter should be the instrument which should win the game for her.

'I think,' she said lightly, 'that he's attractive. He's different, anyway. I shall have him here again.'

'My dear one!'

'Really, Roger. I shall. I like him.'

'Nonsense! You might as well like a whole continent. Damn him for being here when I want to talk to you, anyway. God! I've been through hell since Friday . . .!'

And tucking Pandora and her fur cape under his arm, swinging her along to the little cheap café where they often dined, he told her at length exactly what the nature and extent of hell had been.

Mr Carter, walking home through the winter twilight to his hotel in Bloomsbury, also summed Roger up in one word; his grace and his silver mop of hair, his boyish manner and B.B.C. accent. The word was not 'genuine'; it was a rude wine-merchant word. It relieved Mr Carter's feelings, and he spent the rest of the evening playing billiards in a pub in Tottenham Court Road and wondering when he could call on Pandora again.

It would not be quite true to say that he had fallen in love with her. It was not in his nature to do so serious a thing quickly. He was not susceptible. He had been much run after by women who were anxious to get married, and he had a healthy sense of his own value. He was thirty years old, part-proprietor of a nice little expanding business, owner of a rather pretty house in the suburbs of his home town. He was wary, a little malicious and 'knowing' about attractive women. 'Time enough' he would answer, when his sister said he ought to marry. He never suffered from scruples, remorse, or introspection, but he knew what he wanted his wife to be like, and Pandora surprisingly resembled that image.

He liked her elegance, so different from the ordinary smartness of the girls he knew at home. He liked the gentleness and womanly softness, which he divined, as a 'dowser' divines sweet water, beneath the surface-rock of her culture and poise.

She did not frighten him. All that stuff about books . . . it slid off him like raindrops. He was not interested, that was all. When Pandora and Roger began to talk in a way which he could not understand, he let his mind slip off comfortably on to other thoughts, and it stayed there until the other two had finished.

If Pandora was to be had, he was going to have her.

He determined to telephone and ask her to go to a theatre with him, two days after he had first seen her, but he did not have to take the initiative.

Pandora, steadily following up her plan, telephoned on the day after their meeting and asked him to a party. He accepted: and went in an inquisitive, slightly jeering, completely self-confident mood. 'The Aborigine,' Lallie at once nicknamed him; 'He rather intrigues me,' she said. She attached herself to him, complacently unaware that her nervous mannerisms repelled him and that he thought her dress ugly. She had never met a man with character; she had only known men with personality, and with such she was successful.

Carter had not dreamed that such people existed.

They were the usual over-intelligent, nervously exhausted, witty and tolerant people who go to certain parties, but he thought them 'rotten.' A rotten crew, he thought, steadily watching Pandora, in her coral-red dress, pouring cocktails.

He stood, balancing slightly on his heels, sipping his womanish drink and wishing it was beer; he was as conspicuous as a stone post in that fluid crowd.

Someone's going to take her out of all this, he thought; and his red face looked less expressive than ever as his determination grew.

'Enjoying yourself?' inquired Pandora, stopping near him for a few moments, according to plan. She could see, without looking, that Roger was watching her. Was it going to work, this shameful plot? Was it?

'Fair to middling.'

'Only fair to middling? Well, you are a candid guest, I must say!'

'No offence?' he said cheerfully. His steady stare embarrassed Pandora, who was used to skilfully turning such stares. She could not turn this one. Instead, she turned away her own eyes.

'Oh, none. We all say what we think, here, you know.'

'You do, do you? Well, I've heard a few things tonight . . .'

'You take everything seriously, don't you?'

'Come on, let me get you a drink.'

That was surprisingly neat, the way he turned the conversation, and the shoulder which touched hers as he steered her to the cocktails was hard, yet springy. Roger was watching! He was watching!

She slightly turned her head and smiled up at Carter.

If this was how other women felt when they made a man jealous – no wonder they did it! Pandora felt as though years of good behaviour and sober reticence were sliding from her shoulders. A submerged part of her personality was coming to light.

The next day Carter telephoned and asked if she would do a show with him; and she said 'Yes,' thinking that, of course, he *would* say 'do a show' and that it would be a good opportunity to see some ballet. But there was to be no ballet for Pandora Bland; he rang off before she could tell him that she wanted to see some ballet, and when he telephoned her again in the evening it was to say that he had got stalls for a huge, lush musical comedy, full of primitive humour and legs.

'Well!' thought Pandora, feeling breathless and not at all sure of herself as she sat beside him. 'Champagne and stalls . . . what am I coming to? And not a word about books or music or anything intelligent have we said since the evening began. What have we *talked about*? I'm blessed if

I know.' All the same, despite her disturbed state of mind, and her feeling of guilt and shame at using one man to attract another, she enjoyed the evening. The music was so gay and the girls were so pretty and the dancing so neat: she felt truly grateful as she said 'Good-night' to him and thanked him.

She thought that his manner was different as he said goodnight; he seemed less obviously full of admiration for her.

Pandora was conscious of a tiny feeling of disappointment, which she firmly tried to quell.

'I thought he was going to be a nuisance, but apparently he isn't,' she thought, as she stood by the gas-stove, watching the kettle boil for her dreary little hot-water bottle. 'Well, *that's* a comfort. We can just be friends . . . as I've been with so many men.'

And as she passed through the sitting-room on the way to her bedroom, the coloured print of the 'Friend of Man' looked nobly down at her from its red frame.

Surprisingly, Pandora made a face at it.

It soon began to be rumoured in Pandora's set that The Aborigine was in love with her. This was thought extremely amusing; and everyone waited to see how Roger would react to the news. Some of Pandora's nicer and more sincere friends said that it served Roger right; they had been waiting for five years to see Roger realize what a treasure lay under his handsome nose, and ask Pandora to marry him.

Others, less nice, said that Pandora was losing her fastidiousness as she grew older, and that she must be much more stupid than anyone had suspected, or else she

would not be able to spend evenings alone with that dull
young man.

Roger was, at first, amused, then incredulous, then angry
with her and dismayed because Pandora's spare time no
longer lay at his disposal. When he rang her up, she was
either just going out with Mr Carter, or else she had just
come in from being out with Mr Carter, and they were
just going to have tea, and wouldn't Roger come round?
    He took Pandora's treachery (that was what he called
it to himself) very hard. He had no one to talk to now
about Norah, who was carrying on in the most awful way.
    All his friends, except Pandora, now changed the subject
when he started to talk about Norah. He missed Pandora;
he missed her very much.

At last there came a drizzly, foggy Sunday, on which Mr
Carter had chosen to take Pandora into the country, and
she with a bad cold in the head, and very undecided about
the wisdom of her tactics with Roger and secretly wanting
to stay at home and read a nice book by the fire, but
overwhelmed by the firmness and generalship of Mr Carter.
    He arrived at half-past nine in an old, hired, closed car
which acted as a funnel for all the draughts that blow.
    'Got a cold, have you?' asked Mr Carter, looking keenly
at Pandora's eyes and her little pink nose. 'Ah! . . . a blow
will do that good. I thought we'd go up to Charlton Rings.
Know Charlton Rings? There's a pub there where we can
have a bit of lunch, and we can walk about a bit and look
at the view. What do you think?'
    Pandora thought it sounded quite frightful but did not

dare to say so. She murmured something about having to be home early because Mr Foster (that was Roger) was coming to take her out to supper, and Mr Carter said that *that* would be all right. Part of Pandora's charm for men had always been her willing co-operation in any plan they chose to suggest, and Mr Carter fell under the spell as so many other men friends of Pandora's had fallen. It did not occur to him, as it had never occurred to all the others, that Pandora might not want to bump forty-five miles to Charlton Rings in a draughty car, with a cold in her head. He would be beside her, he would have the pleasure of her conversation and company; and as he wrapped her in a rug (Pandora struggled like one who is being buried alive, but in vain), that was all he cared about.

Pandora quite enjoyed the first twenty miles.

True, the rug smelt of old dogs and was besprinkled with dubious feathers, which suggested that at some time it had been used to nurse chickens on, but it was warm, and she liked (she was just beginning to admit this to herself) being with Mr Carter. Stanley (she thought, glancing at his red, irregular profile, outlined against the drab windscreen of the car), in spite of never having an intelligent word to say, was a restful person to be with.

This was because he knew what he wanted, had made up his mind about most subjects, and was a contented and sensible man, but Pandora could not be expected to realize this, because she had never before met a sensible and contented man. They are rare.

Yes, Stanley was restful to be with, but he could not give her (she mused) the sweet and painful ecstasy which Roger could give. After an evening with Roger, she felt stimulated and alive; after an evening with Stanley she felt soothed, sedate, ironed-out.

What woman (she mused) wants to feel sedate and ironed-out?

But then they began going over patches of bad road, and the car bumped so hideously that Pandora bounced up and down inside the smelly rug in a most uncomfortable manner. Every time her nose came out, it stuck into a steady draught whistling through the window, and when it was plunged into the rug again, it was tickled and made to inhale the ancient and dog-like smell.

'Goes well, doesn't she?' said Mr Carter proudly. 'You'd never think she was twelve years old, would you? She belongs to a pal of mine over here. Aren't getting wet, are you?'

Pandora was getting wet in three distinct places, for the fine rain blew in steadily through the gaps in the car. Her feet were cold, in spite of the rug, and the smells were making her feel a little sick. She looked wildly, curiously, at Stanley Carter. His face was serene. Was this the way, she wondered, that he usually took women out for the day, and did he expect them to like it? But perhaps the young women of his native continent enjoyed this kind of day?

And yet there was something attractive about his serene pleasure! It occurred to her that though he had obviously had a hard working life, he must have remained an unspoiled and simple person if he could enjoy bumping over bad roads in a twelve-year-old car just because he had a woman he cared about by his side.

There was something nice about that. Never mind if it

was selfish, and if none of the many men who called themselves her friends would have done it, there was something touching and attractive about it.

And wasn't it quite as bad to be selfish in more subtle ways; to steal a woman's time and sympathy and energy and give nothing in return but empty charm?

'Here we are!' said Mr Carter, stopping the car with a sickening jerk. 'There's a view for you!'

Like too many views, this one over Buckinghamshire consisted chiefly of being able to see a long way. It was whispered that, on fine days, the gazer could see across four counties, but to-day the only prospect was one of weeping clouds and, far below, fields hidden in mist. One knew one was high up; one thought 'Must be a wonderful view on a fine day,' and that was all there was to it.

'Spot of lunch,' said Mr Carter, leading the frozen Pandora across the brown and sodden turf to a sullen little public house whose door was closed against the driving rain. It stood on a patch of bare ground, backed by twisted thorn trees, and it looked as though it would reopen on the Last Day.

Mr Carter rapped severely at the door.

Pandora stood with her coat collar turned up, staring away into the mist and feeling wretched, cold, angry. If only he had not been so obviously enjoying himself! Look at him now, gazing at her with his head on one side, looking about seventeen and so silly! She was so miserable and felt so forlorn and lonely that suddenly the tears came to her eyes, and she turned away to wipe them, and the raindrops, from her cheeks.

Mr Carter rapped again.

'I could just do with a bit of roast and some Yorkshire,' said the guileless Aborigine, who had no experience of English pubs on a wet Sunday.

The door opened.

A large, fair, dirty, drooping man stood there, with a Sunday paper hanging from one hand. He looked long-suffering, but also a little malicious, as though he were about to enjoy himself at somebody else's expense.

'What about a spot of lunch, George?' said Mr Carter amiably.

The large, fair, dirty man's lips parted in a slow and satisfied smile.

'We don't do no lunches,' he said.

'Here . . . but it says "Lunches" outside,' protested Mr Carter, jerking his thumb at a board in the background.

The large, fair, dirty man looked.

'Ar . . .' he said at last, 'that don't mean nothing, that don't. That's for the summer, see?'

'Then why not take it down in the winter?' demanded Mr Carter, glancing at Pandora, to see how she appreciated his boldness and wit. Pandora was staring away remotely at the weeping landscape.

'That 'ud cost money,' said the dirty man, suddenly seeming to tire of the conversation, and he made as though to close the door.

'Here . . . wait a bit . . . haven't you even any *ham*?' cried Mr Carter, uttering the word which is the hope of the hungry, the last cry of despair from those who seek food on a Sunday in England.

''Am. Well, we may 'ave. If you come in, I'll see. Mind you, I can't promise. We don't get many 'ere on a Sunday in the winter,' and he looked at them thoughtfully, as though he was trying to decide whether they were fugitives from justice.

The end of it was that they ate salt, tough ham in a panelled parlour, without a fire. They had with it some cracked, but moist, yellow cheese; some very new bread which could be pulled out, if the eater chose, like india-rubber; some flat, sour, draught beer; and tinned pineapple, with lumpy cold custard.

'If Roger were here,' thought Pandora, 'how scathing he would be about all this! And he would tell me how much better they order things at the tiniest inn in France; and describe the omelette and the *vin ordinaire*, and the *pot au feu*, all simple, but hot and delicious and nourishing . . .'

And she gently put down her knife and fork.

It now seemed to be dawning upon Stanley that all was not well with the day, and Pandora.

'Aren't you enjoying yourself?' he asked bluntly. Another man would have said, in some embarrassment and guiltily: 'I say, I'm afraid this isn't much fun for you. I'm terribly sorry . . .'

Not so Mr Carter. A note of surprised indignation sounded in his voice; but there was a hurt look in his eyes, too. He did not mind the nasty lunch, the cold and damp and the vague smells. Pandora was with him, and that was all he asked. 'Yes,' thought she, looking at his plain, honest face, 'and he's a nicer and a more spiritual person than I am. All *he* wants is love.' And she did not know what to say, and whether to laugh or cry. 'Oh, dear, why do I have dealings with such hopeless men? Oh, I'm so miserable, I wish I could cry all over him. I wonder what he would do?'

'Yes . . . thank you very much . . . only I'm rather cold that's all . . .' she said; and then wished she had not, because he took her outside, where a stiff wind had blown the rain away, and walked her up and down in it, 'to get the circulation going,' with the kindest warm hand under her elbow. She leaned with a curious sensation of comfort and protection against his hard shoulder, and did not look up, or she would have seen such a transfigured face!

But going home . . . going home was the worst part of the day. It began to rain again. Mr Carter lost the way. The car stuck in the mud for fifteen minutes. Pandora's cold was much worse. She was unromantically hungry. And then he stopped at a noisy, garish tea-place on the outskirts of Richmond, where the wireless blared maddeningly, and there was a stifling smell of high teas being fried. The cakes were stale and sugary, there was no China tea to be had, and the Indian was a deep, rich crimson, in which the spoons almost stood up, and it tasted bitter.

Stanley had some fried fish and chips. He was hungry.

Pandora wanted some, too, but she was so furious, so coldly angry with this boor, this complacent ass who had treated her to one of the most miserable days she had ever spent in her life, that she felt she *must* keep up to her dignity. It would vanish if she greedily ate fish and chips with him in bestial silence and content. And oh! it was nearly a quarter past six, and Roger would be coming at seven o'clock! True, she had put the key in a note under the mat, but he would be so angry at being kept waiting.

Trembling and hysterical with hunger, rage, and the cold

in her head, Pandora was packed into the car again at half-past six, and off they went. She had said nothing for the last quarter of an hour; and once or twice he had glanced at her a little indignantly, but still she would not speak.

He took advantage of a block in the traffic outside Hammersmith Tube Station to ask her to marry him.

'Will you marry me?' he said, in a low, and almost unintelligible gabble, bending forward to stare out at the traffic lights and not looking at Pandora. The glare of lights fell on his face, and the strained look which she knew meant strong feeling.

'*What?* I'm sorry . . . what did you say?' she asked, with a thrill of alarm, of indignation, rushing through her body.

'I said . . . will you marry me? I love you. Loved you ever since I saw you. I'd do anything to make you happy. I can offer you a bit . . . nice little house. Oh, Pandora . .' he turned, facing her, as the light changed to green, and the traffic moved forward: 'Please, I love you so much. I can't sleep.'

This was terrible. With her cheeks burning, she turned her head away. It was impossible to speak while she was looking at that eager, pathetic face, with its touch of self-assurance gone. She said quickly: 'Be careful . . . it's dangerous here . . . let's get out of this jam . . .'

When they were in a quieter road she had got her composure back. She said, still without looking at him: 'I'm sorry. It's out of the question. You see, we've nothing in common . . . our interests aren't the same. It would mean my leaving England . . .'

'Never mind all that, do you love me?'

'No . . . why . . . of course . . . no; I'm sorry. I don't.'

Then came the astounding answer: 'Yes, you do, then.'

'*What nonsense!*' cried Pandora wildly. 'How *dare* you!
How absurd. I never heard such . . . I'm sorry. You must
see it's quite hopeless. You don't understand me, if you can
think I . . .'

'Love me? Yes, I do think it, my girl. I understand you
a long sight better than you do yourself. You don't know
– I do. I know what you want, you see. You think I'm a
rough sort of bloke that doesn't understand about books
and foreign travel and that. Well, I don't. But I know what
makes a woman happy – your sort of woman. And I love
you very much. I've never loved a woman before so's I
wanted to marry her and have kids. Don't mind me. You
think it over. You love me all right. I know you do. I knew
it when you let me take your arm.'

She said nothing, only shook her head, with the tears
running down her cheeks. Oh! it was getting so late, and
Roger would be waiting for her.

Oh! to escape back to Roger, and the familiar life she
loved!

'Please,' she muttered, turning to him, 'could we hurry
a little? Mr Foster will be waiting for me, and I shall be
so late. I'm terribly, terribly sorry, but it's quite out of the
question. Please . . . try not to mind . . . not to be too
miserable.'

The name of Roger made a silence between them which
lasted until he stopped the car outside the block of flats
where she lived.

Pandora looked up at her window, and saw, with a

feeling of dismay, that there was a light there. Oh dear, he was there . . . he had been waiting for her, and he would be hurt and angry!

She turned impulsively to Carter.

'Good-bye. I'm sorry it should have ended like this. I'm so very, *very* sorry. I would give anything if things could be different.'

But all he said was, not looking so wretched as she had feared:

'If you want me, I'm round the corner. At the Edmonstone. I'll be there till Tuesday, early. Don't you fret. Never say die.'

He did not look at her, but drove away in the shocking old car, with his face looking at once set, unhappy, and cocksure.

If she had not been so apprehensive about Roger's state of mind, she would have been in a fine retrospective rage with Stanley Carter as she ran up the stairs.

The first sight she saw was most alarming: her poor little note to Roger, crumpled into a frightful and menacing ball and flung down upon her rubber door-mat. Her heart sank, but her pride sat up and looked angrily around.

Men (she thought, setting her little teeth as she set her key into the lock) . . . great selfish, stupid, cocksure fatheads . . . What a day!

With crimson cheeks and eyes sparkling, she strode down the passage and opened her sitting-room door.

Yes, there he was. Slumped in an armchair. Reading a dreary book by one of his literary acquaintances. His lower lip was sticking out, he had let the fire die down to a grey ghost, the curtains were not drawn, against the sad, foggy evening, and the room smelled of stale cigarettes.

'Hullo!' she said brightly, pulling off her cherry-red hat. 'Sorry I'm so late. We got lost coming home.'

Silence.

'Come on, Roger,' said Pandora, trying to make her voice sound easy and amused. 'Let's go out and feed. I'm frozen and longing for some sherry. I'm sure you must be, too.'

'As a matter of fact,' he replied at last, still not looking up, 'I was just going. I half-promised Lallie I would look in this evening, and it was getting so late; I thought you weren't coming.'

'I know. I'm so sorry.' (She was biting her lip hard to control her rising rage. Queer! She thought that people only did it in novels!) 'I told you . . . we got lost. I've had an awful day, Roger – so boring, and my cold's worse . . .'

He sat up, flinging down the book with a dramatic gesture. The bright cover came off and fell into the ashy grate.

'My God . . . *you've* had an awful day! *You* have! And what about me? What sort of a day have I had, on the top of a hellish scene with Norah last night? This morning I couldn't write a line. My nerves are jangling like a barrel-organ . . . round and round . . . round and round . . . and then I find you still out at eight at night with that coarse, under-bred swine! I've been sitting here in hell. Hell! I tell you I *must* have someone to talk to when I feel like this. I *must*! It's necessary to me, like food and sleep – to talk. The matter with you, Pandora, is that you're selfish. Bone selfish. You won't face it, but you are. Lallie's right;

she always said you were fundamentally cold and self-absorbed. You *know* what I've been through lately, and then you let me down like this. I counted on you. We've been friends, haven't we? I thought there had been something between us, hadn't there? And now you've let me down for this barbarian fool. What were you doing with him all those hours, anyway? Talking? I'll bet you were—'

'SHUT UP! SHUT UP! SHUT UP!' screamed a shrill, furious, hysterical voice. Through the storm of fury and nervous trembling which was shaking and choking her, a shocked Pandora realized that it must be her own. 'Get out of my flat! Go away! I hate you! Selfish, cruel, devilish beast! Go away! Get out, damn you, do you hear? I never want to see you again! I'm sick of you! I've been listening to you for five years, and I'm bored . . . BORED! Go on . . . get out, or I'll *bash* you!'

And wildly looking round for something to bash him with, her eye caught the print of the noble 'Friend of Man', which was resting on the mantelpiece pending the insertion of a new glass. She picked it up. She rushed at him. She saw his face, white, weak, flabby, scared and shocked. Then, reaching up to her full, frenzied five-feet-five, she brought the frame down over his head and shoulders. It hung ludicrously round his neck, like something out of a film by the Marx Brothers. He retreated, saying something she could not hear above her own screams. She saw him go out of the room, heard the door slam. She was alone.

For five minutes she walked round and round, crying noisily, kicking furniture out of her way, beating frantically with her bruised fists on the surface of her beautifully polished table. 'Oh, oh!' she moaned. 'What shall I do? Oh, what is the matter with me? I must be going mad! Oh, oh, I am so miserable! Oh, I want Stanley . . . I want Stanley . . '

And, snatching up her hat, she rushed out of the room, slamming the door behind her.

Down the steps of the building she flew, her feet pattering, with a sound of alarm and furious haste, through the corridors, across the threshold under the shocked and inquiring eyes of the porter. She waved frantically to a passing taxi and fell into it.

The driver was pleased to get half-a-crown from the lady who was crying so bitterly, and well he might be, because the Edmonstone Hotel was only just round the next corner and the strict fare for the ride was exactly ninepence.

'Mr Carter . . . I want to see Mr Carter . . . It's very important, please . . .' Her lips were shaping the words, as a child will rehearse a message, as she pushed open the swing doors of the Edmonstone, but she never had to say them.

Mr Carter himself was there, standing by the fire in the hall lounge, staring rather gloomily into the flames. His short, sturdy figure, his kind red face and clumsy blue suit were seen by Pandora with the most blessed sense of comfort. Now, at last, she knew what she wanted, and here was someone who could give it to her.

'Oh Stanley!' she cried, running at him across the decorous expanse of the Edmonstone lounge hall. 'Here I am. I'm sorry. Please comfort me. I'm so dreadfully miserable. Please love me.'

He put his arms round her cautiously, because, from the first time he had seen her, he had known that she was a delicate and fragile being, who must not be handled roughly.

But she put her own arms closely round his neck, clinging and clinging to him, while the grave and beautiful word 'husband,' drifted across her mind, and then she felt the hard arms, whose touch she had always liked, close upon her tighter and tighter like protecting walls.

Tame Wild Party

A girl whose name was Joyce Cracknell, who lived at Hendon, whose face was neither glamorous nor amusing – a girl like that had been silly to come to a party like this.

Joyce sat gloomily on Miss Josephine Boot's bed, carefully not looking at herself in the black mirror which hung on the opposite wall. She had sat there for an hour. Every twenty minutes a different lady rushed in, flomped down on the foot of the bed, muttered vaguely, 'I say, you don't mind if I 'phone do you?' and at once began an agonized, intimate and lengthy conversation, consisting chiefly of the sentences, 'Darling, do be *sensible*,' and 'Darling, you must *see*.' When this happened, Joyce tried to look like Miss Boot's personal maid, and succeeded rather well. One lady had said to her, brightly and sympathetically, 'Too bad of darling Joey to keep you up.'

Joyce did not get up and go home because, for one thing, she hoped someone would give her a lift home in his or her car. That would save about eight shillings. Also, she had foolishly come to this party with high hopes of enjoying herself and perhaps meeting some people who were interesting and gay, but also kind, and recognizable

234

as human beings by the standards of Hendon and the rest of workaday London.

In both hopes she had been disappointed, but so high had they been that she could not bear, even after two hours of boredom and distress, to get up and go home. Besides, if she did that, she would have to go into the next room, where that man was singing those songs, and find Miss Boot and go up to her and thank her for having her. That was what Hendon (and for the matter of that, part of Mayfair and all of Kensington) did, when it left a party.

But these people didn't. Joyce had watched two of them leaving, an hour ago. The man said, 'Better be getting on, Sue. Don't want to miss it.' The girl said, 'Joey's parties get stickier and stickier. Darling Joey, *there* you are! We must run. *Heavenly* party.' And off they had gone.

The third reason was not a strong one. It was experienced by Joyce Cracknell somewhat hazily, through the mists produced by the one cocktail she had taken. Though she felt sleepy, hazy and miserable, she was conscious also of a wish to discover what was scrabbling about in the next room. She could not, she felt, get up and go home until she found out what was scrabbling.

The next room was dark, and its door was slightly ajar. It was once, perhaps, a powder-closet, for this little house which Josephine Boot had rented was built in 1742, during an age which, like our own, preferred its parties wild.

The scrabbling did not go on all the time. There was a scrabble; and then ten, or perhaps twenty, minutes' silence. Then another scrabble. Then more silence. And so on.

Joyce did not think it was a ghost. She just wondered, though, what it was, and everything, and why it scrabbled, and then kept quiet for some time, and then scrabbled again. She yawned miserably, without troubling to put up her hand, and pushed herself a little deeper into the turquoise blue linen pillows of Miss Boot's large bed. She felt so sleepy. If only she had something to read!

That man had stopped singing in the next room. The gramophone had started again, and she could hear the slithering sound of dancing feet on the parquet floor, the sound of voices talking too fast and too loudly. The bedroom door was half-open, and by looking up the quaint little staircase which led to the living-room, she could see the moving skirts of the dancers, washed with the soft silver of the concealed lighting.

Suddenly one skirt broke away from the moving mass, and its owner came rushing down the stairs into the bedroom, catching distractedly at a tail of hair, which was beginning to uncurl itself down her nape. Joyce was getting ready to say politely, 'Please do,' when asked if she minded if the lady telephoned, but this lady did not seem to want to telephone.

'Awful tragedy,' said the lady absent-mindedly, beginning to paint her mouth, and apparently forgetting about the tail. 'The bar's closed down.'

'Too bad,' said Joyce, rather dryly. She had heard Miss Boot say this, more emphatically, when being ironical with Mr Melnotte, her publicity agent. Said as Joyce said it, quietly and with a hint of contempt, it was effective. The lady turned her head over her shoulder, amused and no longer absent-minded.

'Hullo . . . who are you? You don't approve, do you?'

Her eyes quickly sized up Joyce. Twenty-six . . . well, say

nearly twenty-seven. Lives at Golders Green. Last summer's printed chiffon dress with a 'useful coatee which can be slipped off for dancing, making a delightful evening dress.' Features too large to do anything with, and not enough personality to make them forgotten. Hair unimaginatively dressed. Nice. Very nice, in the older, almost forgotten sense of that word, which meant neat and fastidious.

'I'm Mr Melnotte's secretary,' said Joyce, not rising to the question about her disapproval of the bar.

'Oh,' said the lady, turning back to her face painting but looking in a friendly way at Joyce's reflection in the black mirror. 'Then I suppose you know everybody here?'

'Nearly everybody . . . by sight,' said Miss Cracknell.

'But not to talk to, eh? You must be having a beastly time. Awful . . . a party where one doesn't know anyone. Look here . . .' The lady hesitated, glanced at her own reflection, evidently changed her mind about something, and said, looking a little uncomfortable, 'I mean, why did Joey ask you?'

There was no further pretence between the two. The lady – a Miss Belinda Barker, who designed sets for contemporary smart plays – knew that nothing could be done to make Joyce enjoy a party like this, where everyone 'produced' their own personality as if it were a part in a play, where everybody knew everybody else, and everybody had some parlour trick, some offering of looks, wit, money or mere high spirits spiced with audacity, to offer the world. Another girl, less human, might have enjoyed this party as a spectacle. Not this girl, thought Miss Belinda Barker.

'She *hates* having a big nose,' thought Miss Barker, putting purple paint on her lower lip.

'Yes, I've had a beastly time as a matter of fact,' suddenly said the big-nosed one on the bed, candidly. 'I had one cocktail . . . well, of course I've had them heaps of times before at other places because I dance quite a lot. But this one was quite different. Better stuff in it, I suppose. It's made me feel quite muzzy. And I've only had one dance, and Miss Boot didn't introduce me to anyone. I went to the late show at the Plaza, to fill up time till I got here, and even then I was the first to get here except some little journalist man, and Mr Melnotte hasn't come at all yet, and I don't believe Miss Boot remembers me. I believe she thinks I gate-crashed.'

'But she did ask you?' said Miss Barker, whose face was now complete, and who was beginning to be bored.

'Oh, she *asked* me right enough. She came into the office one day, very pleased about that last stunt Mr Melnotte pulled off for her and she said we must all come to her party after the first night of *Sensible Selina*, and Mr Melnotte said, "Does that include Miss Cracknell?" and Miss Boot said, "Of course," and Mr Melnotte said she meant it, she was so pleased. So I came. I wish I hadn't.'

'Too bad,' said Miss Barker, vaguely. 'Of course, her real name isn't Josephine Boot, you know?'

'What is it, then?' asked Joyce, feeling rather cross at having bared her woes so completely.

'Tranquil Gay.'

'Oh, but it's *pretty*!' cried Joyce.

Miss Barker shook her head disapprovingly.

'It doesn't sound real. Not nowadays, anyway. Now if she'd come to the front about ten years ago, it would have done beautifully. But not now. Nowadays, we're all simple and sincere and bared down to the bone and living on eightpence a week and pretending we enjoy it. The Crisis, you know. So she calls herself Josephine Boot! Bye.'

And Miss Barker, once more kind but preoccupied, floated out of the room and up the stairs, and forgot Joyce completely.

Two minutes later a fat man whom Joyce recognized as Buck Winch, the American film star, came into the room and, smiling a vague apology, fell over the end of the bed and went to sleep.

It was too much. Joyce got up, skirting Mr Winch's legs, and crossed over to the dark doorway of the powder-closet. She was going to investigate the scrabbling noise, which had started again. After that, she was going home. It was three o'clock.

The scrabbling went on.

It was a scratching, scuffling sound. It was like someone shut in a cupboard and trying to get out.

She leaned forward, peering into the darkness, pushing the door open a little wider. The scrabbling went on.

And then, out of the dark, a child's voice came, tremulous with fear but polite:

'Who's that, please?'

'Oh . . .' said Joyce, breathlessly, 'oh . . . it's only me, darling. One of the people at the party. Miss Cracknell. You ought to be asleep, you know.'

Her fingers were feeling round the wall for the switch, and suddenly found them. Light filled the powder-closet room, and Joyce and the little girl sitting up in a small bed blinked at its soft brilliance.

Joyce smiled at the little creature, whose pigtails stuck

out at either side of her head like little horns. She was about seven, solemn, fair-skinned, and blinking with sleep.

'Did you wonder who it was?' asked Joyce, who was not used to talking to children. This, she thought, must be Miss Boot's daughter Selina, after whom the play had been christened. She immediately began to yearn over Selina. There was a thin layer of dust on the dressing-table, the window was shut to the soft spring night air, and the eiderdown was on the floor. These *people*! thought Joyce, picking up the eiderdown and arranging it on the bed.

'Yes. Only I hoped it would be Belinda. She looks so pretty in her party dress. And I heard her talking, only I didn't think I ought to say, "Hullo, Belinda!" 'cos I'm supposed to be asleep, only the music woke me up, and I'm thirsty.'

'I'll get you a drink,' said Joyce, immediately enslaved by the solemn face and precise little voice and those pigtails. 'Isn't there any here? Oh no . . . well, where's the kitchen? Oh, that's where the bar is. Where's the bathroom, then?'

'Upstairs. You go froo the room where the party is. Is Mummy there? Was the play a success?'

'I believe so,' said Joyce, trying not to laugh at the professional tone, 'your Mummy got lots of lovely flowers.'

'Vat's nothing to go by,' said the child of the actress wisely. 'Have the notices come in?'

'I don't think so. They won't be here till about four. You'll hear all about it to-morrow. After I've got you a drink of water, you must go to sleep.'

She lingered a moment, smoothing the bedclothes, turning the pillow to make a cool place for the child's cheek. These small services gave her an exquisitely tender pleasure: she glowed with it, and thought how much she would like to give Miss Boot and Miss Boot's set, a piece of her mind. Just as she was going out of the room . . .

'Al Capone's lost,' murmured Selina, who was half asleep.

'*Who's* lost, darling? Who's Al Capone? A pussie?'

But Selina's eyes were shut. And Joyce, reflecting that in such a mad evening a few more madderies could make no difference, went up the stairs into the room where the party was.

The party had now reached State Three, which is reached by most parties about three hours after they start. Stage Three (following on the Frozen and the Anecdotal Stages) is the Feats of Physical Strength Stage. Someone says, 'Chap showed me a neat trick the other day,' and then everyone tries to do the neat trick, with the help of a chair and a chalk line on the parquet flooring. Then someone else says, 'I say, can you do this?' and everybody tries, with the help of a handkerchief and their teeth.

Joyce pushed her way through a crowd of thirty, all trying to see Elizabeth Dunn do the Walking Stick Trick. Two men were holding down a zebra-skin cushion on to the floor, and on this Elizabeth Dunn's head rested, and the legs of Elizabeth Dunn, wearing those very organdie panties in which five hours previously she had been delighting the first-nighters at *Sensible Selina*, were waving above Elizabeth Dunn's head.

Down a little corridor she went, not a soul noticing her because the couple sitting on the stairs leading up to the hall were too busy kissing, and she went into the bathroom and shut the door firmly behind her.

A young man sitting on the edge of the pale blue bath

looked up at her, and scowled. He was green in the face and a lock of hair fell over one of his eyes giving him a Beardsleyish look which Joyce, who had never heard of Beardsley, found singularly revolting.

'I beg your pardon,' she said coldly, 'I came to get a glass of water.'

'It's in the tap,' he said, 'or was.'

And he leaned back against the wall and turned greener than ever.

Disgusting, thought Joyce. She efficiently fetched down a pale blue mug, rinsed it out, turned on the cold tap and let it run for eight seconds, filled the mug, and turned to go.

But it was no use. She, like most women, could not see a crying child or a shivering old man, or a limping dog, but she must stop and coo over it. She said, still coldly:

'I am afraid you are not feeling well?'

'Never better,' said the young man with frightful irony, opening a pair of swimming eyes. 'Doing this for fun. Love it, really.'

'Can I get you anything?'

'Only a coffin,' groaned the young man. 'Oh God, I feel so ill.'

'Well, it's your own fault,' said Joyce rudely, feeling sorry for him, but so much sorrier for her own disappointment and humiliation and her spoiled evening that she must vent her feelings on somebody. 'You shouldn't drink so many cocktails.'

The young man said nothing, but he stood up. Unsteadily. He advanced, slowly, upon the petrified Joyce. He did not loom over her, because he was not a tall young man, but he looked into her eyes while he said, with awful bitterness, and emphasizing every third word:

'It may *interest* you to know, sister, that I have had *three* cocktails this morning. A Bronx, a Martini, and a Bill's Special. Not an *orgy*, is it, sister? Not exactly making a *night* of it, is it? The fact is, I *cannot* drink. I cannot. Because . . .' and here the young man hesitated, as though there are things which a man may not say to a woman, but finally he said it, 'if I do drink, it makes me *sick*. See?'

And he sat down rather quickly on the edge of the pale blue bath.

'Then, if you know it makes you feel sick, why did you have any?' asked the scornful Joyce, feeling sorrier and sorrier for him, and quite forgetting the thirsty Selina and the mug of cold water in her hand.

He patted the edge of the pale blue bath.

'Sit down, and hear all about it.'

So Joyce sat. She did not want to hear all about it, and yet she did.

'Well, I'm the bartender, you see. Nice, isn't it? Bartender at hot party has three cocktails, and feels sick. *Isn't* sick, mark you. Never is. Just feels like death. And the bar closes down, or rather, that fat hound Buck Winch takes it over, while bartender retires to bathroom to put his head under the tap. Miss Boot's furious, of course, though she never said a word, bless her sweet heart.'

'I don't think it's so sweet,' said Joyce. 'I think she's rather selfish. She doesn't look after her little daughter properly . . .'

'Zat so?' asked the young man, sounding bored. 'Well, everyone has their own methods of dealing with children.

Point is, I let Bill down badly. He's the bartender at Bianchini's, where I go a good deal. Little place in Martin Street, off Leicester Square and he shakes the prettiest cocktails. But he's down with the 'flu. So I said I'd come instead. They'd pay me, and God knows I could do with the money. Bill told me some of his best formulas (on oath, of course) and along I came. Miss Boot knew all about it, of course. It was all square and above board. Only . . . I didn't tell her I can't drink. And she made me have a couple with her (I think she saw I was new to the game and wanted to make me happier) and then I had to have one with another dame with long earrings, and then, oh, God! Oh, Manhattan! I nearly passed out.'

'Well,' said the practical Joyce, who saw no harm done, 'that's rotten, but Miss Boot will understand, if you tell her how it happened. You can't help having . . . having a delicate digestion. Lots of people have.'

'It's not that,' he said, making an impatient little move-ment. He was sitting with his head bent forward, his hands loosely clasped over his knees, the lock of wet hair swinging over his eye.

'What is it, then?'

'Oh . . . everything. This is typical. To-night, I mean. Fact is, I can't stand their pace. They just go too quick for me. They're geared too high: they take everything in top. I chucked a job in a bank to become a saxophonist, because I was so sick of routine and Rugger (that was three years ago – it seems like twenty), and I was wild to get into this kind of life . . . doing good work, you know, but living ten times as fast as most people do, and making life a kind of party. It's no use. I'm finished. I can't stand late nights.

Then I worry if I get into debt. (God! it would feel funny to have something to get into debt with, these days!) I can't stick the uncertainty of not having a regular job. And if I drink, I get sick. So there you are. Funny, isn't it?'

He lifted his head and looked at her, but not as though he saw her. All he saw was a blur of femininity, in a blue dress, who was sitting still, listening to him, and not trying to vamp him, or cut short his own tale of woe and start in on one of her own. It was a restful blur. Soothing.

She sighed, and stood up abruptly.

'I'm afraid I must go home. It must be four o'clock. And mercy! The kiddie's drink! I forgot all about it. I expect she's gone to sleep again, poor mite.'

He stood up too and suddenly gave a huge, miserable yawn, in which Joyce joined. Through their yawn, they suddenly smiled at each other. They were both sleepy, and miles from home, two tame sheep in the heart of a wild, wild party.

'I wonder if we go the same way?' he said. 'Where do you live?'

'Hendon,' said Joyce simply, and her heart warmed at the thought of the place.

'I,' said the young man, equally simply but fully realizing the implications of what he said, 'live at Mill Hill.'

'Then should we share a taxi?' said Joyce, because it was the simple and obvious thing to say, and because she was too sleepy to bother about whether she ought to have let him say it first, and then thanked him prettily.

'We will,' said the young man. And she saw his face grow sad, and knew he was thinking about to-morrow morning, and waking up, and realizing that things were no better for him than they had been the night before. 'Where's your coat?'

She had left it in the bedroom, in a heap with many others, and thither they went to fetch it, the young man picking his own off a crowded peg as he passed.

Everybody was dancing again in the big room, but rather languidly. The party had now reached Stage Five, or Regrets For a Mis-Spent Past; this would be followed by Stage Six, the Belligerent, and Stage Seven, the Amorous or Final. People sat about in clots, regretting. No one took any notice of Joyce or the young man. The notices of *Sensible Selina* had come in, and they were not good, and this, naturally, cast a gloom.

In the little powder-closet they found Selina, fast asleep under the bedclothes. They stood for an instant looking down at her, feeling moved by her innocence and helplessness, as a young man and a young woman can be moved by the sight of a child.

'Poor pet,' whispered Joyce, 'she went off without her drink.'

In the silence, as they stood there, came a sound. To Joyce it was a familiar sound. It was a sound of scrabbling.

'There it is again!' she whispered. 'What can it be?'

'Mice,' yawned the young man, who was bored, wretched, and half-asleep. 'Come on, sister. There's a back staircase down into the mews, through the kitchen. We don't want to go through that room again, do we?'

'*Do* wait a minute. Listen! There it is . . . like little nails, scratching. Oh, I believe it's over here − in the cupboard!' and she darted across the room and turned the glass knob on the door.

The door opened.

Out flew a monkey.

Tiny, brown as a cigar, gibbering with rage and fright, he launched himself at Joyce's chest and clung there, wrapping his hot, dry little black paws round her hands, looking frantically round the room as though in search of someone.

'Oh . . . oh,' she cried, but still remembering to whisper so as not to wake Selina, 'take him away. Dear little thing! Isn't he frightened! *Do* take him away, please.'

But the monkey would not be taken. He resisted the gentle hands of the young man with shivers of fright, and clung hysterically to Joyce, who was stroking the top of his round head with her finger.

'What *shall* we do?' she whispered at last, when all efforts to make the monkey break away had proved useless, 'take him in to Miss Boot? Or shall we leave him on Selina's bed? I wish I dare take him home with me and bring him up to the office to-morrow. Shall I? He seems to like me.' Al Capone had stopped shivering and was pushing himself into the hollow of her neck. He was a most engaging little creature.

So, doubtfully, and feeling sure that she was doing a thing which would let her in for a row to-morrow, Joyce let herself be wrapped in her coat, pulled it over Al Capone, and followed the young man soberly down another narrow staircase and out into the quiet, damp streets.

It was half-past four: the street-lamps looked unreal and the world old and hopeless. But Joyce did not notice this, because she was intent on an extraordinary picture which had suddenly grown in her mind's eye.

She saw the interior of a pleasant Hendonish house and herself

247

sitting by a fire, serene in the knowledge that upstairs a baby lay peacefully asleep. And in the corner of the room, fiddling with a wireless set, was a young man. He was saying in the unselfconscious voice of a happy man, 'It was a good day for me, Jo, when you rescued me from the wild, wild party.' And his face was the face of the untidy, forlorn young creature at her side.

'What's your name?' she asked him dreamily, cuddling the shivering monkey in her arms.

'Reg Mortimer. What's yours? Never mind . . . here's a taxi. In you get. (I want you to take us out to Hendon.)'

So the taxi did.

And suddenly the street-lamps went out. They drove off into a dark world; uncertain, dangerous, where jobs were hard to get and bills harder to meet. And Al Capone suddenly tried to bite Joyce, and the young man laughed, and took her hand and held it while the taxi voyaged out and away to Hendon.

Behind them, in the little house where the wild, wild party was still being held, Selina was sitting up in bed, saying politely to Belinda Barker:

'Thank you, Belinda. I was *very* thirsty. A lady pwomised to get me a dwink, but I think she forgot. And ven, when she came back, I think she stole Al Capone. Any wate, she took him off under her coat. We ought to tell Mummie, don't you think?'

A Young Man in Rags

At half-past four on a fine May morning a young woman might have been observed wandering along the moist pavements of the Embankment.

She wore green sandals, which fact in itself is enough to explain any of the subsequent eccentricities in her conduct. Green as a Cornish sea they were, flat as a Cornish beach at low tide, and decorated on the toes with a chaste cut-out design.

Her face was long and dark, and lit by two large and beautiful brown eyes, and Ingres would have thought that he must paint her when he had time. She had the sleepy, unmodern beauty which attracts painters.

It had attracted in Nancy's case a great many; and Nancy, whose romantic temperament matched her romantic face, dutifully responded by being attracted to them.

She was so used to hearing, 'My dear, I must paint you,' that she often said it instead of 'One to Hampstead, please,' on her way home in the evenings from the Jade School of Art.

For Nancy was learning to be an artist.

She had been granted a studio in Charlotte Street, a latchkey and an allowance. But she dined and slept at home, because her mother believed (and who shall say that the shrewd woman was wrong) that all the things one ever gets to eat in a studio are condensed milk, bananas, and tea with lemon instead of milk.

Nancy drank too much, but only too much coffee. The consumption of large cups of coffee and thousands and thousands of cigarettes seems to be part of learning to be an artist.

So when Nancy had drunk too much coffee the night before, as she often did, and could not sleep, she would get out her little car and drive it all over the more spectacular parts of London, with a wine-red beret pulled down on her wide forehead, and her Spanish eyes sleepily looking for bits to paint.

She always took her palette and brushes and easel, and sometimes she would set it up, and squint at the distance, and make a vivid dab, and scratch it out again, and make another dab and so, squinting, dabbing, and scratching, onward through Life went Nancy, learning to be an artist.

Only it was more difficult for Nancy to learn to be an artist than it is for most people, because she was always falling in love; she did it as naturally and frequently as most people brush their teeth, and all her working hours were complicated by thoughts like—

'Shall I ring up Michael – (or Clive or Harry) – to-day, or shall I leave it till to-morrow? Is he away? Is he angry with me? Does he love me? Do I love him? What is love? I wonder if he's in town?'

It was surprising that she managed to be plump in spite of it. But her soft, drawling, rather high voice, her clear eyes and thinnish lips remained tranquil and unembittered in spite of her agonies.

Perhaps this was due to the anti-banana-cum-milkless-tea crusade waged by Mrs James, Nancy's mother. Perhaps it was due to the romantic sweetness of Nancy's own nature, which recovered from emotional blows like a dark pansy after a rainstorm.

Anyway, there it was, and there was Nancy, twenty-five and still unembittered, walking slowly along the Embankment in her green sandals and black cape at half past four in the morning, looking for something to paint, and miserably wondering if she should ring up Donald or wait till he rang her.

At a quarter to four on the same morning the heavy door of an unusually large house in Portman Square, that square of large houses, had opened, and out came a young man in rags.

He came out thoughtfully, slowly, and stood for a minute staring down the suave, deserted sweep of the square at the green trees of the park, while he pulled the great door to after him, and considerately closed it with a moderate click.

It had passed through the mind of the young man in rags that it would have been a fitting conclusion to his night's work had he slammed the door with a tremendous, hollow and reverberating slam, which would have echoed not only through the remote attics, cisterns, cellars, and incredible number of unused bedrooms in the house in Portman Square, but also sent waves of sound flapping endlessly down Portman Square itself.

But then he had considered the excitable and nervous constitutions of the numerous foreign attachés, ambassadors and consuls at present slumbering more or less peacefully in the numerous Embassies in Portman Square.

He thought how the repose of many of these gentlemen must be haunted by just such a sound as he had contemplated making with the front door, which would have resembled, to their sleep-dazed minds, the exploding of a catastrophic, endlessly consequential bomb in the Balkans or somewhere else temperamental. And he decided not to slam the door.

But once the door was shut there was no doubt that it was shut. And the young man, shivering and blinking sleepily in his greenish rags, looked up at the door, and smiled at the brass lion's head, worn with polishing, which was the door knocker.

He smiled his famous whimsical smile, which he had already decided to abandon, because the smile was becoming popular and people, especially women, were beginning to talk about 'Tony's lovely little crooked smile.'

It was bad enough, he had frequently thought, to be landed with such a puckish, temperamental and heart-breaker's name as 'Tony,' without making the situation worse by handing around a whimsical smile.

He therefore stopped smiling and looked at his hands instead. He spread them out in front of him, turned the palms upwards, and looked at the backs, and before he knew it, he was smiling again, but this time the smile was not whimsical. It was rueful, with the corners of his mouth turned down.

Then the young man in rags, turning his back on the

shut door of the house in Portman Square, spent an indus-
trious two minutes in rubbing his hands up and down the
railings until he had produced what he fondly imagined
to be an imitation of that deep-sunk, ageless and slightly
cream-coloured ingraining of grime which is only acquired
(as any tramp would have told him) by many years of
fleeting and accidental contacts with water.

Then the young man in rags, putting his newly-soiled
hands in his pockets (whence the fingers protruded with
heartrending obviousness), turned up his coat collar and
set off at a brisk pace in the direction of the Embankment.

'How hard – how very hard' – mused the young man in
rags, fretfully, 'How more-than-bearably-hard is a seat on
the Embankment when one is lying on it for the first time!'

And he shifted himself over sideways, so that his weight
rested on his shoulder and his hipbone, instead of on the
nape of his neck, as had previously been the case. He
crumpled a copy of an evening paper into a ball, and his
cheek was pillowed upon it, most scratchily and unsatisfactorily, and he had already had time to discover that the
beauties of early sunlight are best seen through one eye,
from an adequately warmed bed.

'Still, I'll do it properly,' he mused, 'I'll beat her yet,
the old humgruffin. She's a silly, melodramatic old woman.'

He turned over on his left side, and his long-suffering
spine obediently adjusted itself to the change of position.
A draught of air, blowing briskly up through one of the
spaces in the seat, found the centre of his ear with surprising
accuracy, and he shifted his head impatiently, pulling his
newspaper pillow over the hole.

He lay with closed eyes, trying to sleep, and quietly rejoicing that his seat was unoccupied save by himself, so that he could at least extend himself almost at full length.

And then something small, hard, round and cold was stealthily inserted into his half-open hand, and, opening his eyes, he saw Nancy James tip-toeing away from him with the exaggerated caution of one who fears to be detected in the act of doing a good deed.

The young man in rags did not, of course, know that the back view of a large black hat and black cape belonged to Nancy James.

All he knew was that a queerly dressed girl had given him half-a-crown. He could see it, a narrow rim of silver, glittering in his half-opened hand.

And the young man in rags, not for the first time in his life, felt a sweep. In fact, so familiar was the mixture of shame and resentment that swept over him that it required all his willpower (and alas! he had not much) to raise himself on one elbow and call, hoarsely:

'Hi! Lady!'

The hoarseness of his voice was at once assumed by the romantic Nancy to be due to the ravages of consumption.

'Hi . . . lady! Is this 'ere for me?' repeated the young man in rags, fervently.

Nancy turned reluctantly, nodded and smiled her sweet, dark smile, and was all in favour of hurrying on. But the air of the young man in rags was so forlorn, his rags so ragged, and his face, in spite of a surprising growth of stubbly hairs, so unlike the faces of those to whom Nancy habitually gave half-crowns, that she hesitated, and was lost.

As for the young man, his heart was like a singing bird.

He had walked out of a house in Portman Square straight into the arms of romance. Who could ask for more?

'Well, lady, I can't take it,' he said with decision, swinging his feet down onto the ground, and sitting upright. 'I can't, and that's straight.'

'Oh – but why not? I'm sorry if I've offended you,' faltered Nancy. 'You shouldn't be proud, you know. We all have our ups and downs. Won't you even take it as a loan?'

The young man shook his head firmly.

'Sorry, lady, but it can't be done. Wot I eats, I earns. That's my motto. Sometimes I changes it to "What I earns, I eats," but that's only in the summer, when I'm choppin' wood for home-made cakes and pies. Low I may have sunk, but charity – no, lady.'

He thrust the half-crown towards Nancy and coughed hollowly.

Nancy's dark eyes grew moist.

'You've got a terrible cough, if you don't mind my saying so,' said she. 'If you won't take this as a loan, would you – would you perhaps take it as payment for sitting to me? As a model, I mean? As a matter of fact,' stammered Nancy, 'I saw you asleep, and thought what a good composition you would make.'

'Wot – paint me? 'Ere?' cried he, and the scandalized note in his voice and his shocked expression convinced the horrified Nancy that he thought she wanted him to sit for the altogether at five o'clock on a May morning on the Embankment.

'Oh, no – you don't understand. I don't mean that sort of picture at all,' cried Nancy, almost wringing her hands with dismay. 'I mean . . . I should like to paint you as you are, asleep on the seat, and then I would pay you for it, as though you were a real model.'

''Ow much would you pay me, lady?' asked the young man, with a sudden shrewd narrowing of his eyelids, jutting out of his jaw and general assumption of cupidity that fell coldly upon the heart of the charitable Nancy.

But she looked at his rags, considered his cough, his hoarseness and his youth, and made excuses for him.

'Would seven-and-sixpence be enough,' she asked gently, 'for two hours?'

'Make it 'alf-a-guinea, and we'll call it a go,' said the young man in rags, with a most unmistakable gleam of triumph in his eyes.

Nancy, the weak-minded, the romantic Nancy, felt a pang of disappointment that her protégé should haggle thus over half-a-crown, especially after he had so nobly refused her charity a few minutes ago. But she looked again at his face and meekly agreed to half-a-guinea.

No sooner had her murmured 'Yes' faltered out on the morning air than the young man's feet swung briskly up on to the seat again, his head fell dramatically upon his newspaper pillow, and, with one hand falling pathetically down by the side of the seat, he fell, apparently, into picturesque slumber.

Nancy, trained in the severely realistic school, disapproved of his unnatural pose, but was afraid to say so for fear of hurting his feelings. She therefore crossed the road to the car, and unpacked her painting materials, first making sure that she had a pound in silver in her purse to pay her model.

For the next half-hour or so her brush dabbed, hesitated

and swept in silence. Once or twice she timidly asked him if he would like to relax his position and rest, but received no answer save a peculiarly unconvincing snore.

It is not possible to produce much of a picture – even a satisfactory rough sketch – in under an hour unless one is a far better artist than Nancy was ever likely to be. She looked at her picture at ten minutes past six, sighed, and put down her brushes.

For the past few minutes she had been conscious of the grins of passing gangs of workmen, the delighted stares of tramcar conductors and the condescending but protective attitude of strolling policemen.

Her model, secure in the knowledge that he was earning his half-a-guinea, had apparently fallen into real sleep.

Nancy, feeling hungry and discouraged with the result of her dabbings and scratchings, decided to call it a day.

She opened her purse, counted half-a-guinea into her hand, and, bending forward, gently touched the shoulder of the young man in rags.

'Eh?' said he, opening his eyes. 'I say, you haven't finished already, have you? Stout work!'

And even the ears of the dreamy and unobservant Nancy could not fail to recognize that the purest B.B.C. accent was not more pure than the accent of the young man in rags.

She stared at him curiously, and he lowered his eyes and yawned profusely behind his soiled hand.

'You're a worker, lidy,' said the young man in rags. 'It's a pity there ain't more about like you. Now, if it's all the same to you, I'll take me money and get a bit of breakfast.'

He rose from the seat and stood smiling quizzically down into her puzzled face.

'You know, I'm sure I've seen you before somewhere,' said Nancy slowly. 'But I can't place you at all.'

'I was shover to Lady Pennruddock before I come ter this. Drink, it was,' responded her model, glibly and with relish. 'Terrible thing, drink. I carn't keep orf of it.'

And even the dreamy and unobservant eyes of Nancy could tell, from one glance at the clear eyes of the young man in rags, that whatever had been the cause of his downfall, it was most certainly not drink.

'Oh . . .' she said, uncertainly. 'I know Lady Pennruddock slightly; she's a friend of my mother's. Well I'm – I'm sorry . . . it's terrible, as you say, when one can't resist anything.'

And Nancy sighed, thinking of how she could never resist falling in love.

'There you are . . . and thank you very much,' she added, giving him the money. 'I will leave you my address and 'phone number, and then you must come to my studio some time to-morrow, and I will try to finish the sketch. It's not very good, though, I'm afraid.'

And she looked doubtfully at her incoherent masterpiece, while the young man in rags carefully counted his half-guinea – which Nancy thought extremely rude of him.

'I say,' he said, without looking up, 'is that your car over there?'

'Yes,' said Nancy, trying to speak haughtily, and only succeeding in sounding alarmed.

'Well, if it's not taking you terribly out of your way, would you give me a lift to Portman Square? Where do you live?'

'H–H–Hampstead,' stammered Nancy, who was a snob, like many people with romantic souls; she shrank from the prospect of driving the young man in rags through the London streets in an open car.

'Well, be a dear soul, and give me a lift? It's quite important that I should be at Lady Pennruddock's house by breakfast time.'

'Of course, I shall be very pleased,' muttered Nancy, with her heart melting once more.

'He's going to fling himself on Lady Pennruddock's charity,' she thought, with a glow of sympathy.

'Thanks most awfully. Let me pack up for you,' said the young man in rags.

And in less time than it takes to tell, the easel and brushes were packed safely into the car, and Nancy and her model were off to Portman Square, Nancy marvelling whence her companion's Cockney accent had fled since she paid him his half-guinea.

And, on closer inspection, his white and regular teeth, his hands and his hair, seemed to hint at a devotion to cleanliness which was strangely out of keeping with his greenish rags.

He yawned suddenly, and coloured as he met Nancy's large and inquiring eyes, under her red beret.

'Sorry,' he said. 'Terrible of me, but I've been up all night.'

There did not seem to be anything to say to this except: 'Have you really?' so Nancy said it.

He nodded.

'Didn't get away till three,' he went on, confidentially, 'and then when I got home, would you believe it, the old humgruffin was sitting up in bed, playing chess, and waiting for me!'

'Your wife?' faltered Nancy, aware of a distinct pang of disappointment in the region of that susceptible organ, her heart.

He laughed.

'Heavens, no! I'm not married . . . not yet, anyway,' and he threw a shamelessly flirtatious glance at the already captivated Nancy.

'No. Lady Pennruddock, I meant.'

'But surely,' said Nancy, with all the outraged gentility of a real Bohemian in her voice, 'Lady Penruddock doesn't interview her chauffeur while she is in bed?'

'I'm not her chauffeur; I'm her nephew . . . or was,' said the young man in rags, calmly. 'You see, darling Nancy (I saw your name on your easel), I cannot work, and to beg I am ashamed. And I will stay out all night at low parties instead of staying at home and learning how to stand for Parliament. So when I rolled home at three this morning from a fancy dress ball there was Auntie, sitting up in bed in a robe all over Chinese dragons, waiting for me. Gave me the fright of my life, I must say.

'So we had a nice, quiet chat for half an hour, and then Auntie threw a pawn or a bishop or something at me, and told me to clear out of her house, and not to come back until I could show her half-a-guinea, honestly earned. (She made it half-a-guinea because, when she was a girl, guineas were all the go, you know, and she still thinks in 'em.) I don't suppose for a moment that she meant it, but I thought I'd better take her at her word, and give her a fright. So I went. And the rest – as they say in the last chapter of detective stories – you know.'

'So you're not a tramp!' said Nancy, in whose heart all the rhododendrons had suddenly burst into blossom.

'Not on your sweet life, Nancy darling,' said he. 'I'm only a sweep . . . a bit of a sweep, anyway. But when we're married, I shall work like three sweeps, in a select residential neighbourhood . . . whoa! Here we are. This is the humgruffin's den.'

As the dazed Nancy pulled up in front of Lady Pennruddock's house, a window at one side of the door was opened, and the fierce, handsome white head of London's most redoubtable dowager herself was thrust into the early sunlight, set off admirably by the red and green dragons on her dressing gown.

'Morning, Auntie. I've earned my half-guinea by sitting to this lady as a model,' said her nephew cheerfully. 'Can we come in, and I'll introduce you, and then we can have some breakfast? Here's the picture' – and he waved it at his aunt.

'Come in, Tony, and don't make such a noise,' said Lady Pennruddock crossly. 'You know I never mean what I say when I'm interrupted in the middle of a game of chess. My dear, you are Nancy James, aren't you? I know your mother, as I expect you know. Come inside, and we'll have some breakfast and you can show me the painting . . . which looks very bad from here I must say.'

'As for you, Tony, go and change your clothes.'

And the white head and brilliant dragons vanished with an almost audible snap, while Tony, tucking Nancy's hand under his arm, led her up the steps of the house in Portman Square.

Cake

'*O-Lan, you are the earth.*'

With the simple words from the Chinese farmer the film of *The Good Earth* came to an end. The light slowly went up, revealing the pale, dazed audience, and Rickey Roscoe sitting in the front row of the dress circle with his wife Jenny, slipped a little flask that had been full of whisky back into his pocket and said thickly:

'You know, Jen, if you were to die, I couldn't say that sort of thing about you, could I? She was such a doormat wasn't she? I mean, no ideas of her own at all, except sticking to her husband and brats. Not your type. They don't make 'em like that nowadays.'

Jenny did not reply, for she was glancing down at the little mirror on her knee to see if she wanted powdering.

'Could I?' he persisted, louder, leaning over her. 'That was all I meant, Jen. Just that she wasn't your type. A woman like that, now—'

'Come on, I'm late.' Jenny snapped the flapjack shut, got up, and began pushing through to the gangway.

'Oh, what's the rush,' he said loudly, stumbling after her. 'After all, it's our last evening together, isn't it?'

Several people glanced up, surprised, then smiled. That

263

thick-set fair chap was a bit 'on', and the woman with him was trying to look as if she didn't know he was. Heaven help him when they got home.

'All I meant was,' explained Rickey again, saying each word carefully as though he were not sure what was coming next, 'she was a b. doormat. That's all I meant, Jen.'

His wife walked ahead of him, through the foyer and out into Regent Street. The green, scarlet and blue electric signs were already winking through the spring twilight. Several men turned to look at her, and as she waited for Rickey to catch her up, it occurred to her that the difference between a successful woman and a failure lay in just that masculine turn of the head. The women men did not turn to look at might have succeeded at their jobs, but they had failed as women. But she had succeeded in both fields. Her bank-balance told her that she had won as a worker; her mirror told her that she was an unusually attractive woman.

'Let's have a drink, Jen,' said Rickey, trying to take her arm. She pulled away a little.

'I can't, Rickey. I haven't time.'

'Oh, come on, Jen. Be matey. Just a little drink, Jen. Shan't ever have a drink together again, p'raps.'

'Don't be such a fool,' she said, quietly but very angrily. 'We shall probably all three be the best of friends this time next year. And you've had enough.'

But when he turned in through the doors of a brasserie she followed him.

When they were sitting at a table for two and he had ordered, Jenny's expression suddenly softened. She smiled across at Rickey, sitting opposite to her and looking red, crumpled and sulkily miserable, and said:

'Didn't you like the locusts, Rickey?'

'What?' He looked up stupidly, then smiled. 'Oh, in the film. Yes . . . marvellous.'

He swallowed his drink, looking wretchedly at her.

'I knew you would.'

They smiled at each other, across the table smeared with wet and fluffy with ash.

'That's why I wanted you to see it with me.'

'The Last Flick Together, was that it, Jenny darling?'

'Something like that.' Jenny finished her drink, and opened the huge black bag swung from her shoulder on a black cord, with the initials 'J.R.' in brilliants.

'I'm glad we saw it together, Jenny.'

She did not answer.

'I say, though, this is a funny sort of way to spend your last evening with your wife, isn't it, Jen? I say, Jen,' staring at her, as his eyes slowly filled, ludicrously and yet unbearably, with tears. 'I can't believe it's *us* this is happening to, can you?'

'Rickey *dear*,' she said, repressively, shutting her bag, 'we don't want to go through all that again, do we?'

'I suppose not.'

'Get the waiter, will you? I must go.'

'I don't care a damn about her, not a damn,' he said suddenly, slumping down in his chair. 'For two pins I'd call the whole thing off. She's only someone to—'

'Now you see why I've got to go on by myself,' said Jenny quietly. 'When you can say a thing like that. You're like a boy of nineteen. And I'm grown up. That's all there is to it.'

She caught the waiter's eye; he came up, and while Rickey was paying she sat with her hands clasping the black bag, watching.

For three years she had watched Rickey paying waiters, while her salary from the Advance Advertising Company rose from two hundred and fifty pounds a year to two thousand, and her ambition, fed on success, rose with it.

The steady soaring in their standard of living, and the equally steady decline in their married happiness as her ambition grew stronger, 'were the outstanding features of the years 1935 to 1938,' thought Jenny drearily, as though she were reading a bad advertisement. And this evening, their Last Flick Together being over, Rickey would catch the boat train from Victoria at eight o'clock, and with him would be Margot Faulkener, a free-lance and a feather of the blue, kind and friendly and unambitious, who loved Rickey more than a little and did not at all mind being Jenny's grounds for divorce.

The arrangement was sensible, friendly and only a little sad. Jenny and Rickey were still fond of one another, but both had been able to see (Jenny rather more clearly than Rickey) that their marriage would no longer work.

Rickey wanted a child; that was the real cause of its failure. Jenny did not want one, because a child would interfere with her work, which she loved and which had satisfied her completely until Rickey had come bounding at her (suggesting to the unsentimental eye a Saint Bernard dog) and bothered her into loving him.

All their mutual friends had been very surprised when

Jenny married Rickey (note that they did not say 'when Rickey married Jenny'). The last man on *earth*, they all said. Dear old Rickey, kindest of men, making an adequate income in Insurance, easily satisfied and unambitious, sociable, yet domesticated, and *not* at all the right husband for Jenny.

Having decided this, they all went about their affairs with the pleasurable anticipation at the back of their minds that the Roscoe *ménage* might blow up any time. And now it had.

Jenny was not surprised at herself for marrying Rickey. Her personality was outwardly a little hard and cool, but her secret nature was sensitive and affectionate. She suppressed these qualities with her strong will, because they do not help a woman to succeed in the world of Business, but she knew quite well that she had married Rickey because he was her complement. He did not suppress his natural warmth, and his simplicity refreshed and comforted her, like a walk in the country.

He was not at all a fool, but he was not the slave of a passion for making more money. At first this had attracted Jenny. But when she discovered that he looked on his work, too, as a means to an end, and that end a peaceful, amusing, slow-timed living, she got impatient.

He could not understand her ambition. He came of a large, comfortably-off family that rode life as easily as corks; resilient, cheerful, healthy people. But Jenny was the only daughter of an unsuccessful painter, and had been brought up in an intense, anti-social atmosphere poisoned by thwarted ambition; and ever since she could remember, her strongest longing had been to get on, be a success, make more money than anyone else, be elegant and fashionable and first-class at her job, too.

She was without creative power, but she was so pretty, had such a steel will, and so much common sense and intelligence and untiring appetite for work that she was bound to succeed at any job she undertook. Men liked her unfailingly fresh looks and cool good humour, and women liked her unemotional kindness. She was a bit greedy, as a matter of fact, but it didn't show. Only Rickey knew that she was greedy. He called her 'Greed-pot,' the name his mother had given his fat youngest brother when they were children.

The little name, that Jenny at first found charming, gradually became the symbol of her husband's failure to understand the deepest need of her nature; and the Roscoes began to have rows, while Rickey started drinking so heavily that it caused comment even in a circle that took heavy drinking for granted. Matters grew steadily worse, and when he drifted into an affair with Margot Faulkener, Jenny was so angry that she took it as an excuse to suggest a divorce.

Rickey took it hard. He protested that he loved his wife as much as ever. Margot was only a bit of fun, and not so much fun, at that. If Jenny had been nicer to him (stated Rickey) he would never have gone near Margot.

No, said Jenny, it wouldn't do. It was not only Margot, it was everything. They had given marriage a fair trial and it had not worked. Now there was no reason why they should not cut free from one another, and start all over again. It was done every day, and in their case, thank heaven, there were no children to make things more difficult than they were already. Jenny stood firm for divorce: and she was going to have her way.

The marriage thus outlined had not been undertaken in a solemn spirit by either party, and had not worked itself out along noble steadfast lines. But in the circle in which Jenny and Rickey moved, nobility and steadfastness were out of fashion; indeed, all over the modern world these two virtues are fighting for their lives, armed only with wooden sticks. And if the Roscoe marriage did contain the roots of these outmoded virtues, they were buried so deep under money-mania, speed-mania and work-mania that the tips of their noses never even showed.

When Rickey put Jenny into a taxi and gave the man the address – 'Aster House, Baalbec Road, Highbury—' she said flippantly as she leaned out of the window:

'I'll be late. Still, one doesn't send one's husband off on a trip like this every night in the week, does one?'

'No, I suppose one doesn't,' said Rickey, wretchedly. He added, staring at her, 'Good-bye, Greed-pot. Sorry I couldn't make a go of it for you. You're the only girl for me, you know, always, in spite of everything.'

'I'm sorry too, Rickey. Good-bye.'

She tried to say something more, smilingly shook her head, and sat back without dignity as the taxi started. She did not watch him out of sight.

As the taxi moved steadily northwards through the quiet Bloomsbury squares, the light coming through the window showed a slender young woman of twenty-eight, dressed in about a hundred and fifty pounds' worth of clothes. Every trace of exuberance, childishness and indecision in her manner had been planed away, and replaced by an

expensive quietness in dress, and the simplicity of a sophis-
ticate. Her black broadtail coat and Mainbocher suit
matched her low voice, small movements and unaffected
glance. She was a very perfect specimen of the Successful
Careerist, 1938 Model, and she was all her own work.

She was dark-haired with light grey eyes. This evening
her face was painted a pleasing ivory and her lips a natural
red, for she knew that Miss Maude Allworton, the feminist
and former Suffragette, would disapprove violently of a
painted face. So Miss Allworton must see this particular
face without realizing that it was painted.

The idea had been Jenny's, as so many of the Advance
Advertising Corporation's ideas were. She had suggested a
series of interviews with six famous pioneers of the past
fifty years, to appear as full page displays in the most
important dailies. The old people would say, in phrases
carefully edited by the copywriters of Advance Advertising,
exactly what they thought about the modern world and
particularly about the altered standard of living. It was to
be an indirect appeal to the shopping-consciousness of
millions of men and women. Dignified, wise, strong faces
would look out candidly from the page of Mrs Johnson's
favourite newspaper and tell Mrs Johnson how much better
the Present is than the Past. For this the dignified, wise,
strong faces would get twenty-five guineas each.

But some of the ageing pioneers had not made much
money out of their spadework and were living in what
the papers delicately call 'retirement' in unfashionable parts
of London; while others were irritable, others were deaf,
and still others were not coherent upon the telephone.
Therefore Jenny, who had a talent for the personal touch,

had been chosen to interview all six. Miss Maude Allworton was fourth on the list.

She had been a red-hot militant in the exciting days just before the Four Years War. She had hunger-struck and been forcibly fed, poured paraffin in letter boxes, chained herself to railings, carried banners, tackled hecklers, insulted Cabinet Ministers, hidden for days in friends' coal-cellars while wanted by the police, and generally had a whale of a time. She had been a Public Figure, not to say a Public Nuisance, whose storm of red hair, flying necktie, and large feet in low-heeled shoes were familiar to all readers of the picture papers in 1913.

That was twenty-seven years ago. Between the 'Fighting Maudie' of those days and the Miss M. Allworton of to-day lay the Four Years War and the changes it made. And the tide of publicity had quietly receded from her; a generation was out in the world, working and playing, that did not know her name. Sometimes her signature appeared under a letter about some feminist problem in *Time and Tide* or *The Times*, but only older people remembered who she was. She lived in Highbury on a small income left to her by her mother, with a woman friend, and her temper was rumoured to be vile. Jenny was not looking forward to the interview.

As she sat in the taxi, now going along the Holloway Road, she tried hard to relax . . . and felt too wretched to smile at the idea. She never lied consciously to herself about her feelings, and she admitted that she still loved Rickey. It was unbearable to think of him with Margot; she wrenched her thoughts away from the picture. She would not have married him unless she had felt that he

was the one man for her; and he still was. That was the
hell of it. And now it was too late to mend matters.

*Ah, money doesn't buy happiness, they can say what they
like*, thought Jenny with miserable flippancy, huddling
herself into the broadtail coat and forgetting to relax. Oh
well, there's always the job, thank heaven.

The taxi stopped outside a gate with 'Aster House'
glimmering dingily on it. She glanced at herself in the
mirror before she got out, to make quite sure she did not
look painted. Old people flew at one like panthers about
paint; a reporter friend of Jenny's had been told by a famous
old actress: *Your eyes are painted. I can't give an interview to
a bad girl*, and had had to scrub her black Irish lashes with
a clean handkerchief to convince the old witch they weren't.

Now for Fighting Maudie, curse her.

She told the driver to wait, pushed open the gate that
hung on one hinge, and went down a narrow weedy path.
These houses had long gardens running down to the road,
which was badly lit, quiet and decaying. There were dripping sooty laurel bushes, rank grass with a spring flower
glimmering here and there in the starved earth, worn stone
steps leading up to pillared porches. Jenny pulled a bell,
newly varnished with some black stuff that ruined her
antelope glove, and waited, staring ruefully at the black
smear. What was Rickey doing now? Moving about their
flat, a double whisky following him round the room from
the built-in bookcase to dressing table, as he collected his
traps and packed . . .

She rang again, impatiently.

Depressing hole, she thought, staring at the faint lights
in the house opposite. Thank heaven for money, youth,

brains, central heating, electric cleaners and refrigerators. *And* for flats that have only been up six months. I suppose this house must be seventy years old. Time it came down.

Why doesn't someone come? She jerked at the bell again.

Must be pretty bad to come down to this, after thinking one was going to set the world on fire in 1913. But then they were all such fools, those Suffragettes and Women's Movement people. All suffering from chronic masculine protests, dressing like men yet hating men, giving up all the fun of being a woman (she moved her shoulders gently inside the Mainbocher suit) and putting people's backs up. They were bonny fighters, I suppose . . . but *what* fools! Didn't know the first thing about having their cake *and* eating it.

Now my generation has brought cake-managing to a fine art. Man–jobs, man–salaries, and all the fun of being a woman into the bargain.

We certainly are the lucky ones.

But as she turned to face the opening door she did not feel very lucky.

An old woman, neatly dressed in a white apron and black frock, stood peering up at her.

'Come in, please,' she said at once, in the unmodulated voice of the hopelessly deaf, 'Miss Allworton's expecting you.'

Jenny followed her down a long dim hall with a tiled floor that was deathly cold, past enormous dark landscapes in tarnished gilt frames. Everything was clean, but the house smelled shut-up and dead.

'In here.' The woman opened a door and Jenny went in. 'Miss Maude'll be down in a minute.'

Now this room is a really charming shape, Jenny thought, glancing round at the arch dividing the apartment in two, the french windows at one end, the low ceiling, and niches for bookshelves on either side of the iron basket grate. It could be made delightful. At present it's appalling.

And not clean, she decided a minute later in disgust, noticing the film of dust that lay on the shapely Victorian sideboard and centre table, the dull brass trays and bowls on the mantel-piece, the grubby loose covers, the two saucers with soppy bread and milk in the grate. An improbably large cat was curled in the biggest arm-chair, and another, not quite so enormous, on the rug in front of the broken gas-stove in the charming old grate. There were newspapers tossed about, and a big desk in one corner overflowed with papers. A thoroughly 'lived-in' room, thought Jenny. So long as I don't have to live in it, I can bear it.

I'd forgotten that there were rooms like this all over London. One gets used very quickly to success and the sort of rooms it buys. This is the room of a failure.

While she was glancing at her diamond fob watch, the door opened suddenly and a woman came into the room. She was small and thin, with grey hair pulled tightly from a shiny forehead, protruding grey eyes and a tiny twitching mouth. She wore a grey skirt that was too short and showed her skinny legs almost to the knee, and a white blouse under a grey wool cardigan.

She came towards the staring Jenny with a peculiar tripping step, rubbing her hands over each other as though they were cold.

'Oh, how do you do?' (The voice coming softly and

agitatedly from the pale lips was unmistakably that of a lady.) 'I expect you think I'm Miss Allworton, don't you, but I'm not, I'm her companion, Miss Urse.' She hesitated, pressing her hands together as though in prayer and staring at the floor. She had not once looked straight at Jenny while she was speaking; her glance wandered about the room in a suspicious frightened way. She went on:

'I just wanted to see you *before she did*. Of course, I don't know what you've come to see her about, she wouldn't tell me, but the maid told me she was expecting you this evening, and so I just wanted to see you and *beg* you not to believe anything she says about me and Mr Saville.'

'Oh. Yes? Mr Saville?' Jenny kept her voice quiet and gentle, humouring the poor little creature and trying not to feel repulsion at her manner and face, as she almost whispered the next words.

'Yes. Miss Allworton's fiancé. You see, *many* years ago they were engaged to be married. He used to come here, when we were girls (Maude and I were at Girton together, you know, and I came here to live with her and her mother when my own mother died), but though of course I knew he was engaged to Maude and I *assure* you there was never a word passed between us that a third person might not have heard . . . I always knew that it was really me he cared about.'

'Yes,' murmured Jenny, still gently. A feeling of horror came over her. This was what happened to women who grew old without husbands or jobs. How absurd, she thought a second later, there must be millions of them who grow old successfully without either . . . provided that they've got private means and don't starve to death.

'So I just wanted to warn you,' the soft voice went on, 'that Miss Allworton has always been very jealous of me and of course when she realized Mr Saville cared for me but was too honourable to break off his engagement to her, that made it much worse. I have *always* been a loyal friend to her, Miss . . . I'm afraid I don't know your name . . .'

'Roscoe,' muttered Jenny.

'Miss Roscoe, and I have given up *many* chances of a happy married life and children to stay with her. I have really given my *life* to Maude, Miss Roscoe, and now that she is getting on, and her temper gets really worse every day, I assure you it does, she frightens me sometimes, she gets in such terrible rages—'

She glanced nervously at the door.

'And I just wanted to ask you not to believe anything she says about there being anything wrong between Mr Saville and me. That's all. We both behaved *perfectly* honourably, Miss Roscoe, I assure you. It was a difficult time, and we both suffered, but we did what was right, and I have never regretted it.'

She gulped nervously.

'And if she mentions a *letter*, Miss Roscoe—'

'Makin' friends with Miss Roscoe, May?'

The deep voice came from a woman who had quietly opened the door and now stood looking at them and laughing silently. The little woman gave a sort of squeak, embarrassing in its frank terror, and darted out of the room like a rabbit. The woman at the door stood aside to let her pass, slammed the door on her, then came over to Jenny and held out her hand.

'How do you do, Miss Roscoe?'

'How do you do?' Jenny's fingers were crushed and her hand hurt by the pressure of a big signet ring.

'Sorry to have kept you waitin',' Miss Allworton went on. 'Smoke?' She held out a crushed packet in two fingers stained dark yellow with nicotine.

'I don't, thank you.'

Miss Allworton raised her bushy white eyebrows.

'Old-fashioned, aren't you? I hope you're not prejudiced against women smokin'?'

'Oh no,' said Jenny, feeling irritated, and just preventing herself from informing the Pioneer that it was new-fashioned, rather than old-fashioned, not to smoke. 'I just don't happen to care for it.'

'I see. Well, Miss Roscoe, sit down, sit down. Make yourself comfortable. Now what do you want me to tell you? Somethin' about the good old days before the War, eh?'

She gave a violent, jovial laugh. Behind her long splendid blue eyes loneliness walked up and down, up and down, like an old lion. She was dressed in a tweed suit that (like Miss Urse's) was too short for her, a shirt blouse and brogues. She was very handsome, with her straight nose, long firm mouth and fine profile; and Jenny found herself thinking that a family of ten might have been borne by that magnificent body and left the mother plenty of energy for living. *What a waste*, she found herself thinking. And the next instant, *Why waste?* She did what she wanted to do, didn't she?

'Yes, if you will . . . and something about the good new days, too, if you will, by way of contrast. That's what we really want to bring out, you see, Miss Allworton, the contrast between the standard of living for the average family before the Four Years War, and the standard now. It's a sort of an indirect appeal to the shopping public. We want to persuade them to feel they're lucky to be alive in 1938.'

Jenny said this with cool assurance, but as she thought of the headlines in the papers that morning she had a feeling that 'they' might be a little difficult to persuade.

Miss Allworton looked disappointed. So the interview was not to be a feast of reminiscence! She was not to tell the millions of fools living in the new suburbs how much more fun life was in 1913. She had got to praise the postwar world, which she feared and loathed. She said roughly, crossing her legs:

'Well, I don't know much about the standard of livin' for the average family nowadays, Miss Roscoe. My own family consists of myself and that fool May Urse, who gets crazier every day, as you doubtless saw, and the old woman who let you in; she's deaf as a post and has been with me thirty years. May and I don't go out much. I can't afford it, to be candid with you. I run down to Girton once a year, and sometimes to my Club if they've got an interestin' speaker (fools, most of them. No *drive*). But I don't go out much nowadays, or to these cocktail parties. The fact is,' she ground out her cigarette, not looking at Jenny, 'most of my friends are abroad or dead and I'm too old to make new ones. I don't like the young, Miss Roscoe,' looking arrogantly at the girl opposite her, 'I don't understand them and they don't understand me. I suppose if I were truthful I should say that I lived in the past. All old people do. Of course, if they've got grandchildren they have a stake in the future, but . . . I haven't any grandchildren.' She lit another cigarette. There was a pause.

Jenny felt that the interview was going badly, and she was too tired to pull it together. Her thoughts strayed miserably to Rickey. She checked them resolutely, and said:

'But you wouldn't mind our saying in the ad – in the statement, Miss Allworton, that you think the modern woman has a better life of it than the woman of even twenty years ago?'

'I don't mind your *sayin'* it, Miss Roscoe, because I'm givin' you this interview for money and I've got to earn the money. But I don't *believe* it.'

'Oh . . .' Jenny suddenly felt too exhausted to start an argument with the magnificent and tiresome old egoist. 'If you really don't mind our saying it, then I shall. I'll introduce something about the modern woman having reaped all the benefits that you pioneers sowed, shall I?'

To save her life she could not have kept the sarcasm and spite out of her voice. She wanted to cry. She was so tired that she could hardly speak. Miss Allworton, the marooned Pioneer, the bitter frustrated failure who had started out with such high hopes, was the last straw. Of course, none of we moderns'll ever be like that, thought Jenny, but what an Awful Warning. Just didn't know how to manage her cake . . .

'You can say what you please, Miss Roscoe.' Miss Allworton stood up, leaning her arm on the mantelpiece and looking down at the girl in black with the tan chiffon scarf tucked at her neck, sitting groomed and young and successful in the shabby old chair. 'I leave it to you . . . entirely.'

There was an uncomfortable pause that Jenny found herself unable to break. It went on until it was unbearable, and still it went on. Jenny stared at the cat. At last she looked up, quickly, and met Miss Allworton's miserable eyes, full of envy and a sort of wonder, looking straight into her own.

Miss Allworton spoke quickly.

'Mustn't mind me starin' at you, Miss Roscoe, and forgive my bein' rude. You see, you interest me.' Her voice was almost shy. 'You're not a bit like a feminist to look at. You're well dressed (oh, I know how a woman ought to look, though your sort of clothes never suited me; I'm too big) and I like that little hat, and you . . . I don't know. Thirty-five years ago there simply weren't women like you, Miss Roscoe, anywhere in the world.'

'Weren't there?' said Jenny, oddly touched.

'No. Women were either fools or feminists. But you don't seem to be either.'

'Thanks,' said Jenny, demurely.

Miss Allworton suddenly smiled, a broad schoolboyish smile that gave her a strangely youthful look, and Jenny realized that thirty-five years ago all her high-collared, long-skirted, earnest friends had called that smile, '*Maude's ripping grin.*'

Then Miss Allworton's face suddenly grew solemn, as though she were going to talk about God. She said off-handedly, examining her cigarette:

'Like your job?'

'Very much.' Jenny answered simply. Here, surely, they could meet on common ground.

'Married?'

'Yes.' Her eyes met the older woman's eyes steadily, and no change betrayed the misery that suddenly swept over her. *That's marriage, that was.*

'Any kids?'

Jenny shook her head.

'Luck or judgment?' Again the grin.

'Judgment,' said Jenny, laughing a little. It occurred to her that had she known Miss Allworton in 1902 she might have liked her.

'Plenty of time eh?'

Jenny nodded again, for to her dismay she knew that if she spoke she would start to cry. It was not because she regretted having no kids, but because it was impossible – now – to have Rickey's kids, and she felt she would never want anyone else's.

'Well' – Maud Allworton crushed out her cigarette, stood up, and moved restlessly about the room – 'I don't know that I've ever regretted not havin' any. They're a great tie when one's the type that wants work too . . . I could have, you know!' sharply, turning to Jenny. 'I made my choice deliberately. I had to choose between marriage and The Cause, and I chose The Cause.'

Jenny said nothing, but she thought: Then you were a fool. If you'd managed your life sensibly you could probably have had both.

'Yes . . . I chose The Cause,' repeated Miss Allworton, standing in front of a light red mahogany sideboard that Jenny had admired earlier in the evening, and picking up a photograph in a silver frame that glittered. It was the only well-kept object in that dismal room.

'This was the man who wanted to marry me.' She crossed the room abruptly and held the frame out to Jenny, who took it and looked at the photograph. 'We'd known each other since we were children, and when I was thirty-five we became engaged. We were not children or fools. I had been working for The Cause all my life, and he was an intelligent man and he knew what it meant to me. Of course I was looked on as a hopeless old maid by all my kind fools of relations, but not by him . . . he'd waited for me, and I was prepared to risk havin' children . . . no joke at that age, in those days, Miss Roscoe, no joke even nowadays when I'm told it's made as easy as . . . it can be.'

There was a pause. Jenny was studying the photograph of a charming face, sensitive yet masculine and humorous, an Edwardian face with thick moustaches that did not hide the full lips of the natural lover. Killed in the War, of course, she thought.

'He was perfectly willing to *share* me with The Cause,' went on Miss Allworton bitterly, 'but that wasn't good enough for me. I wanted to be as free as though I were not married, free to give *everythin'* for The Cause. But George didn't see it like that. So I broke off the engagement. He enlisted when the War broke out, and before he went to France he came to see me for the last time and asked me to marry him . . . and I said no.'

She flung back her head, standing in the middle of that dismal room and staring back into the far-off days of 1914. But Jenny stared at George Saville's face. His mouth was like Rickey's.

'And then he was killed,' ended Miss Allworton abruptly and harshly. Silence fell.

So that's that, thought Jenny. Her man killed, and all the things she fought for accepted as commonplaces by a new generation that's never heard of her. No wonder she's bitter . . . and she probably knows it's partly her own fault and that makes it worse. Cake! Not one woman in a million knows how to have it and eat it too.

'. . . so that's why you interest me,' Miss Allworton went on. 'You seem to have managed the impossible; a happy marriage *and* a successful career.'

Jenny said nothing. There was no question in the older woman's voice; she took her visitor's happiness for granted, yet Jenny, sitting there and staring at the cat, suddenly felt bitterly ashamed of herself. I'm no better than she is, really, she thought fiercely. I've had my chance to make a happy marriage and I've mucked it . . . *just like she did. God, what shall I do?*

Suddenly a blazingly simple idea struck her. She stood up quickly and glanced at her watch. It was half-past seven . . . nearly twenty-five minutes to eight. There was still time to catch Rickey, make him understand, say that she was going to give in. He should have his child, and she would have her cake . . . but this time she would manage it properly, as a modern careerist should, not muddle it away like a careerist of thirty years ago.

'Miss Allworton,' she said rapidly, 'are you on the telephone? No, of course you're not . . . I tried to find you in the book and couldn't . . . how stupid of me to forget. Look, you must forgive me, I'm afraid it sounds shockingly unbusinesslike, but I've just remembered something I simply must attend to . . .'

'At home?' asked Maude Allworton, smiling mockingly but with a touch of sympathy. 'Kettle boilin' over?'

'No . . . husband,' said Jenny simply. 'Miss Allworton, I must go at once. It really is . . . important.'

'Off you go, then. But I'm sorry, I rather hoped that you'd stay to dinner. I've got some very amusin' stories in my book that I'd have liked you to hear, my book of memoirs, you know, Hewett and Worsley are considerin' it . . . particularly one about Tommie Lascelles (she was Iris really, but never anything but "Tommie" to us) and the P.M.'s mother-in-law . . . but of course if you really must go . . .'

'I must. But I'll come back, Miss Allworton.'

'Will you? Will you really? There are so many things I'd like to talk to you about.'

'I will. I promise.'

She held out her hand, and winced as it was shaken.

'I'll come to the door with you . . . no. Better let May do that. She'll be wantin' to ask you if I said anythin' about her and George, poor thing.'

Jenny, in an agony of impatience, waited while she opened the door and shouted, 'May!'

'Did you call, Maude dear?' inquired Miss Urse, popping out of a door like the White Rabbit.

'Sounded like it.' Miss Allworton grinned at Jenny. 'See Miss Roscoe out, will you. Good-bye, Miss Roscoe. Thanks for comin'. You can say anythin' you like about me in your advertisement, I don't care. And come again soon.'

And as the door shut Jenny was almost sure she heard her add, 'And good luck, my dear.'

Miss Urse pattered ahead of Jenny down the hall. At the front door she paused, her fingers slowly turning the knob that opened it, and looked round at Jenny, her pale eyes glancing suspiciously from side to side.

'Did she say anything?' she whispered.

'Not a word,' Jenny whispered reassuringly. 'I expect she's forgotten all about it. I shouldn't worry if I were you.'

Miss Urse shook her head.

'Oh no, she hasn't. But I'll try not to worry. And thank you so much for being so kind. Can you see your way? Sure? Good-night.'

She slowly shut the door, and Jenny, free at last, raced down the path and tore open the taxi door.

'Anything wrong, madam?' asked the driver hopefully, getting out. He looked ready to fight a gang for her.

'Nothing, but I *must* be at Victoria just before eight o'clock. Can you make it? There's a fiver if you do.'

'*Can* I!' said the driver. 'You're there.'

He slammed the door very hard to show that he did not care what became of the taxi, climbed in, and away they went at a satisfactorily increasing speed.

For a minute Jenny played with the idea of telephoning to Rickey at the flat, but then she realized that he would already have left for Victoria. She leaned back and tried to calm her thoughts. There was a good chance that the taxi would make it; and she must think what to say.

Then she thought: there's nothing to say, except, 'Rickey, I've been a fool. Let's try again, on your terms.'

Yes, that's what I'll say.

If he'll only believe me, and if only I can get there before Margot does!

It's hard luck on her, but it won't be the first time a man's let her down.

Suppose Rickey does the heroic, and insists on going because he *can't* let her down?

He won't. Thirty years ago, if he'd been George Saville, he might . . . but not nowadays. Our generation makes fools of itself, but not in that particular way.

She glanced at her watch again. It was a quarter to eight and the taxi was hurtling through Bloomsbury.

We'll do it!

She looked affectionately at the back of the driver's head, huddled into his overcoat like a gangster.

It won't be easy (she was thinking again about the rebuilding of her marriage) but I can do it, I know. And Rickey will make it easier for me because he'll be so grateful and so blissfully happy that I've seen sense!

Just for a minute she felt painfully lonely. It was not much fun being an adult, in a world full of children. Even Rickey was a child, though he weighed thirteen stone and stood six foot in his socks. Then she remembered how narrowly she, Jenny Roscoe, the successful careerist, had escaped being as childish as the rest of the world, and her sense of loneliness passed. They, she and her generation, were all fools together. It might be an humiliating feeling, but it was certainly not a lonely one!

The taxi screamed to a stop in front of Victoria Station.

Jenny climbed out (it is only in thrillers that people 'leap' in and out of taxis), unpinning her platinum and diamond fob watch.

'Wait here,' she said, tossing it to the driver, 'and I'll give you your fiver when I come out. I haven't it on me now. Trust me?'

'Sure,' said the driver. Five years ago he would have said, 'You bet,' but time has to march on.

He watched the young lady run into the station.

Ten minutes later, when he had just begun to examine the watch a little more seriously, the young lady re-appeared with a tall fair chap who looked like a thundercloud and a pretty little dark bit in a fur coat. The little dark bit was the only one who was smiling. All three stopped in front of the taxi. The dark bit said, cheerfully:

'Well, happy days, you two. Give me a ring some time and let me know how it's working out.'

'Thanks. We will,' said the other young lady . . . his young lady. 'You think it won't, don't you?'

'Oh no,' said the pretty dark bit. 'I know my Jenny. I'm sure it will work. You'll see to that . . . now.'

The big fair chap swore loudly.

'All right, all right,' said his young lady, hastily. 'Good-bye, Margot.'

''Bye, Jenny. 'Bye, Rickey. You've got my number if ever you want me again.'

The big fair man looked at her, but said nothing.

'Here's your fiver,' said the driver's young lady, counting out notes and money. 'Home, Rickey?'

'I suppose so,' said the big fair chap, and gave an address. The pretty little dark bit had sprinted into the station, evidently to catch a train.

Jenny and Rickey sat side by side, in silence. Presently

Rickey, apparently coming to a decision, leant over and smacked Jenny rather hard in the face.

'Rickey you *beast!*' she gasped, beginning to cry. 'What's that for?'

'For playing me up for three years and making me look six kinds of a fool in front of Margot. If I didn't love you I'd do it again, too.'

'I'm sorry. I deserved it,' said Jenny equably, mopping her face with care. 'You ought to have done that two years ago and then I guess we'd have been all right.'

'We're going to be all right from now on. But if ever I feel you need it, I shall do it again.'

A few weeks later a cheque for twenty-five guineas went to Miss Allworton, accompanied by the swaggerest cake that Bond Street could supply and an invitation to drink sherry with Jenny one evening that week. This meeting was the first of many for which Jenny, who was not so busy at the office these days, managed to make time; and when the Roscoe heir was born, amid the cheers of Fleet Street and Bloomsbury, Miss Allworton was invited to be his godmother and accepted.

To be godmother to the baby son of a woman a generation younger than oneself does not exactly crown a frustrated life with romance, but it was admitted by all observers that Miss Allworton seemed to like it.

Mr Amberly's Brother

Serene amidst a group of trees, Mr Amberly's house faced the gliding Thames.

The lawns, their green uniformity broken only by square, brilliant beds of flowers, and by a rock garden immediately under the drawing-room windows, were smooth and unmarred by daisies, by the prints of careless high heels, or by any stray bone deposited by the sort of stray dog who buries treasures in the gardens of men less wise than Mr Amberly.

The flower beds were filled at this season of the year by a rare type of tulip (flame colour, streaked with dark brown) which Mr Amberly had discovered during a visit he had made to Holland.

He had commissioned his head gardener to fill the beds with the flowers in the autumn; and it pleased him to glance occasionally through his dining-room window, as he sat at lunch or over his coffee in the evening, and to reflect that no other man in England save him, Conrad Amberly, possessed beds full of tulips of flame colour streaked with dark brown.

Above his head, as he sat thoughtfully sipping his Turkish coffee, gleamed through the summer dusk the dim moons of his collection of old pewter plates and dishes, ranged along the walls on shelves of oak.

His feet, in shoes that were made for him by a bent ill-tempered old man in Shepherd Market who was a master of the shoe-maker's craft, rested on a Persian rug three hundred years old.

Silence – soft, rich, filled with the noiseless rippling of the river and the last callings of the birds – floated through his house from attic to garden.

Perhaps Mr Amberly appreciated the power of his money to buy silence more than he appreciated any of the other luxuries that money can buy. Silence in the house of the poor is usually the silence of exhausted sleep, and in the houses of the middle classes it is often the silence of boredom. But in the house of a connoisseur, a collector of pictures, of pewter and old lace and Japanese carvings, silence is like the soft breath of all these beautiful treasures stirring in their sleep, and the wise man inhales it gratefully and never willingly breaks it.

And it was only a lengthy wail, discontented, ear-piercing, floating across his expensive silence that brought home to Mr Amberly (and not for the first time) that all men and women – women, especially – were not so wise as himself.

Impassively Mr Amberly extended the tip of his shoe and pressed it against a rise slightly to the left of the silky edge of the rug.

Impassively, perhaps half or three-quarters of a minute later, a large, correct butler stood in the opened door, saying:

'You rang, sir?'

'Shut the windows, Willis, if you please.'

The butler crossed the room like a sleek, gross cat, stooped creakingly, and unhooked the French windows, which he shut.

The wailing sound dimmed to a distant rumour which a wise man could ignore or pretend to ignore.

'Shall I draw the curtains, sir?'

'No, thank you. That will do.'

'Very good, sir.'

When the door had shut under the butler's careful and lingering hand, the silence crept back into Conrad Amberly's dining-room again. The blue smoke from a Russian cigarette floated upwards in a pure, unwavering column, fraying out at the top into a flat cloud. The black, syrupy coffee slowly cooled in the tiny cup. And he sat, with his head bent on his breast, listening to the muffled wailing floating across from the garden next door.

He was thinking thoughts that he seldom permitted to disturb the cultured peace of his bachelor life, but they were not the thoughts that sentimentalists might suppose to be passing through the mind of a middle-aged, unmarried man, sitting alone, listening to a child crying.

He was reflecting, irritably, that unpleasant, disturbing noises, indicating poverty, violence, discomfort and all the qualities he most disliked, had been floating across his privet hedge ever since Mrs Massereene had moved into the house next door a year ago.

He was thinking about the puny baby that lay in a shabby pram in the garden, and cried; the timid, plain girl of five or six whom he had discovered stealthily insinuating a struggling rabbit through a hole in the hedge 'to look at the flowers, 'cos we haven't hardly any in our garden';

and the regiment of boys (it seemed impossible that only two of them could make so much noise) who played in the garden in the evenings.

He was remembering Mrs Massereene when she had been Nesta Phillips; very pretty, in spite of her wild, untidy ways, with a habit of grinning at him and remarking, 'Conrad, you're an old maid. Miss Constance Amberly, you should have been. I shall rumple your hair!'

He was remembering – oh! so much more vividly than he remembered the thrill of purchasing his first piece of plate at Christie's – the touch of Nesta's rough little hands all over his head as she thoroughly carried out her threat.

He was remembering how he had weighed the advantages and disadvantages of making Nesta mistress of the beautiful house he had just inherited, at the age of twenty-nine, from his father. His waverings and hesitancies, and the sudden decisions which were made only to be revoked in a panic a second later, now seemed to have taken place in the mind of a young man who had died a hundred years ago, or who had never really lived at all.

And while he was hesitating on the brink of marriage, assuming in his self-centred pride that he had only to offer and Nesta would accept, the news came that Nesta had married someone else.

She had run away, in just the impulsive, untidy, emotional way Conrad had always disliked and feared in her, with the usual poor and handsome cad who haunts the outer fringes of a candle-flame of beauty such as she possessed.

And Mr Amberly, sitting with his head sunk on his breast in the slowly-darkening room, could still feel the shock of confused emotion he had felt a year ago, when he heard that Nesta's husband was dead and that she was coming back to live next door to him in the shabby house where she had lived as a girl.

She came back as a woman of forty, with four children, and with the lamps of beauty behind her eyes almost extinguished by years of unhappiness.

But just as Nesta had disturbed the calm of Mr Amberly's youth by her contemptuous honesty and her living beauty, so she now disturbed the calm of his middle-age by the suggestion of noisy poverty that drifted across to him from her untidy garden and her two rosy sons and the wailing baby that she was always trying to soothe.

'The child can't be well,' thought Mr Amberly irritably – so irritably that the thought passed his lips in a scarcely audible, impatient mutter.

He rose heavily, and crossing over to the french windows, stood looking moodily down on the motionless beds of tulips, almost colourless in the twilight, and the stealthy onward sweep of the silver river at the foot of his garden.

As Mr Amberly stood there, unconsciously straining his ears for the wailing sound that had now stopped, he became slowly aware that the scarcely perceptible reflection cast by his own body on the window glass was thickening, and growing darker and more solid, until, scarcely daring to draw his breath, he was looking out through the window into the eyes of a man who stood facing him on the path outside.

And yet, though this man had grown out of the thin, twilight air before his eyes, and now stood, dark and solid, where a moment ago there had been nothing but indifferent evening landscape, Mr Amberly was not afraid.

Indeed, he was conscious of extraordinary happiness and relief pouring into his mind.

The man outside was smiling at him and motioning him to open the window, and Mr Amberly, his fingers trembling with eagerness, unfastened the catch and pushed the windows wide.

The sweet smell of the garden floated in with the dark figure as he stepped into the room, and Mr Amberly was so intently studying the stranger's face that he did not even murmur a protest when he saw the rough patched boots tramping across the silky surface of his Persian carpet.

The stranger sank, uninvited, into a chair, and took a cigarette from an old silver Persian box lying on the table, and lit it. But at the first puff he made a grimace, crushed the cigarette into Mr Amberly's coffee-cup and drew out an old pipe.

Mr Amberly switched on a soft light.

Neither man spoke. A cloud of rank smoke slowly floated into the room, blown here and there by the light wind blowing in from the garden. Mr Amberly, his hands on his knees, sat leaning forward, staring at the stranger's face with a look of wistfulness and bitterness in his eyes.

'I thought you were dead,' said Mr Amberly, slowly, at last.

'If I'm not, that's not your fault; you've done your best to kill me for the last forty-six years,' retorted the other. 'I'm only here to-night because, for once, you forgot to think about your pewter pots and your precious bits of lace and the rest of your rubbish. I'm here because you were thinking about another human being.'

A shadow of distaste passed over Mr Amberly's face at

the contemptuous 'rest of your rubbish,' but he did not
pause to gather his resentment into a speech full of delicate,
satirical reproof. He said, looking at the grim, dark face
that was a replica of his own, but older and stronger:

'I've often wondered . . . Did you run away to sea, after
all, and see with your own eyes all the places we used to
talk about together when I was young? Did you see Thebes,
and Java, and Popocatapetl?'

'All of them,' replied the stranger. 'All of them, Conrad.
All the places that were once mere names to us; the places
that you have allowed to become only names to you. I
have smelled their dust, picked their flowers, slept in their
sunshine, worked in their mines. All this –' and he waved
a big, condescending hand round the sober beauty of Mr
Amberly's dining-room '– all this is so much lies and sham
compared with the things that have happened to me. You
know that, don't you, Conrad? You know, in your secret
heart, what I always told you when you were a young
man: that lace is made to wrap round the shoulders of a
breathing woman, not to be kept in cases for half-men to
finger. Men! What do you call yourself, at forty-six?'

'You always hated my love for beautiful things,' said Mr
Amberly. 'When we used to talk together, long ago, you
always sneered at me, because I wanted to collect beauty,
to imprison it, and keep it so that I could look at it, in
peace and solitude, for as long as I lived. All *you* wanted
was life – more and more life; strong, fierce, terrifying.
What do you know of culture and art, and the life of the
intellect? Nothing! Less than nothing! You were right when
you said that I have always tried to kill you. I have tried
to kill you – only *you* know, perhaps, how hard I have

tried. You deserve death. You're a barbarian from the outer darkness. I set myself, in my youth, to crush you. I thought I had crushed you . . until to-night.'

'But I wasn't crushed, Conrad, I only escaped,' said the stranger. 'While you were poring over your trinkets and your first editions, I was working by the side of the men who made your trinkets in India and China, talking with the men whose thoughts and passions afterwards lay between the covers of your books. I lived the adventures you only read about. I loved all the women you faintly admired on canvas, or from a distance on the stage.'

'You loved Nesta,' accused Mr Amberly, in a low voice, his head bent upon his breast as it had been earlier in the evening when he had sat remembering his youth.

'That's true. I loved Nesta . . . as well as you did,' admitted the stranger. 'I did not need to tell her I loved her, nor to ask her to share my life, because she knew I loved her, and because she shared my life already, in her love of colour and beauty and adventure. Nesta has always been my dearest friend. I went to Nesta, and consoled her in her misery, when you were afraid to go to her. Nesta knows I'm still alive. She knows I'm your brother, Conrad; your other self, crushed down, silenced, ignored though I am by your conscious self.'

'She knows about you?' whispered Mr Amberly.

'Of course she does. That's why she still cares about the selfish mask that you've become during the past fifteen years. She knows that in your heart, almost buried under a load of beautiful, useless trifles, and selfish fear of facing real life, I dwell – I, your brother, the man that you might have been.'

'It isn't true,' whispered Mr Amberly. 'I could never have become like you. I've always wanted to stand aside, and watch, and let life slip past me like a lovely dream. You're lying. You're not my brother, my second self. You're a ghost – a ghost I killed years ago.'

'Then if I am a ghost,' thundered the stranger, and as he spoke, he rose from his seat, and towered over Mr Amberly like a menacing dark cloud – 'and if you killed me years ago, why are you afraid to meet my eyes? Why are your own eyes full of discontent, and fear, and envy?'

'Go away – leave me,' muttered Mr Amberly, shrinking back in his chair and covering his face with his hands. 'Why did you come here? You know our meetings always end in the same way; at first I am glad to see you, because your coming seems to release me from something that holds me captive – and then you begin to mock and taunt me with all the things I've missed in life . . . because I'm afraid. I've always been afraid, and you know it. I shall never change now; I'm too old. Go back into my secret heart, and hide there until you die.'

He stopped speaking, and cowered back, glaring up at his brother.

But as the dark, solid figure seemed to shrink in upon itself, and to draw nearer to his own body as though to be absorbed into him, Mr Amberly's eyes showed no triumph or hatred.

He watched the face, so like his own and yet so much finer, fading, thinning, dissolving like a candle flame in the light of the sun; he felt the familiar load of secret ambition and discontent slowly fill his mind again, and slowly sink beneath the waves of custom and cowardice.

And then he stood alone in his softly-lit and elegant room, and shut his eyes to close out the emptiness, and stopped his ears to shut out the silence, the rich, perfect silence that he had been drinking like rare wine only an hour ago.

But suddenly, Mr Amberly turned and blundered across the room, across the cold, silent space of his hall where a gilt clock ticked. He opened the front door, and hurried through the warm darkness down the path of his front garden, between the beds of white geraniums.

The unpainted, rickety gate of the house next door creaked under his impatient hand, and he strode up the weedy path towards the light burning behind the fanlight.

Nesta Massereene, opening the door a moment later to his knock, looked up into his pale, moved face with amazed eyes, and laughed, an echo of the rich, soft chuckle he remembered.

'Why, Conrad!' she said. 'If it isn't you! What's the matter? You look as though you'd seen a ghost!'

'I have,' said Mr Amberly. 'May I come in and tell you about it, Nesta?'

Absent-mindedly he picked up a pair of shabby, muddy little boots that had been left outside the sitting-room door.

With his glance resting on Nesta's silvering hair, he followed her into the room.

www.vintage-books.co.uk